**Praise for John Ridley's novel**
*Love Is a Racket*

"Smart and edgy and even moving; if Richard Ford wrote genre fiction, it might read something like this."

—*The New York Times Book Review*

"[A] knife-edged, taut thriller . . . Closer to the edgy, pulp fiction world pioneered by Nathanael West's *The Day of the Locust*, Jim Thompson's novels, or James Ellroy's *L.A. Confidential* . . . Ridley delivers a series of twists and turns at the end that will leave one breathless with suspense and in awe for a fine story, deftly told."

—*Emerge*

"Ridley fills his novel with a dark circus of characters we enjoy spending time with. . . . Ridley does a skillful job at letting us play the voyeur, allowing a vicarious walk in the shoes of those caught in the tragic tar pits of life from which there is no escape. . . . *Love Is a Racket* is an entertaining story, filled with bits of sharp humor and a myriad of plot twists."

—*Milwaukee Journal Sentinel*

"John Ridley writes with a fresh voice, one marked with anger, humor, and a stark reality that burns through each word. It is a voice demanding to be heard."

—LORENZO CARCATERRA
Author of *Sleepers* and *Apaches*

"A strangely haunting drama . . . Suspenseful as a slow-burning fuse . . . [*Love Is a Racket*] first shocks and then stimulates the imagination. . . . Told crisply and without wasting a monosyllable, the story moves deftly to its well-concealed denouement."

—*Library Journal*

Everybody
Smokes
in
Hell

## ALSO BY JOHN RIDLEY

*Stray Dogs*

*Love Is a Racket*

# John Ridley

---

# Everybody Smokes in Hell

Ballantine Books • New York

A Ballantine Book
Published by The Ballantine Publishing Group
Copyright © 1999 by International Famous Players Radio Picture Corporation

http://www.randomhouse.com/BB/

Library of Congress Catalog Card Number: 00-104179

ISBN: 0-345-42147-7

This edition published by arrangement with Alfred A. Knopf,
a division of Random House, Inc.

Manufactured in the United States of America

First Ballantine Books Trade Edition: August 2000

10 9 8 7 6 5 4 3 2 1

to the Yoshidas

Chuck   Jean   Kathy   Arlene


and a quick nod to m' man

Ernie Pandish

sorry Gayle this one's

for

Kaila

major props to the following people in a semi-particular order:

Adam Fierro

Arthur Pine    Richard Pine    Gideon Pine
Lori Andiman    Sarah Piel    Catherine Drayton

Sonny Mehta
Paul Bogaards
Leyla Aker
Jonas Karp

Gina Centrello
Peter Borland
Emily Grayson

Paula Shuster    Marie Coolman

and
especially

Frances Ryan

and a big fat thank-you to the following in the meadows:

Eddie Millan    Jennifer Gray

Hal Welch
Linda Martin    Leslie Dennis    Bonita Spurgin

Ben Siegel    Steve Wynn

# Everybody
# Smokes
# in
# Hell

The overall picture, as the boys say, is of a degraded community whose idealism even is largely fake. The pretentiousness, the bogus enthusiasm, the constant drinking and drabbing, the incessant squabbling over money, the all-persuasive agent, the strutting of the big shots (and their usually utter incompetence to achieve anything they start out to do), the constant fear of losing all this fairy gold and being the nothing they have never ceased to be, the snide tricks, the whole damn mess is out of this world.

— RAYMOND CHANDLER in a letter dated
January 12, 1946, to Alfred A. Knopf

*H*OLLYWOOD was what the sign said. Said it in giant white letters. Said it big as every dream of every dreamer who ever came Tinseltowning. Said it for all the world to see, when anyone could see it at all through the overcoat of smog that kept the city of Los Angeles bundled up tight.

HOLLYWOODLAND was what the sign used to say. Not anymore. A bunch of decades ago the "land" part, having fallen into a state of disrepair, crumbled up and tumbled down the hills, the Hollywood Hills, with all its palatial Hollywood Hills houses. The three-million-, five-million-, as-many-million-dollars-as-you-want-to-spend houses of the movie stars and the movie stars' wives and the movie stars' mistresses and the movie stars' personal trainers who fucked the mistresses while the movie stars were out making movies about a guy who loves his family.

Drop down some more and you come to Los Feliz with its smaller, but still kinda big and still very nice houses that were more for the middle class, if you consider middle class a family that rakes in two-fifty to half a mil a year. It was LA middle class anyway.

And keep dropping down the hills,

down,

down,

like you were taking the express to purgatory's basement, you hit Hollywood. Dirt, soot, traffic. The homeless. That's what you see without even looking hard. The rest is just Mexicans cruising in their low riders, crackheads passed out in the street—maybe passed out, maybe dead—and an urban rainbow of gang-ready kids. And, of course, there was the occasional movie studio.

It was night. The movie studios were closed. The cruising Mexicans and the gang kids were in full effect. Hollywood belonged to them.

And then there was the white guy. Not just white like you call your average pink-fleshed guy white. This one was dead-pale white. Hold-him-up-to-the-light-and-see-his-kidneys white. Too white for most twenty-somethings in a land of beach and sun. Shaggy hair—dirty and tangled like a ball of yarn used to clean floors—hung from his head, obscuring his face. He moved in a hophead/dope-fiend slow dance, a drug/booze mix his unseen partner, and therefore went just-another-junkie unnoticed as he swooned and swayed his way across the parking lot into the 24/7 Mart, past the counter. The counter is where the clerk, a black guy sporting an official multicolor 24/7 Mart top, rang up an old Russian Jewess who, along with her husband, had sur-vived the massacre at Zagrodski by the SS *Einsatzgruppen* to one day come to America, to California, to Silver Lake, where her husband got shanked to death over fifteen bucks and change one night when he was walking the dog. The clerk behind the counter didn't know any of this. Didn't care. Couldn't even pronounce *Einsatzgruppen*. What he cared about right then was the pair of thirteen-year-olds trying to snatch a copy of *Penthouse* from behind the counter—not particularly because they wanted to see chicks in the buff, they peeped naked chicks on cable for free, but because it was more of a challenge to steal shit from behind the counter than from anywhere else in the store—as he rang up the old Russian woman who he didn't like because she was always whining about something, not knowing about Zagrodski or her husband or that she had every reason in the world to whine because the world had not once ever done anything right by her.

He swatted at the two young boys. The clerk swatted at them with his hand and sent them scattering, sent them running past Emilio and Carmen, who were huddled by the dairy case at the back of the 24/7 Mart. Emilio had his right hand up Carmen's sweater. Emilio was work-ing her left tit out of her bra. Emilio was getting to some serious fondling like he usually did with Carmen by the dairy case at the back of the 24/7 Mart 'cause that was one of the few places he could fondle Carmen 'cause Carmen's father hated Emilio 'cause Carmen's father thought Emilio was a no-good, lazy so-and-so whose sole intention was to fuck his daughter.

Carmen's father was right.

Carmen's father should've kept a better eye on Carmen.

Emilio's left hand massaged Carmen's full Mexican ass. Emilio loved Carmen's Mexican ass, and whispered with his sexiest voice in Carmen's ear how much he loved her Mexican ass, which really pissed Carmen off as Carmen's family was from Ecuador.

Emilio got his face slapped. Later him and her would freak in the back of his tricked-out Chevy, but for now Carmen stormed off, shoving her tit back into her bra as she went, with Emilio begging and pleading right behind.

They brushed past Buddy and Alfonso. Buddy and Alf were like a latter-day Abbott and Costello—Buddy being kind of short and kind of dumpy while Alf was tallish and decent-looking, at least to those who went for the slicked-back-hair-and-five-o'clock-shadow look. Most likely the same six people who never missed a rerun of *Miami Vice*. Alfonso was in the middle of sliding a forty from the Mart's beer cooler, popping it open and slurping it down. Twenty-eight years old and Alf still got the same schoolboy high from stealing a beer as the thirteen-year-olds did trying to snatch the *Penthouse*.

Buddy wasn't getting any kicks. Buddy was just nervous. Nervous because Alfonso was stealing the beer, nervous about what was going down tonight. Nervous because he didn't want to come off as nervous. Buddy was tired of being a nervous guy. He wasn't going to be a nervous guy much longer. Buddy had convinced himself that soon, real soon, courtesy of Alfonso, he was going to be a hardass.

Alfonso finished the beer, moved for the counter. He grabbed up a pack of Twinkies along the way and tossed them down before the clerk who wore the official multicolor 24/7 Mart top and a name tag that read "Paris," and who happened to be Buddy's roommate.

Not even checking the price, Paris rang up the Twinkies same as he'd done with tens of dozens of Twinkies and Ho-Hos and Ding Dongs and Slim Jims and Chocodiles in the thirty nights and counting he'd been working at the 24/7 Mart.

"Three oh three," Paris said.

"For a pack of Twinkies?" Alfonso said back.

"And for the beer you drank." Paris pointed to one of the convex mirrors that hung near the ceiling.

Alfonso looked at the mirror, then back at Paris. He got with a smile. The smile said: "Fuck you."

What Alfonso said was: "Well, ain't you Convenience Store Man?

Another couple of years of this, and maybe they'll let you start working during the day."

"Three oh three."

"What if I don't got it?" His smile went on saying "Fuck you."

Buddy: "Give him the money, Alf."

Alfonso just kept staring at Paris, kept smiling at him, kept waiting for him to do something, the something he knew Paris would never do except stand there while a guy cracked wise at him.

Buddy, again: "Just give him the money!"

"Fucking wimp." Alfonso looked straight ahead, but he could've been talking to either of the roommates; to both of them.

Buddy clawed for his wallet. "Here, take it." His fingers moved so quick they were barely able to dig free some bills and fumble them to the counter. "Just take the money."

"Fucking wimp." This time, for sure, it was meant for Buddy.

Buddy to Alf: "We don't need any extra drama. Not tonight."

Paris to Buddy: "Why you getting messed up with this guy?" It was a rhetorical question. Paris knew Buddy well enough to be hepped to his aspirations of becoming a hustler and a player; a man who was connected and respected. Like every other nobody in LA, he wanted to be somebody.

The dude Buddy had chosen to apprentice under, Alfonso, was none of the things Buddy wanted to be, but he mimed the banter and faked the rest good enough so that being in Alf's proximity made Buddy feel like he was moving smooth and steady along the road to Mack-dom.

And it's not that Paris much cared what Buddy did or who with, but Alf was such an obvious fuckup he had to ask his roomie: "Why you wasting time with him?"

"How about you just worry about your own shit?" Alfonso stepped in to cover for Buddy.

"Wasn't talking to you."

"Well, I'm telling you . . ." Alfonso pressed himself up against the counter. It was all that separated him from Paris, and there was nothing but empty air to keep Alfonso from reaching out and giving Paris a great and mighty ass-kicking if he wanted.

Paris took a slight but obvious step back.

"Worry about your own shit, or I'll give you some shit to worry about."

Shared stares. Alf's angry, Paris's anxious, Buddy's scared. Eyes flinching around the room, sweat streaking over his forehead, Buddy was a long way from quitting his nervous-guy ways.

He inched for the door: "I'm . . . I'm gonna . . ."

"Do yourself a favor, Buddy. All this guy's going to bring you is trouble."

"What are you, his mommy?" Alfonso cutting in, not giving up the press.

"What are you? Nothing but a wannabe hood."

Reflexively Paris flinched in anticipation of the automatic punch to the head that was likely to follow that brand of smart mouth.

But the remark didn't so much bother Alfonso as give him something else to fuck-you smile about.

"Oh, yeah," he said. "I'm nothing. Why don't you say that again while you're ringing up a Big Guzzle. I'm nothing . . . and you're nothing but a loser."

For a real quick second a picture flashed in Paris's mind. A picture of her screaming those same words at him, the memory of it a bitter sting like a bad scar that won't fade away.

"Shut up!" Paris yelled back.

"How's the world look from across that counter? Better get used to the view."

"Get out of here!"

Alfonso got out. He took all the slow-groove time he wanted doing it. Buddy tagged along behind.

Paris was left standing right where he was, kept close company by the shame of so readily accepting the humiliation he'd been handed.

A beat later the filthy white guy took up the space at the counter Alfonso had previously filled, his arms brimming with frozen burritos. Frozen burritos were a popular item with late-night hopheads. The filthy white guy opened his arms and the burritos thudded on the counter cinder-block heavy.

Without putting thought to it, Paris scanned the burritos as he'd done with tens of dozens of frozen burritos and frozen pizzas and frozen burgers and frozen chili dogs he'd rung up in the thirty nights and counting he'd been working at the 24/7 Mart.

Thirty nights.

One month.

Happy anniversary, Paris.

Paris said: "Eight dollars."

Filthy White Guy dug gangly hands in his pockets; pale fingers pulled out a bill. A hundred-dollar bill. Filthy White Guy just held it up for Paris like it was nothing but ordinary for a filthy white guy to come around a 24/7 Mart in the middle of the night buying frozen burritos with a hundred-dollar bill.

Paris took the bill and looked it over careful, as if he would know a fake one when he saw it. After going through the motion of giving Ben Franklin all the attention he felt he deserved, to Filthy White Guy: "Welfare been good to you, huh? I always knew even poor white guys was rich."

Barely Paris made change, gave it back to Filthy White Guy. Filthy White Guy jammed the fistful of bills in his pocket with all the care of someone who'd gotten back used Kleenex for their cash.

Scooping up the burritos, Filthy White Guy carried them—dropping a few along the way, they bounced off the linoleum—over to the complimentary 24/7 Mart microwave and put them, all of them, inside.

Paris, who had watched this one-man "Just Say No" campaign, came around the counter. "C'mon. One at a time."

It was just then the two thirteen-year-olds, who had been laying in wait for the perfect op, reached over the counter and grabbed the *Penthouse* they'd been eyeing all night.

"Hey!" Paris moved for the kids.

Filthy White Guy turned on the microwave.

The overstuffed machine groaned and flashed and popped and spewed radiated burritos all over the store.

The kids made it out the door.

Everywhere, burrito parts dripped and slid and oozed in downward patterns.

Paris caught a glimpse of himself in one of the Mart's security mirrors. His body, draped in the multicolored uniform, distorted by the curve of the glass, made him look very much like a pathetic circus clown.

"I can't deal with this," the clown muttered. "I can't deal with it."

**M**r. Bashir was a very understanding guy. "It is the type of decision a manager is faced with every day," he said. He said what he said even in tone, reassuring, despite having lost a microwave oven.

Paris couldn't recall having ever seen Mr. Bashir pissed. It must be, he figured, because Mr. Bashir was from the Middle East or the East or from one of those terrorist-filled, war-torn countries *over there*, and once you got the hell out of *over there*—alive—any other kind of shit life threw at you was nothing but a foot massage.

Bashir went on: "The magazine or the microwave. You tried to stop the children from reading, and meanwhile my microwave is burned up like my wife's tandoori chicken."

Could you ever sound real pissed, Paris wondered, with that kind of singsongy accent anyway? Come on, even if you were screaming to beat the devil, everything out of your mouth would come off like you were yapping on helium.

"I'm sorry. I only turned around for a second and—"

"Life is learning, and what you have learned is that, if little boys want to give themselves erections, then so be it, but save the microwave."

"I don't . . . I'm sorry."

"Tomorrow is a whole new day, and with it come whole new opportunities. Next time you will do better."

Kind words from Mr. Bashir: Tomorrow. Next time.

Tomorrow. Next time. Kind words that were like a slap in the face. How many tomorrows did Paris have to look forward to as night boy at a 24/7 Mart? Thirty down, a lifetime to go?

"Yeah. I'll see you tomorrow, Mr. Bashir."

Outside. The parking lot. Paris walked to his car, a 1976 AMC Gremlin. It was a bad knockoff of the Ford Pinto, which itself was as awful a piece of mechanical engineering all the great brains in Detroit had ever devised and could still get away with selling to the public. Rusted holes you could jam a fist through, peeling green paint fell away like flakes of snow; just in case the car had some value, those kept it from having any.

And something new: Filthy White Guy, on the ground, propped up against the driver's door.

This Paris most definitely did not need. "Awwww, come on. Hey!" His foot poked and nudged at Filthy White Guy. No way he was going to touch that shit with his hand. "Hey . . . Hey! You're sleeping on my car. Come on, man. Move."

He did. Filthy White Guy responded to the foot nudges by sliding along the side of the car until his head smacked ground.

"You okay? You sick or something?"

Sick or something, Paris thought. Try high or something. Hopped up or something. Crack, blow, smacked up or something.

Paris, forgetting his feet, shoving the guy now with his bare hands: "Move it, okay, pal? Time to stroll on back to Bumville."

Filthy White Guy, lips barely moving, voice little more than a whisper: "I . . . I want to go home."

"You and me both, so you want to slide over?"

Filthy White Guy gave Paris just enough room to squeeze into his car, just enough room to back the Gremlin out without crushing the white guy's skull under the tires. Paris fired up the engine and was ready to do just that: Back out. Head off. Go home.

But he didn't. What he did was look around the parking lot, around the Hollywood surrounding it: dark, empty. Empty except for punks who looked like bangers, and addicts who looked like killers. And here was Filthy White Guy one-half passed out and—as Paris recalled—pockets swollen with cash. He was no better than bleeding brill waiting for sharks to pick up the scent.

Rolling down the window, Paris leaned out of the car. "You can't stay around here, man. Someone's going to roll you."

Over the sputtering Gremlin engine Paris heard: "I want to go home."

More looking around the parking lot. Still just as dark and deserted except for the bangers and the addicts, only—and maybe this was Paris's own paranoia—the bangers and the addicts seemed to have circled in closer, waiting for Paris to split the scene. Waiting for him to leave Filthy Half-Passed-Out White Guy all to them.

Engine off.

Paris wasn't a particularly good person, and that was by his own figuring. It's not like he hung around soup kitchens doling out freebies, or gave a damn when dykes were outside Mayfair Market in WeHo collecting money for the AIDS Walk, but he was one of those "There but for the grace of God" guys; one of those guys that thought if you went out of your way to ignore someone else's bad shit then that same bad shit was liable to boomerang around and smack you in the head at some point. So, from time to time, Paris found himself doing things that weren't really in his heart, but were just a way, like a gambler's ritual, of keeping more trouble from his already troubled existence.

This was one of those times.

Paris knew the feeling, the need to slot himself some good karma, and frankly the feeling didn't feel good.

"Damn it."

Out of the Gremlin. Grabbing Filthy White Guy under the arms, Paris dragged him toward the passenger side.

"And you better not have AIDS or some shit."

AIDS. Paris thought: maybe he should have been nicer when the dykes were out collecting.

"You fucking stink," Paris ranted.

This is craziness, Paris thought. But he engaged in the craziness anyway by driving Sunset after he asked Filthy White Guy where he lived and Filthy White Guy replied with a limp finger pointed westward, and nothing more.

So Paris headed the Gremlin westward. Filthy White Guy draped the seat next to him in a semilimp, semiconscious way as he produced an odor that was a museum-quality collection of puke, piss, funk, and general body reek.

"Fucking stink," Paris ranted on.

Filthy White Guy responded to that by letting his head thud against the glass of the window.

"I'm not going to get that smell out. And don't tell me about driving around with the windows open. Drive around with the windows open all you want, it's the kind of smell that don't go away. Ever."

Between rants Paris had begun to notice something, vaguely, as he wasn't always quick with his observations. He had driven west like Filthy White Guy had finger-pointed him to, and they had gone from the scummy part of Hollywood across La Brea to the kinda nice part of Hollywood on past Crescent Heights/Laurel Canyon to the nice part of West Hollywood way past Doheny to the very ultra-beautifully nice part of Beverly Hills. So intent was Paris on the Gremlin's new aromas and what he was going to do about them he hadn't paid much mind to his driving.

"Where are we going, man? I'm not taking you all the way out to Santa Monica. You even got a place, or you just—"

Here's a thought, thought Paris: What if Filthy White Guy isn't as messed up as he seems? What if he was faking his daze to get a ride with some Too-Nice Guy dumb enough to drive him and drive him until they were somewhere quiet, secluded, like Will Rogers Park, where has-been pop stars went to jerk themselves, and where a filthy white guy could do all manner of unpleasant things to a guy who's been real nice, and there wouldn't be anyone around to know about it?

Here's another thought, thought Paris: Aren't most serial killers filthy white guys?

"Here!"

The word, coming loud and unexpectedly as it did from Filthy White Guy, made Paris jerk the wheel, pulling the Gremlin into oncoming traffic.

A blaring horn and flashing lights from a speeding Jag.

Paris jammed on the brakes while he screamed: "Don't you touch me! Don't you fucki—"

"Here. Turn here."

Paris looked off to his right, where Filthy White Guy wanted him to turn—a spot Paris had passed how many dozens of times, but had never turned off into because he never had any reason before, and would never have figured if he did have a reason it would be to take some bum home. It was a street called Bellagio. It was the west gates of Bel Air.

"You live here?"

Weak, tired, but with no hint of acknowledging the oddness Paris found in a homeless guy wanting to get taken to some of the slickest pads in town: "Yeah."

Paris sat in traffic for a second, Benzes and Beamers honking away as they had to drive around him. He was way skeptical about what Filthy White Guy was asking, but eventually got to where he "what the hell"-ed himself. He'd traveled this far down the road, why not take it just a little further?

His voice shrugged. "I guess if you've got to be a bum might as well be a bum in the best part of town."

The Gremlin signaled right and went into Bel Air.

Paris drove up Bellagio and up Chalon and all the way up Roscomare and kept going up until they were just barely south of Mulholland, barely south of the top of Los Angeles, where Filthy White Guy pointed Paris toward a pair of huge iron gates that secured a long driveway which disappeared into a thicket of trees.

For Paris the joke had run its course. Filthy White Guy? Living in there? No. No way.

Except, Filthy White Guy hopped out of the Gremlin and tap-tapped a couple of numbers on a keypad. The gates slowly opened, as if backing away from his presence.

Filthy White Guy got back in the car.

Paris, near astonished: "Okay, so what's the punch line?"

"None. It's mine." Filthy White Guy was making a nice recovery from his intoxication. The kind of recovery that comes from being very used to recovering from being intoxicated on a regular basis.

"Your parents rich or something?"

Now it was Filthy White Guy who was astonished, but in a very amused way. "You have no idea who I am."

"From looking around, I'd say you're the pope of skid row."

Filthy White Guy smiled, but he didn't laugh. Not that he didn't want to. It was more like he didn't have any laughter in him.

Paris drove through the huge gates toward what else but a huge house. It was a big, stone, English-countryside-looking thing, what style Paris didn't know other than it being the biggest house he'd ever seen. Seen up close, anyway.

It wasn't just the house that was impressive, but the yard as well. Yard? Acre. Meadow. Lush, emerald grass, trees . . . a pond. All that, and not even done yet. Landscaping equipment, shrubs with their roots wrapped, bags of fertilizer. How much more perfect, Paris wondered, could you make a piece of land?

Around a drive to the mansion's front door. Did mansions have anything as blah as a front door? Or did they have a west door? A receiving door? A main reception area off the garden?

Whatever it was, whatever it was called, Filthy White Guy got out of the car, opened it, and went into the house. Not a word to Paris, just out and in.

The door stayed open.

Just a crack. Just a hint. Open and inviting. A casual flirtation same as the smile and glance from a passing woman. A silent proposition to the curious waiting to be acted upon.

So Paris had choices. He could turn the Gremlin around, drive away, know nothing more about what happened this evening than what happened: he had given a ride to a drunk Hollywood vagrant who wasn't quite that, but more like a drunk Bel Air vagrant who wasn't vagrant at all. Paris could turn, drive away, leaving all this for what it seemed to be: more of the craziness that passed as commonplace, everyday LA.

Or . . .

The door was still open. The flirtation was ongoing.

Paris turned the key. After running on a bit, the Gremlin's engine sputtered out. He followed Filthy White Guy into the house.


Inside. Huge, of course, and lots more styles and designs Paris didn't particularly know but had seen in period movies he'd watched while working those couple of weeks in that video store. African crap and Indian-looking stuff and some junk he thought he remembered from a Kurosawa film. And not separated or grouped. All the styles were blended up and mixed together to form a thing all its own. It was a . . . What was it? It was a mosaic woven of the world. A tapestry held in private. A museum for one. Like in *Citizen Kane*, Paris recalled. That Kane guy had a private museum.

That Kane guy was also a lonely, miserable wreck.

Paris wandered around looking for Filthy White Guy. He wandered into and out of room after room after room. A room filled with books. A room with a pool table. A room with a pool. Finally, in a room with a big leather couch and a bar—just a couch and a bar—Paris found Filthy White Guy.

No preamble: "Want something to drink?"

"Yeah. Sure."

From the bar Filthy White Guy grabbed up two bottles of Dewar's, one for Paris and one for himself. He grabbed them up no different than if he were grabbing up a couple of beers.

Paris spun the top and took a sip.

Filthy White Guy gave himself a long and healthy swig. To him it *was* a bottle of beer.

Paris said: "You were surprised I didn't know who you are, like I should."

"Yeah, you should."

"So, who are you?"

Again from Filthy White Guy the amused look. A look that was almost grateful, as if anonymity was a new and good sensation; a first kiss.

He walked to a pair of double doors, stopped, looked back at Paris, and gave that humorless smile one more time. A hesitation, a dramatic pause that asked: "Ready?"

From Paris the silent question got a nod.

Filthy White Guy pushed the doors open.

Inside the room the four walls, floor to ceiling, the shelves and bookcases, every inch of space was covered, filled, crammed, and overflowing with statues, awards, plaques, certificates, trophies . . . Gold records, platinum records, multiplatinum records, Grammys, American Music Awards, Billboard Awards, radio-play certifications . . . Awards to the point awards didn't mean anything anymore and were no longer hung on the wall or carefully placed in some semblance of order on a shelf, but were just put in this corner or that. Not even put. Thrown, and not thrown very well.

Paris stepped to one of the framed RIAA multimillion-sales

awards, one that was obviously received early on enough that it got a spot of honor on a wall.

Reading from it: "Will of Instinct. You in that band?"

"I'm the lead singer."

Paris blank-stared him.

"Ian Jermaine."

More blank stare.

"You've never seen me on MTV?"

"Don't know. I guess. Grungy white guys all kind of look alike to me. That Alternative shit's sort of played out anyway. No offense."

Indignant: "And what kind of shit do you listen to, Rap?"

Indignant right back: "No, I don't listen to Rap. What, I'm black, I gotta like Rap?" Paris headed into the other room, the room with the couch and the bar, taking more than a few hits of Dewar's on the way. "And if you're such a big-ass rock star"—he got back on the offensive—"how come you're crawling around Hollywood at three in the morning?"

"I was out celebrating. Got a little wasted." Ian was behind the bar. Another bottle got opened. "It's my birthday."

"Happy birthday."

"What's so happy about it? I'm turning twenty-five."

"So?"

"So?"

"Yeah, so? You're twenty-five. So what?"

Ian found Paris's naïveté blatantly entertaining, the way that wheelchair science guy would find a man who couldn't add hi-fuckin'-larious. "You know when you hit twenty-five you're closer to fifty than you are to the day you were born."

Never having given an idea like that much thought, Paris just shrugged.

"Closer to fifty." Ian underscored his words as if syllabic emphasis would make his point clear. "I'm rollin' on fifty."

"Sure. You're practically feeble. Maybe you ought to trade in this joint for a room at the home."

Paris was giving a pass at sarcasm, but Ian just went with the idea.

"Not a rest home. Somewhere else."

"Where?"

"Someplace wonderful."

"Vegas?"

"Ever heard of this dude Yukio Mishima?" Ian knew that Paris hadn't, so he didn't bother waiting for an answer. "He was a Japanese author. *Temple of the Golden Pavilion, Sea of Fertility* tetralogy. You should read him sometime. Read much?" Ian knew that Paris didn't, so he didn't bother waiting for an answer. "So Mishima—right?—he thought the problem with the world was that people let themselves get all old and decrepit and shit. He thought that back in ancient Greece heaven must've been flossin 'cause everybody kicked real young, dig?"

Paris followed, but he wasn't sure what he was following. "Die young, stay pretty. That kind of thing?"

Ian put the Dewar's down—he drank some first, then put it down—and crossed the room to a *katana* that hung on the wall.

Paris didn't know it was a *katana*. All Paris knew was that it was one of them Japanese-looking swords like the one in the *dojo* he worked out in back when he was trying to become the next Jet Li. Jet Li must've worked out like a bastard, because Paris went at it twice a week for almost four and a half weeks and never got any better.

Ian took the *katana* from its mounting, unsheathed it from a lacquered scabbard. The tempered-steel blade was accented with a 24-karat gold electroplate, the handle covered with an elaborate blood-red braiding. For an instrument of death it was a beautiful thing.

Light hit the blade, polished up like a mirror, and reflected with a near-blinding brilliance. Slowly, gracefully, Ian did battle with the empty air.

As he slashed his phantom opponent: "He had a philosophy, Mishima: Art and Action. The completion of a great work of art's got to be followed by a great physical action. Then the two are forever joined by ritual suicide. Death at your greatest moment. First you become immortal, then you die."

"Like, you write a really good song, then do that knife-in-the-stomach thing?"

Ian did a disappointed head-shake. Paris's ignorance was killing him.

*Katana* back in the sheath, back up on the wall.

Ian: "Ain't simple like all that, you know? Nothing easy about death. You gotta go strong, and you gotta go memorable: Marilyn and Jimmy Dean. Any motherfucker can live. Only legends die good."

"And that's what you're planning to do? You turn twenty-five and you're going to check out big-time?"

Ian's answer was another pull at the Dewar's bottle.

Paris matched it with a sip of his own. "Yeah, well, I've heard that Alternative shit, and it sure as hell ain't worth dying over."

With his chin Ian pointed. Over there, across the room on a table: a DAT player. Small, like a pack of smokes. Maybe a little bigger. Headphones hooked up.

Paris looked at the player, back to Ian, who again did the chin point, then crossed the room. Headphones snug over his ears. A finger to a button: Play.

Music.

Paris listened.

Eventually the tape ran to its end. The player cut off.

Paris lifted the headphones. To Ian, one word—the only word—that expressed everything he'd just heard simply and completely: "Wow."

"Wow," he said again.

"I recorded that myself."

"You and your band?"

"No. I've got a studio in the house. That right there is all me."

"It's . . . That was . . ." Known adjectives seemed meaningless to Paris, inadequate and a feeble form of description. "Wow."

"My last will and testament. Forget about Alternative, or Grunge, or being so cutting-edge you got no edge at all. That right there is something pure and special and right on. That is magic most holy. That is art most phenomenal. *That* is what I'm leaving this stinking world. All that remains is the action. Maximum evolution, dude. I'm taking my shit to the *ooother* level."

Ian preached like a surfer Dalai Lama.

He preached on: "Death is life. The bigger I die, the larger I live, and I'm about to blowuptuate more than anybody ever knew how. You see how powerful I just came?"

A couple of nods from Paris. "Yeah, I get it. You're a spoiled, rich white kid who pays for his burritos with hundred-dollar bills, thinks he's the next James Dean, and wants to off himself 'cause he's turning twenty-five and nobody sang him 'Happy Birthday' loud enough."

Same as a big fat fuck-you Ian took Paris's words. Same as a slap to the face. He moved at Paris, Paris just then thinking it might not've been a good idea to wise-talk a drunk rock guy, as drunk rock guys were unpredictable. Sometimes they trashed hotel rooms. Sometimes they beat the shit out of their supermodel girlfriends. Sometimes they just wrote a new song that sold a couple million copies, but usually it was one of the first two. But Paris realized his mistake after he'd said what he'd said, so the thought was punctured-condom useless.

"As if someone like you could ever dig where I'm at." Ian's hand shot out to Paris. Paris flinched, but all Ian did was grab at that little plastic name tag Paris wore, rip it from his orange-and-green and Smoothie-stained uniform, and flick it back at him so that it thwapped against his face with a mild sting. Injury to the insult. "A guy who wears a name tag to work and rings up Doritos and Yoo-hoos for a living; how the hell could you understand? You're nothing but a loser."

That picture flashed up in front of Paris again; the picture of *her*. And with picture came sound: "You're a loser!"

Sharp, hot, Paris screamed back: "I'm not a loser!"

Ian turned away. Not pushed away by the force of Paris's words, but simply turned away like a guy who couldn't stand the sight of what he was looking at anymore.

With his back to Paris: "What are you, then? Huh? You know what I've done in my time? I have stood before the multitudes and sung my heart as they chanted my very words back to me. I have made love to the most beautiful women to walk this earth as the sun rose and set, then rose again. I have been a poet, a voice of my generation, a living legend . . . and then I turned twenty-five. What have you ever done, dude? And you rap to me about a wasted life? I may die, but you, brother, you ain't never even lived." Collapsing on the big leather couch, Ian curled up with the Dewar's: a booze teddy bear. "The time of my departure has come. I have fought a good fight, kept the faith, I have finished the race. That's God talking. Thanks for the ride, friend. Maybe it's time you took one yourself."

With that, like a TV with its cord yanked, Ian faded and shut off.

Paris just stood, immobile, held in place by the singer's pointed words and feeling his every wound. Eventually he collected his freshly slapped-around self and slow-limped for the door that would lead to the long hall he would walk to his car that would drive him back to . . . back to a wasted life.

Halfway there a soft call halted him, turned him. It wasn't a voice that beckoned. It was a feeling.

On the table: the DAT player. The music.

The same feeling that had turned Paris around now articulated ideas. Take a ride, the feeling said.

Eyes to Ian. Passed out.

Eyes to the player. The music.

Eyes to the next room. All those multiplatinum, multimillion-selling awards.

The feeling said: Take a chance.

And then the player was in his hand. Paris couldn't even recall his actions or any philosophical debate over right and wrong, should or shouldn't. There was just the player suddenly in his grip. And even as he contemplated the rapidity with which the act of stealing had taken place, the act had itself become a relic of the distant past. Already he was outside the house, already he was yanking open the Gremlin's door and throwing himself behind the wheel. Already he was speeding away from the home of the artist formerly known as Filthy White Guy back to Hollywood.

Paris stopped trying to play catch-up with his actions and just let them happen, just rode a wave of occurrences. By the time his body and mind were back in sync, the Gremlin had parked itself outside his apartment.

Paris sat, the car's motor coughing itself out, looking down at his hand. He hard-stared at the DAT machine, but it was to Ian he said, and to her: "I'm not a loser."

*B*uddy drove a Continental. Big. Old. A '63. Same as the one Kennedy got his head opened up in. Buddy had bought it on the cheap off a girl doing a quick-sell for some get-me-to-Canada money. He didn't ask questions when they swapped cash for car. Even though the Continental was probably stolen, or involved in a crime, or had some such history riding with it, Buddy didn't ask nothing. He didn't care. He just liked the car.

That was Buddy's problem. One of them. He didn't ask questions. His other problem, another of them, was that he usually paid for his ignorance by getting undertowed into some bad incident he could have avoided if he'd made a few inquiries up front.

He thought about that, Buddy did, his two problems, two of his problems, as he angled the Continental across from a Watts tenement.

"You ready?" Alf asked, meaning: You ready to commit a felony? You ready to mix it up with other criminals? You ready to get dangerous?

"Sure" was Buddy's answer. One word, and it stumbled its way out of his mouth, tripping over fear and jitters. Was he ready? Hell, no. But he was going to fake readiness as much as the next I-never-stole-anything-in-my-life guy who wants to be a player.

But Alf was all right with the answer. "Yeah, see. I knew you was cool."

". . . I'm cool."

"Not like that roomie of yours. That boy's straight *bee-atch*," Alf said, trying to talk like a brother, which is the way white guys talked when they wanted to sound cool. Didn't work. Not for him. Not for any white guy. "He ain't nothing, and ain't never gonna be nothing but nothing. Working for minimum at a goddamn juice stand. He better ask somebody. Shit don't get handed to you."

"I know."

"You want something, you got to reach out for it."

"Yeah. Yeah. I know."

"Reach out and make it your own."

"I know. Yeah."

"Uh-huh. I knew you was cool."

"I'm cool." Buddy paused, then: "I just—"

"What?"

"I just—"

Alf looked all disappointed. "You ain't going punk, are you?"

"No, I—"

"Last minute, and you decide to go punk?"

"I'm not a punk!" Buddy jacked up his tone and volume, trying to approximate manliness, and got fairly close with the effort. "I just want to make sure everything is—"

"I got things worked, all right? I got things figured." Looking over at the tenement: "He's nothing but a doped-up addict who deals on the side. Small time, but enough to start us on easy street. I go in, take what I want, we're gone. That simple, so save the punk act."

Simple. Yeah.

"I'm not. . . . Just making sure."

Alfonso got himself out of the car. His hand dipped under his jacket. It came back out gripping a gun.

Buddy had to work overtime not to wet himself. Hardasses didn't piss their pants at the sight of heat.

To Alf, fronting like a man of action: "Let's get it on."

Alfonso yeah-baby smiled to that. He wasn't smiling on the inside. On the inside Alfonso was worn out, because on the inside Alf knew Buddy was a bitch and it took a lot of effort to pretend he wasn't. Too much effort, he thought, just to jack heroin. It ain't worth it. He should've had his own wheels. If he had his own wheels he wouldn't need Buddy and his traveling girlie show. Alf marked that top of list of things to do with his H money: get wheels, dump the bitch.

Alfonso crossed for the tenement.

Buddy sat in the car, working out his fear and kinda beaming to himself. He did it. He wasn't a punk. He was a man. He was there, wasn't he? Wasn't he backing Alf up? Even though he was just sitting in a car with the motor running across the street from the action, wasn't he doing what he was supposed to be doing?

Punk?

Naw. He wasn't no punk.

Buddy spun some thoughts on that, on his new self-approved nonpunk status, while he shaky-handed a cigarette to his lips, then managed to fumble on the car lighter, waited for it to pop out, and lit up his smoke.

Meanwhile, time didn't move. It just sat on its ass doing nothing when what it should have been doing was passing, racing along so Alf would come strolling out the door of the tenement, smile on face and smack in hand. A brick of it, a kilo. Isn't that what Alf had said?

Buddy didn't know drugs, he didn't know the metric system, but he knew enough to know that a kilo of heroin was a heap. Cut that shit up, mix it with some baby powder or baking soda, sell it on the street, and it was worth . . . well, it was worth a lot. Alf had said it was, so it must have been.

And there was a whole gang of things Buddy could do with that kind of money, there were plans he had. He could . . . he was gonna . . . well, there were a lot of things he was gonna do. Buy some junks, for one. Go out, buy shit, and not even look at the price tag while he was doing it.

And chicks. There would be chicks. Where money is concerned, chicks aren't far behind. And with the chicks would come the sex: abundant fucking inspired by the shine of gold and the glitter of diamond. Precious metal and stone pressed to flesh; that was the only foreplay a good woman needed.

Yeah, Buddy was going to be a man with money, and don't nobody not respect a money man.

Time had apparently died because it still wasn't moving, it lay like a corpse. That, or Buddy had just sucked down his cig in two draws. Either way he needed another smoke. One got fished from the pack and put to his lips. He pushed in the lighter. When it got hot enough it popped back out.

Buddy, the lighter; he lifted it to the cigarette in his mouth. Just as the coil touched the paper, as the heat lit the tobacco, that's when time came alive, and with great rapidity shit began to happen. All manner of shit.

Across the street. The tenement windows got lit with muzzle flashes. The building echoed with pops. Loud pops. Loud enough to jump the lighter from Buddy's hand. Loud enough to make his heart triple-pump. Loud enough to make his body shake and his bladder want to spill.

"Shit," came squealing out of him. "Oh, shit." Forget all the tough-guy, big-man talk he'd been slinging. Buddy was on the non-stop to Bitchville. All he was missing was a pretty dress and fuzzy pink slippers.

Buddy had the desire to move, to duck and hide, or, better idea, to put foot to gas and get the hell gone. But he didn't. He didn't move. Fear was a concrete overcoat that held him right where he was.

All he could do was what he had done before, so he did it again: "Shit."

Tenement door. Alfonso came sleepwalking out.

Buddy shrugged off the fear just long enough to get from the car, go to Alf, prop him up. All that was reflex. If Buddy had put a second's thought to what he was doing, put a thought to the fact that the muzzle flashes he'd seen and pops he'd heard could come again and this time come for him, he would have been curled up on the floor mats of the Continental weeping.

"Alf! Alfonso, what happened?"

Alfonso mumbled.

"What the hell happened?"

The mumbles turned into words. ". . . They shouldn't have been there. . . ."

"What . . . what are you—"

"Those motherfu . . . shouldn'ta . . ."

Buddy walked/dragged Alfonso to the car, to the backseat, threw him in. Moving quick to the front, Buddy got himself behind the wheel. The dash lights lit his hands. They were soaked with a liquidy redness that dripped and ran down his forearms.

Buddy looked to Alf.

Blood gurgled from a bunch of holes in his body.

Panic: "Oh, Jesus . . . You're . . . Oh, shit . . ."

Faint, from the backseat: "Dri . . ."

"I-I . . . Oh, shit. Oh fucking shi—"

". . . Drive . . ."

Drive?

All Buddy was good for was sitting and shaking. "I . . . Fuck! I can't deal with this shit!" A breakdown was coming. It was coming fast, it was coming hard. "I CAN'T DEAL WITH IT!"

". . . You gotta drive. . . . You gotta . . ."

Drive.

Buddy focused up on the word. It planed the edge off his panic; gave him something besides shot-up people and flowing blood to concentrate on.

Drive.

Yeah. He had to drive.

Hand to the key, a twist. He ground the motor that was already running. Jerking the gearshift up and down the PRNDL, Buddy finally found the D slot. Heavy-footing the gas, the tires screamed: rubber on asphalt. The Continental got itself on into the night, fishtailing wide and wildly as it went.

From the backseat, barely: "Shouldn't . . . shouldn't have been there. . . ."

"No shit, we shouldn't have been there. What the hell were we—"

"They shouldn't have been . . ."

"They? Who?"

"They shouldn't have—"

"Who was there? Who?"

Hard turn. Buddy's hands slipped over the steering wheel. The mix of blood and sweat stole his grip. The Continental's front tire kicked up over the curb, the fender clipped a light pole. Metal ground metal and threw up a jizz of sparks.

". . . I got it." Blood filled Alf's lungs. He sounded like he was slowly slipping underwater. "Don't think I didn't get it. Got . . . got them too . . . bitches. . . ." Some coughs. Alf slipping further under. Inches from the deep end of forever.

Billboards of circumstance whipped past Buddy. Signs advertising events and eventualities: Alfonso in the backseat bleeding would lead to Alfonso in the backseat dying which would result in Buddy having to get rid of a dead Alfonso.

Panic into anger: "Don't you die on me!" Buddy didn't care so much about Alf as he cared about being stuck with Alf's body. "Don't you fucking die on me!"

"Got them . . . fuhh . . ."

"No you don't! You don't die!"

The Continental rode on, furiously, with no destination in mind.

Buddy went on admonishing Alf, despite the collection of five bullets he carried in him, for having the audacity to slowly, painfully, horribly bleed to death.

To the east, the sun was getting with the sky. It lit up the empty blue, set on fire the morning smog like a match to kindling, and turned the pollutant shroud a magnificent gold. So magnificent you almost wanted to thank God for all the millions of cars that had donated their exhaust to make the display possible.

Ian faced east, faced the sun. He felt the first of its warmth creeping across his flesh. He felt calm, and relaxed. He felt serene. He felt the barrel of a shotgun butt-up against his chin.

He'd settled on a shotgun suicide, Ian had, because he thought it ironic. His brain, his organ of creation, after giving birth to the most magnificent piece of music that mankind would ever attend, was to be scattered in a fine purée that would seed the garden beneath the very balcony where he stood. From that moment on, the flowers that grew, the life that pushed its way up from the ground, would bear his essence. Then, in the crowning achievement of the most perfect self-inflicted death, by acts of nature—the pollination and cross-pollination of countless plants—Ian would be reborn ten times ten thousand times throughout the world.

The image of the end he had planned was a very beautiful thought. He rushed through thinking about it because Ian didn't have time to think beautiful things. He was way behind in a schedule that called for him to splatter his brains at dawn. The booze had kept him sleeping late. The sun was already pushing up past the horizon. No chance to change clothes, hook up some cooler gear to be found no longer living in. No time to write a suicide note. The music would serve as good-bye. The music on the tape in the player on the table where he'd left it last night. Where he was pretty sure he had left it last night.

Last night . . . ?

All the drink had taken an eraser to his short-term memory. The sun, going from warm to hot. It didn't just light the smog now, the sun cooked it, turning the atmosphere into a noxious gas that would slow-choke Los Angeles and all its air-kissing troglodytes for the next twelve hours.

Now was the time. . . .

Ian's finger gripped the trigger of the shotgun.

. . . The time to evolve to the next level. To a higher plane . . .

A slow steady pull.

. . . Art, action, and ritual death . . .

The sound of the hammer scraping back against its casing.

. . . The door was opening. Ian was stepping into immortality. . . .

The click of the trigger. The snap of the hammer. The sound of firing pin hitting shell.

There was nothing. Not a thing. Misfire. The shotgun didn't go off.

How about that, Ian thought.

He started up again.

Again he pulled at the trigger.

. . . Evolution to the next level. Art, action, ritual death. Immortality . . .

Click. Snap. Hammer to shell.

More nothing.

What the hell!?

Ian jerked the trigger twice. Click. Snap. Nothing. Click. Snap. Nothing one more time.

Goddamn it!

Quick, he broke the shotgun down. Loaded. Two shells in the barrels. Firing pin sharp and striking. Then what the hell is the problem?

Shotgun back up under his chin.

. . . Evolution, art, immortality . . .

Click. Snap.

Fucking shit! What the fuck? God-fucking-damn it.

Out from under his chin, Ian shook the shotgun. Rattled it. Jerked the trigger, jerked the trigger.

The sun moving well up into the sky. The sounds of people and commuters and Shadow Traffic copters all swirling together to spoil a glorious moment. It was do-or-die time. Die-or-live time.

Click. Snap.

Aw, Jee-zuz . . .

Shakin' and jerkin' and swingin' the shotgun.

What does a guy gotta do to kill himself? What the hell does a guy gotta—

Like a pair of lions, the shotgun barrels roared. Buckshot tore away Ian's right foot, leaving a shredded pulp of knotted bone and blood-sloshing flesh.

"Ooooooooh shiiiiiiiit!" The shotgun flew from Ian's hands and up into them jumped the bloody meat-dripping stump of a foot broiling with a pain so severe and intense that, truly, Ian felt nothing at all. It was the idea of having a foot shotgun-blast-amputated into a useless half-mass that caused him hurt. "Oh, Christ! Oh, fucking Christ!"

Clutching his foot, Ian did a one-legged cartoon hop—something Larry might do after Moe dropped a bowling ball on his toes—that did nothing to dissipate the mounting agony. What it did do was cause him to lose his balance, send him tumbling against the beautiful and recently installed frameless all-glass balcony doors, the crash of his body into the glass more than slightly drowned out by the sound of shards embedding, ripping and tearing human flesh.

"Aaaaaaaah, Jesus! Jesus, shit!" Like some fucked-up acupuncture, the glass skewering his back quite effectively redirected Ian's thoughts from his missing foot.

More hopping around now, but with some contorted groping: Ian trying to pull the pieces of the door from his back. Hopping, writhing, reaching. Screaming. The floor of the deck slick with blood. A hop and a slip, a skid. A thigh hitting the balcony railing and a body flipping into the open, empty air. Empty except for the sound of the girl-like screech Ian let out as he piloted for the ground.

Had he not done that, had he not opened his mouth to scream, he might have survived the fall onto the bags of soft, moist fertilizer the landscapers had piled beneath the balcony. Instead the impact forced the fertilizer down his throat, into his lungs, bloating and choking them with manure. At the same time a cloud of refined Milorganite shot up into the air, settled over Ian's body like a burial shroud. A very stinky burial shroud.

The door had opened, and he had stumbled and tripped and fallen through it to immortality. This was the last of Ian.

$\mathcal{B}$uddy flipped his back to the east and jammed up his hands against his face to keep the sunlight out of his eyes. He didn't want the light. He didn't want to see what the day had in store for him. For sure he didn't want to peek in the backseat of the Continental.

But he did.

He took his hands down and turned and looked on the off-chance that everything that had happened the night before hadn't happened.

Buddy had heard the phrase "pool of blood" get tagged with bodies that had been shot up or stabbed and allowed to slow-die. But that's all it was: a phrase. Hyperbole, Buddy would have called it if Buddy knew what hyperbole meant. And yet, there in the backseat, Alfonso's drained-pale body floated in a real-live honest-to-God pool of blood.

Buddy went back to jamming his hands to his face, but a couple of minutes of that and he came up with the notion all covering his eyes would do was keep him from seeing the cops when they showed up. And they would show up. Cops got a thing for murder. And drug-related mayhem? They positively loved that.

So Buddy got himself together as best he could and got out of the car. That didn't amount to much, it didn't at all improve the situation, but getting out of the Continental was more than he'd been able to manage for the last five hours. Beyond that he hadn't worked out a plan of action, so Buddy settled for standing around like a dumbass with a stiff in his ride. That he could handle just fine.

On the overpass, above him, the morning traffic zipped along slower and slower as the road filled up with Angelenos off to day labor. Below the overpass, around him, was a small graveyard of abandoned cars. Other people discarding the trouble in their lives? A dog lay near a concrete support. It was sleeping, or dead. The flies that buzzed around it said dead.

In the time it took Buddy to analyze his surroundings, he was able to stitch together another piece of the plan he was forming moment by moment. He would check on Alfonso. Appearances to the contrary, there was the possibility that somehow Alfonso had been able to survive the bullets and the bleeding and was still—

Buddy opened the back door. Alfonso moved like he was trying to get out of the car without using his legs; his torso kept leaning until it wasn't leaning, it was falling. The body kept falling until its head stopped it by smacking the pavement, hard, same as if Alf was trying to drive nails with his skull. The accompanying thud was just as loud.

Buddy took that as confirmation, along with the bullet holes and that pool of blood, that, yeah, Alfonso was in fact dead.

Buddy stared at Alfonso some. When he finished that, he delivered a eulogy to his extinct pal.

"You son of a bitch! I told you not to die on me! I told you not to die!" Buddy blessed the body a few times with kicks to its chest and head. The carcass resonated spastically at the end of each blow. "Now what am I supposed to do? What the hell am I supposed to do now?"

The final benediction, very quietly: "I told you not to die."

The body's hand moved, a last twitch caused by the firing of a dying axon, or the tightening of muscles as they went into rigor. Or maybe it was just one more spasm left over from Buddy's flailing foot.

Buddy looked at it, the hand, and what it clutched: a package wrapped in brown paper. A brick of heroin. As freaked out as Buddy was, he wasn't so freaked out that the sight of the dope couldn't slap him steady, couldn't get his brain working proper: Take the dope, sell the dope, take the money, get hidden. Stay hidden. Maybe he was the last man standing in a drug/murder fiasco, but LA churned those out every hour on the hour. It wouldn't be long until people forgot which drug/murder fiasco in particular Buddy was wanted for and stopped caring if he ever took a tumble for it or not. But until then . . .

Quick, Buddy reached down and grabbed the package. Hard, he yanked on it, trying to pull it free of Alf's rock-solid death grip. Foot to the body's chest for leverage, one more stiff tug. The package came loose, the body skipped backward.

Buddy, a demon of the night trying to outdistance the sun, ran.

The sun did its goddamnedest to punch its light through the eastern windows of Chad's house. It didn't come close. Not even. The drapes he'd hung, the design stolen from ones in the rooms at Caesars in Vegas, were thick enough to keep out the light of an atomic blast.

Chad dug the dark.

The drapes, the ones he had, cost a little more than most drapes would have a nerve to. Anti-atomic-blast drapes ain't cheap. But thanks to a little creative financing, Chad was able to afford them. Creative financing is what got him his house, too. Thirty-three hundred square feet. Thirty-three hundred square feet in the Palisades. Nothing but creative financing could get you a house like that in a part of town like this. Same with the car in Chad's driveway. BMW 750iL. The big Beamer. Chad would have been much better off with the Five series. The Three would have been fine. Even that roadster was cute. But every D-girl in Hollywood drove one of those roadsters, and kids who worked at The Gap somehow rated Threes. And there wasn't a Beverly Hills doctor or Santa Monica lawyer who didn't roll in a Five. The Sevens were the ones that set you apart from the crowd. The Sevens were the ones that got you looked at right when you pulled up to Morton's or Orso. Sevens were what the big boys at ICM, WMA, CAA— all the power 10-percenteries dominoed on Wilshire Chad aspired to ascend to from the mid-level, boutique, not-as-respected agency status in which he currently found himself mired—rolled in. And if you want to be there, in that club, The Society of Big-Dicked Agents, then you gotta front like you belong.

So a Seven is what Chad wanted and, thanks again to creative financing, a Seven is what he got himself.

The problem with creative financing is that making payments is a motherfucker. Not because the nut is particularly high—not only because of that—but because it's got to be made on time, all the time. Got to be. Must be. Has to be. If anyone were to take a serious gander at things . . . If someone were to check a few facts and recheck a few figures . . . If anybody had enough snap, crackle, and pop to see that two and two wasn't adding up to four . . .

That was the other problem with creative financing. When you were sitting around minding your own business trying to relax and enjoy your creatively financed life, all of a sudden ideas would start to creep into your brain box about all the everythings that could go wrong at any moment.

But there was Ian and Will of Instinct and the new album they were due to start recording that would probably ship at two million units for starters. And a tour. Can't have a new album without a tour, and a Will of Instinct tour would sell out all of the eighteen cities it was booked in.

Twenty-three.

Better make it twenty-three cities. And all that—the new album and the tour and some merchandising thrown in for good measure— all that would take care of any creative financing problems.

And with all that cash-generating superpower of Will of Instinct squarely in his pocket, Chad rarely ever thought about all the everythings that could go so very wrong. Rarely ever, except for every single quiet moment he was alone with himself. Chad went to a whole lot of trouble not to catch himself alone with his panicky thoughts. Instead, there were clients to hang with, parties to attend, aspiring songstresses to "talk business" with.

Except for last night. Last night found Chad without a client, or a party, or a chick who thought she could make it big in music if only she met the right people, so when he should have been sleeping he was sitting up thinking.

The phone rang, rang him out of his closed loop of nervous notions, and Chad was thankful for it.

"Hello," he said, clearheaded from being so very awake.

Marcus, who was on the other end of the line, was a bit surprised at Chad's alertness at the early hour, but was glad as the things to come would require much sharp thinking.

Marcus said: "It's Ian."

That was all Marcus said. All he needed to say. Chad knew. When you get a call first thing in the morning from one of your assistants

about one of your volatile Alternative rock–star clients and all your
assistant says to you is "It's Ian," you've got a pretty good idea of the
craziness the day's about to bring.

"Where?" Chad asked.

"His house," Marcus answered.

Chad hung up.

Chad got up and went into his newly remodeled bathroom and
showered and shaved and dressed in an Armani suit, not being particular about which one. After that he went down to his 750iL and started it
and drove to Ian's house.

Through all that, the showering and the dressing and the drive,
Chad's little head was filled with nothing but very troubled thoughts on
creative financing.

Daymond Evans was not trying to deal with any muthafuckin' sunshine. It was too goddamn late in the day for that. Early is what it was, but Daymond hadn't crashed yet, so as far as he was concerned it was late in the day. Too goddamn late in the day for sunshine.

But the sun never-minded Daymond and came on anyway, pouring light down on Baldwin Hills; on the big houses and fancy cars up in there. So big and so fancy you'd think you were in Beverly Hills, except you weren't, and you'd know it 'cause Baldwin Hills is where the big houses and fancy cars are owned by blacks. African Americans. Call 'em what you want. They don't care. They're rich and they'll buy your ass if they don't like you.

They were the "smart" blacks. The "well-spoken" blacks. The black executives and professionals and some of them entertainment people who'd gotten themselves all monied up, but instead of moving west where the rest of the LA money cribbed, they kept themselves close to their roots.

They were keepin' their shit real, that's what they'd tell you. They'd tell you they stayed in the Hills to keep connected with where they were from.

But what it was, was this: living in Baldwin Hills made them feel good. It don't matter who you are, what color; it always feels good to be able to look down on where you came from; down on all the suckers who didn't make it—couldn't make it—to up where you're at. That's what hills are for, aren't they—for looking down?

Daymond wasn't an executive, or professional. Wasn't an entertainment big to-do. He got his money the old-fashioned way: he sold drugs for it. And with his drug money he got himself a big-ass house up in the hills, and the execs and pros and them didn't think much about how Daymond paid for it, 'cause Daymond didn't sell around the neighborhood, and for all they knew Daymond was a rapper or some such something.

That didn't make Daymond happy, his bougie neighbors thinking he was a rapper. Why's a young brother with ends gotta be a rapper? Why couldn't he be a white-collar brother like them?

Yeah, okay, he wasn't a white-collar brother, he was a crack dealer, and rappin' is a big step up from sellin', but he could have been an exec. Could have been if he'd made it past seventh grade.

Daymond wasn't happy about his neighbors not giving him props. He wasn't happy about the goddamn sunlight. There was a whole gang of shit Daymond wasn't happy about, and Omar and Kenny knew it.

"One a y'all muthafuckas wanna school me on some shit?" Daymond yelled.

It wasn't the yelling that hipped Omar and Kenny to Daymond's pissedness. Daymond was always going off on something. They knew he wasn't right 'cause he was yelling about drugs, and when drugs were involved Daymond could get a serious mad on.

"So what da fuck is goin' down?" Daymond yelled on.

Omar: "Don't know."

"Don't know? What da fuck you doin' on my dime when you don't be knowin' shit? I can git bitches for free dat don't know shit."

Omar didn't say anything to that, not right away, and neither did Kenny, who never had a whole lot to say for himself. Kenny didn't like to talk, 'cause he didn't like the sound of his voice. It didn't sound good courtesy of a bullet in the throat at age six, caught one night while he was sitting at the dinner table. Bullet right through the wall, right through his throat. Half of a part of an inch to the left and the slug would've snapped his spine. Killed him. He was lucky, is what he got told.

Yeah.

What a lucky muthafucka Kenny was to take a bullet in the throat between spoonfuls of generic peas and government cheese, which was just about all his family could afford on aid. It left Kenny with a gurgle of a rasp that he blames for slowing up his sex life. He didn't get laid a first time until he was thirteen. Four years ago. So, with all that working for him, Kenny wasn't a talker. He was good with his nines, though. Three dead muthafuckas'll tell you all about that.

Omar was still taking a moment to not respond to Daymond. He looked over at the two skeezes on the couch bookending his boss. There were always two of them on the couch, at least two, and Omar thought them skeezes because that's what they were. Money girls, like flies on Daymond's green, spendable shit. Were they any more honorable of women, Omar would have acknowledged such. Omar had much love for women, having been raised in a house with three of them: his sister; his mother, who was only fifteen years older than his sister; and his grandmother, who was just twenty-two years older than his mother. Three strong sistas getting by on their own. Yeah, Omar gave women their props. But these two on the couch, like the two who occupied their space the day before, and the others who had done the same days before that, were hos and nothing but. Good-looking, though. One was—the light-skinneded one—and the other was not entirely ugly, and both had asses that were full and tight and worth having them around for.

Daymond, Omar gave up, had done very well for himself, moving from clocker to pusher. There was one time Omar knew of Daymond got bitch-slapped by another seller and the seller got six caps for his trouble. Round this part of the world props came from the end of a gun, and Daymond had bought his self six bullets' worth. So he quit selling and started supplying and carved more territory and bought more lead-lined respect along the way, and it wasn't long before he had broke himself off a bunch of space just north of Torrance. Yeah, Daymond was a regular captain a muthafuckin' industry. It wasn't much after that he turned twenty. Twenty and a stone killer, and it showed. Young and young-looking, there wasn't anything youthful about Daymond. The light in his eyes was a cold one. The blood in his veins was like battery acid. His innocence—that got buried right next to the first person he ever murdered.

Somewhere in Los Angeles there was a potter's field of interred young souls. A generation first neglected, then shoveled into a mass grave.

Omar stopped thinking, stopped looking at the high yellow's ass, and got back to talking. "Bentley and them went to take the shit over to Martin's. We didn't never hear back."

"Bentley best not've run off with my shit."

"They ain't fools. No way they'd play you like that."

"Martin probably shootin' da shit up. Goddamn powder cost me a grip. What da fuck do I let him move my shit for anyhow? Ain't nothing but a crackhead."

"He yo cuz," Kenny pointed out, sounding like he was talking through a foot of gravel.

"Dat's wha's fucked up 'bout havin' family: they always wantin' ta be breakin' off suma yo shit. Goddamn junkie. Every other muthafucka in town dyin' off dat shit 'n' Martin keeps goin' like dat shit is spinach ta him or sumthin'."

No ceremony. Daymond reached over and grabbed the girl's tit. Not high yellow's, but the darker one's. Daymond rubbed it, squeezed it, fondled it. The girl didn't do nothing about it. Nothing meaning nothing. She didn't try to stop him, and she didn't enjoy it. She just let her tit get grabbed 'cause she knew, far as Daymond cared, that was her sole reason for living.

The action of the rubbing and the squeezing and the fondling seemed to have a calming effect on Daymond; a race memory activated, telling him that the tit was the source of life and nourishment. It was a pacifier. That, and it made him think not so much about his missing drugs and more about having sex.

Daymond: "Do work. Git yo asses over there. Find my shit!"

Marching orders. As always, without question, without hesitation, without thought, Omar and Kenny started marching.

As they got to steppin' they heard, in the middle of her tit massage, the dark girl saying: "Oh, baby, I wants you bad. Let's get some buck wildin' on." She said it just about like she meant it.

Ian was still stretched out where he had left himself, on and with a throatful of the manure pile. The only changes of significance were that he was substantially more dead than previously, and that Chad was now present to view the body along with his assistants Marcus—the assistant who had phoned up with the dead-Ian news—and Jay, the other assistant. Chad referred to them, respectively, as the black one and the cherubic one: cherubic in body and reddish-cherubic in face. Usually Chad substituted the word "cherubic" with "fat."

Early on, when Chad lay around jerking off to fantasies about his big-time Hollywood-agent career, he never envisioned himself with a male assistant, let alone two of them. Traditionally male underlings were reserved for females and gay males. What real man would ever have anything other than a chick taking his dictation? But in the PCified world Chad found himself living in, having a couple of guys working for him was a safe bet. All it took was one duty-bug in a skirt conjuring up a story involving some dirty joke, salacious look, or untoward move, then running down the halls of the company screaming like a bitch who ended up on the bad end of a back-alley gang bang, for all of Chad's career dreams to come crashing down around him.

Worse, all it took was one femme assistant to get past her shock and over her fear of being blackballed from Hollywood forever and report one of Chad's actual dirty jokes, salacious looks, or untoward moves for Chad to get kicked to the Wilshire curb. So a couple of boys in the outer office it was.

Chad made a quiet sound, a wisp of breath hiccuped from him as if his body was working its way up to the release of his sorrow. "Ian . . . Ian, Ian . . ." The mantra, then came the grief. It came and came hard, but it was not for Ian. The sorrow Chad felt was for himself. For Ian there was only rage.

"You stupid son of a bitch! You had to die!"

Jay shuffled nervously. Marcus just stood.

Down to the body, grabbing it by its tangle of hair, Chad yanked up the head. Air was expelled from its chest, clearing the lungs of a good portion of the fertilizer that filled them. Again with the yelling: "You had to fucking die, didn't you?"

"Time to check out, it's time to check out." Hands folded before him, head down slightly, Marcus was a preacher delivering a sermon of the obvious.

Chad spewed: "It was not time for Ian to check out!" Chad dropped Ian's head. More manure dribbled from the mouth. "Not when Will of Instinct owed the label another album! They were supposed to put out one more album. We had a contract, for Christ's sake. We had a contract and this little fuck broke it." Chad gave a kick to the body, as if, despite its shot-off foot, the razors of glass stuck in its back, the fall that forced it full of processed shit, the body hadn't done its fair share of suffering in passing and was now taking collection on the balance.

Jay kept up his shuffling. Stared down intently at his feet to make certain they did the job correctly. "Well, Will of Instinct can still put out a new—"

"Will of Instinct!? That's Will of Instinct right there, laying face-down in a pile of crap." Chad, for the record, indicated he was talking about Ian with another swipe of his foot.

This morning, in Los Angeles, there was a whole lot of dead-body-kicking going on.

Chad: "He wrote the songs, he sang the songs . . . Nobody gives a good goddamn about the rest of those long-haired faggots."

A mild spike from Jay, a little body jerk, before he went back to the studious business of shuffling some more.

Chad, to the body: "One fucking album, then for all I care they could find you buck naked in a ditch with a needle in your arm."

Hands still folded, head still bowed, Marcus asked: "What do you want us to do?"

"What?" Chad asked back. He was looking at Ian, but thinking of creative financing.

"About Ian; what do you want us to do? Call the cops?"

"Screw the cops. Call the papers. Call *Entertainment Weekly*. At least let's try to sell the shit that's already in the stores." Chad shook his head at the lifeless sprawl. "One album. Selfish bastard."

Unaware of himself, Chad wandered into Ian's house.

Jay quit his shuffling. "That was . . . Okay, he's upset, but that kind of language . . ."

"Something about your star act offing himself does that to a man."

"I understand that. Nobody's happy when their act dies—"

Marcus raised his head for the first time; his hands unfolded themselves and one extended.

Jay dug in his pocket, gave over his StarTAC. "I'm not thrilled Ian's dead either, you know, but that doesn't give him the right to say—"

"To say what?" Marcus tossed off, uninterested and otherwise occupied trying to recall a phone number. He remembered. He dialed.

"He just . . . I mean, I know he's upset. . . ." Jay driveled his words, trailed off into silence, picked up his shuffling at the exact point he left off.

On the other end of a cell line the party Marcus was calling picked up.

"Yeah, hello, let me have Features. . . . Your damn cover story, that's what it's regarding."


Inside Ian's house Chad wandered. He looked at, without really seeing, the ornate fixtures, the art. All there was, everywhere he gazed, were things. So many things. Very expensive things. Why in the hell would Ian want to cut out when his life brimmed until it sloshed with so much stuff? As much stuff as Chad could ever conceive. And not just monetary things. Sure, Ian had durable goods by the busload, but he had the other stuff too. The unseen things that permeated the house with a thick aroma: the envy of people, the love of masses, and the lust of women. Most importantly that. The endless variety of female delicti—mouth, ass, vagina—presented, given, gladly handed over in an equally endless march of shape, size, variety, and color. Ian had a stew of fame and notoriety to chow on day in and day out, but it did not satiate. It hadn't been enough for him. What does a man need to fill himself? What more did this man need that he didn't have?

Or was it something else? A concept crawled spiderlike through Chad's mind in the shadow of incomprehension. Maybe it wasn't that Ian wasn't full up. Maybe he was too full. Maybe he had completed himself to the point life was no longer worth, or in need of, living.

But if it ain't fame and it ain't money and it ain't women, then what is it that completes a man?

Across the room: a table. A space on the table. An emptiness that echoed of past occupation, a vacancy where unknown to Chad a DAT player had but hours ago sat.

And the void sang a siren's song that called Chad, gravitated him toward it.

From underfoot a sound: a light crunch. A knee jerk brought Chad's foot up and the same reaction brought his head down. From the floor he picked up a name tag. 24/7 Mart, it said. Beneath that: Paris.

## INT. VIDEO STORE—MORNING

The girl behind the counter was nineteen and white trash distilled to its purest form: uncontaminated, unaffected, undetrashified by the many and various, the endless variety of ethnicities in the city she'd migrated to—the city of Los Angeles—from whatever Wal★Mart-ized portion of lower Middle America she once called home. The girl was white trash by virtue of the pumps she wore with her Levi's and the halter top that drooped from her shoulders, exposing creamy pink afraid-of-the-sun flesh. She was white trash because of her hair—dirty blond despite its bleaching—which had been teased and permed, blown out and curled. . . . It had been everything except properly introduced to a comb, or at least to a comb that was anything like familiar with current hairstyles.

The store was open but empty. Too early in the day for anyone to be renting videos. The girl filled her time thumbing through a Hollywood fluff rag, not bothering with the simple-worded articles, but lingering in rapture over all the pictures of beautiful movie-star people hanging out in beautiful movie-star places doing nothing more significant than looking good. Manufactured glamour shots were just about as heavy-duty a concept as this chick could handle. All the more she'd ever aspire to.

Pure. White. Trash.

In fact, the only matter of substance that ever complicated her uncomplicated white-trash mind was where to put her chewing gum while she fucked. At the moment not even that germ of a thought was present.

Enter Paris.

"Nickel around?" he asked.

The girl didn't look up. She yelled to a room in the back of the store hidden, not much and not well, behind curtains. "Nickel, Paris's here."

"He alone?" Nickel's bodiless voice questioned.

This time the girl looked up, lifted her head. Lead it was made of, the way the effort seemed. A tired gaze at Paris. Her head back down. "Yeah," she hollered.

Nickel: "Send him back."

"Go on back."

"Thanks."

Paris went off to find the man behind the curtain.

In the back of the store was a room. In the room were rows of metal shelves. On the shelves were VCRs. Hooked up to each VCR—one next to another, forming an electric wall of moving images—were dozens of televisions playing the same grainy, shaky, more-than-slightly-out-of-focus picture.

At a table was a man. The man was Nickel. Nickel was kind of short and pretty much middle-aged in appearance. He might have been younger, but he was balding and overweight and it was kinder to think of him as a typical middle-aged guy rather than a younger guy who didn't look so good. At his table Nickel was very diligently affixing labels—Xeroxed-down one sheets—to cassette boxes. He looked like Baldy, the pituitary-impaired elf, doing chores for Santa.

Paris said: "Hey, Nickel."

Nickel said: "Hey, man." A nod of his head toward the electric wall. "Just running off some new Spielbergs."

"How'd you get that? It's still in the theaters."

"Sent a kid in with a camcorder. Taped it off the screen."

"Off the screen?"

"Yeah. Except for when the kid laughs and jiggles the camera it ain't too bad."

"It looks like shit," Paris differed.

Nickel was the kind of guy where there was only a thimbleful of things he was defensive about. When you're overweight, balding, and spend your time in a cathode-lit backroom you're not much in a position to take life too personal. But this, what Nickel referred to as his trade, what the world called bootlegging, was his little illegal corner of the Empire Entertainment. He took his corner very seriously.

"Hey," Nickel growled, angry displeasure squeezing out through narrow eyes. He stood for effect, but coming off the stool to his feet only made him shorter. "You want it on DVD with THX surround sound, you can wait eighteen months and pay thirty bucks. You want it first, you want it fast, you come to me." He slapped another miniature one sheet crookedly onto a video box. "Now, what can I do you for? Want Coppola's new flick?" Nickel jerked his head at some more TVs that were copying images of fuzzy blobs doing something up on the silver screen.

"No," Paris said. "No, I was looking to make a little cash."

"You and the world, baby. What's the plan this week?"

"A tape. Can you move it for me?"

"What you got?"

"It's not video. Audio."

"Music?" Nickel scratched at his face, fingernails catching on his acne scars. When you got it bad in the looks department, you got it bad all the way. "I don't bootleg tunes much anymore, but I could probably get it out. Anything good?"

"Ian Jermaine. That guy from Wish of Instant . . . whatever."

Nickel exhaled himself a scoffing laugh. "Oh, man. You crawling out of the woodwork with the rest of the slugs?"

"The rest . . . ?" Paris wasn't quite following.

"Everybody's going to be trying to pass that shit off now. What do you got, a concert or something?"

"No, it's . . . Nobody's ever heard this—"

"What?"

"What do you mean, crawling out of the—"

"Nobody's ever heard what?"

Paris and Nickel locked in a French kiss of miscommunication, transmitting confusion back and forth.

Paris said: "I just figured it might be worth something. We copy up a few tapes, get it sold—"

"Wait! What are you talking about, what you said before—nobody's heard this?"

It's new stuff. I got a new tape."

"New—" Nickel sunk a little deeper into noncomprehension.

"Yeah. New. He just made it. Like I said, nobody's heard it before. I figure, we bootleg it, we can make a few hundred."

A video box, the tiny one sheet meant to adorn it, seconds ago slipped from Nickel's hand, his fingers having lost their grip, lost all normal sensation. Nickel had become preoccupied with a new and stronger feeling, one that came around with the stink of money. It was the tactile sense of greed.

"A few hun . . ." Nickel flustered out. "You're shitting me, right?"

"You don't think we can get that much?"

A beat. Disbelief at what he was hearing sat Nickel down. He got himself together for some explaining. "What are you doing, hibernating? You hiding out somewhere? He's dead."

"Wha . . . ?"

"Ian Jermaine is dead."

The news flash hit like a wife beater and staggered Paris just the same. "Ian—"

"Is dead. Yeah, you're getting it. Dead and gone. He killed himself."

"Ki . . . When?"

"I don't know."

"What time?"

"I don't know. What did I say? I said I don't know. It was just on the news. Jumped into a pile of shit or something. Weird."

"I didn't think he'd really . . . Jesus," Paris gasped.

"Jesus two times. Guy like that takes himself out, he isn't just another stiff, he's pure legend, know what I'm saying? Hendrix and Morrison and Joplin. Christ, dying was the best thing that ever happened to John Denver.

"And you've got Ian Jermaine's music, you got something no one's heard, and you want to know if you can make a few hundred? Try it again. Try millions."

In breathless repetition: "Millions . . ."

Nickel looked at Paris. Nickel looked at him, and as he did, the shadow of money lust eclipsing his face, Nickel changed. Slightly and subtly, barely to the naked eye, he morphed from being just a guy into a guy who wanted something from another guy and wanted it with a voracity. It was an alteration you had to look for carefully, but once found, you knew was there. The change was hardly at all, but total and complete. Just that little, and just that much.

The new Nickel asked: "Where you got this tape?"

The new Nickel took a step toward Paris. A moment ago it would have been a step taken, just a step, and nothing more than that. But in the moment that had passed, the moment in which Nickel had become as unrecognizable as he was familiar, his soul alien-snatched and avarice-replaced B-movie style, the step he took was more like a haunting, threatening creep.

Paris matched Nickel's move, but backward toward the door: "I . . . I don't."

"You said—"

"I've got . . . I know someone who could get it. Let me talk to him."

"Wait a minute, man!"

"I'm just going to talk to him."

Paris stumbled, made gimp by the disjuncture of thought and action. His mind was pondering a DAT and a dead Ian and a word Nickel had said: "millions." His body was concentrating on getting the hell out of the store. The result was a herky-jerky dance by Paris from the backroom into the main room, a shelf knocked over along the way. Bootlegs of a shitty Hollywood movie—*another* shitty Hollywood movie—skittered across the floor.

Nickel, his voice, chased Paris as he bolted outside and up the street: "Paris . . . Paris!" Then, knowing what he'd just lost: "Damn!"

Through all of that—Nickel with his yelling and Paris with his knocking things over—only once did the white-trash girl with the perpetually dirty-blond hair look up from her magazine. A beat later she went right back to the hearty business of doing nothing more than looking at alllll those pretty pictures.

Pushing mid-morning.

The sun was heading into round two of its daily struggle with the smog. Losing. Getting the crap kicked out of it. Getting beat down behind gray soot drapes that hung over the city and greenhoused it. It was going to be hot downtown. It was going to be killer in the Valley.

That's what the organism LA, 8.7 million strong, was gearing up for: The heat, how to deal with the heat, how to survive the heat until sundown, how to sleep through the hot night. How to handle the heat all over again tomorrow. What the organism LA wasn't much thinking about was abandoned cars under overpasses, or a particular car under a particular overpass Alf's body was half in, half out of.

Omar and Kenny were thinking about it—the car, Alf's body. Its blood coagulated so that even it no longer moved and flowed in ersatz life.

"Dat's the ride," Kenny talking, "huh? Like Martin described."

Omar nodded. "Held on just long enough to drop dime. One time in his life he ever toughed anything out." Nodding at the Continental: "Didn't get very far."

Omar walked to the body, gave it a close visual inspection. He knew well of the dead, having early on taken the clinic on shot-up bodies LA gives away daily to its urban youth. "Looks like they got him."

"So muthafuckin' what?" Kenny talked loud and tough. He talked loud and tough when he was away from Daymond, and even more so when he was around Omar. Omar was quiet and smart. He had stayed in school past the tenth grade. For around the way, he was a goddamn genius. Kenny couldn't compete with quiet and smart. He couldn't compete with Omar's non-fucked-up-by-a-bullet-to-the-throat voice either. All he could do was make a lot of noise and be hardass about it so no one would correct him on his dumbness. "He kilt two a Daymond's boys, his cuz, and ran off with Daymond's shit. So what if they got him?"

"All I'm saying is they got him."

A *phhhht* sound and a wave of his hand to dismiss Omar's logicalizing. "They got his ass, but they didn't kill him. Not right off. Don't mean shit if they don't kill somebody. This ain't no muthafuckin' game of tag 'n' shit. We ain't in the gettin'-muthafuckas business, we in the gettin'-muthafuckas-dead business."

"They couldn't've known they were gonna get hit. That was a last-minute drop. Whoever jacked Martin and them was small-time, nickel-and-dime—trying to take Martin for whatever little bit he was holdin'. Bet they don't even know what they got."

"That ain't the point. Them muthafuckas Daymond sent fucked up. You droppin' drugs from yo boss ta one of his dealers, you best be expectin' shit, have yo gats ready ta get ta cappin'." Omar lectured like he was giving a weekend seminar at the Ramada on gang-banging. Using his patented loud-and-tough style, he lectured more. "Dat's yo muthafuckin' job: protect da muthafuckin' drugs. You gotta be expectin' shit. Any muthafucka on da street can walk around not expectin' shit. What we do, shit got ta be expected."

Omar continued his analysis of the crime scene, surveying the car.

"Bled all up in the backseat. Somebody drove him here."

"Then somebody be a dead muthafucka. Stolt Daymond's shit. Daymond gonna have a serious mad on."

Getting all quiet and solemn, Omar looked around, saw the graffitied walls of the underpass. The abandoned cars. The dead dog and its convention of flies. He closed his eyes, and other things became apparent to him. "Trouble's coming, bro. It's all around. I can smell it like a summer storm. Yeah. Trouble's coming . . . and it's going to rain vengeance."

Kenny, loud, tough: "Whatever."

The early edition of the LA *Times* was late enough that it had a piece on the short life, questionable significance, and bizarre death of Ian Jermaine. Paris got himself a copy, quarter tossed to the newsy who worked the stand along Cahuenga.

Paris whipped through the article, his brain feeding only on the words it needed: Dead. Manure. Agent. Chad Bayless. Continental Talent Agency. After that the paper wasn't good for nothing but tossing.

Ideas, big ideas, thrashed in Paris's puddle of a mind. Ideas born of one word from Nickel: "millions." Driven by the word, his every other instinct faded away until one remained: Do this. Do this for *her.*

End of the street: a pay phone. Paris went for it, digging change from his pocket.

Chad's teeth worked at a thumbnail. Bit it, whittled it, shaped it in a thoughtless way. He had canceled all meetings and shunned the inevitable calls from *Variety* and the *Reporter* so that he could spend the morning with himself. Ten minutes of his own company reminded Chad he was the last person in the world he wanted to be alone with. Eleven minutes into his retreat he found out that the thumbnail thing was just enough activity to keep him from going completely bonkers.

The intercom buzzed police-siren-loud and Chad gave a frightened start same as if it was. Smacking at the phone with his fist, the whole plastic unit skipped across his desk like a slapped puppy.

"Chad . . . ?" His secretary, Jen; her voice coming through the speaker.

"What?"

"Chad?"

Chad's fingers punched futilely at the buttons on the phone, trying to make the intercom work. Mind numb, he was useless with himself: a retard trying to type Shakespeare. "What?"

"Hello . . . ? Chad . . . ?"

Yelling: "What!" Screaming: "What!"

Jen heard him. Through the door, not through the phone.
". . . I . . . There's a Paris on two-three for you."

"Paris? Paris who?"

"He didn't give a last name. He told me to tell you he has the last
of Ian. Doesn't that seem an odd thing to say—the last of Ian? I'll tell
you what I think. You want to know what I think. . . ."

Jen went on with theories about how Paris probably worked for
the *Globe,* or the *Star,* or worse yet *People* magazine, and was trying to trick
Chad into an interview. Maybe, though, she considered because of this
"last of Ian" remark, Paris might be either an obsessed fan or Ian's gay
lover because she was always convinced that Ian was gay regardless of
the statutory-rape charges that were . . .

Chad heard zero of that. His secretary was just verbal Muzak.
Paris, he mouthed. He mouthed it again. Paris.

Realization hit. Hands all over himself. The name tag. Found it. The
pin bit into his finger as he pulled it from a pocket. The name: Paris.

"Put him through."

"What . . . ? Hello . . . ?"

"Put him through the goddamn phone!"

That Jen got.

"Hello . . . ?" a voice came across the speaker, male this time.

Chad fumbled up the receiver. "Hello?"

"You Chad Bayless?"

"Yes. And you're Paris."

"Yeah."

Some quiet. Some labored and nervous breathing got mixed
together over fiber optics.

Across the way from Paris, on the other side of the street, a guy
and a woman were talking. Just standing, talking. Then the guy pulled a
gun from his pocket. Real casually he pulled it out, showed it to the
woman no different than if he were showing her a watch on a fob. He
didn't do anything with it except show it to her, and Paris couldn't tell
if he was showing it to her to scare the woman, impress her. Maybe he
was just showing it to her to show it to her, showing it to her as if to
say: Hey, you know how everyone else in the city has a piece? I got one

too. After that the guy put the gun back in his pocket, and him and the woman walked on.

Chad asked: "How are you, Paris?"

". . . Okay."

"Good. That's good."

Sweat sandpaper-scraped its way down Chad's temple and, simultaneously across town, didn't flow much easier over Paris's flesh. At this moment, in the entire world, were there two more desperate men, or would a more desperate man already be watching the hammer fall on the gun in his mouth?

"Well, Paris, is there something you'd like to talk about, or did you just want to breathe at me?" Chad was getting his bullshit cool back. He had the advantage: he knew how to work a phone. It's what being an agent was all about. That and all the back-stabbing and ass-fucking 10 percent could buy. Play things nice and easy. See what the boy's got to say, Chad thought—the first clear one he'd had in a while. See what this Paris is all about.

"I've got the last of Ian." Paris talked like words were new to him, halting and unsure.

"That's what you told my secretary. The last of Ian. What does that mean?"

"I've got his last tape. I've got the last songs he ever sung."

"What do you mean, his last—"

Riding on a lava of frustration: "What are you, stupid? He's dead, man, and I've got the last stuff he ever did."

"The last songs Ian Jermaine ever recorded are on sale at Tower Records. I don't know who you think you're scamming—"

To the mouthpiece of the phone Paris put the DAT machine. The play button, depressed.

After a short while Paris turned the tape off again.

In the wake of the music, against himself, against his own inability to articulate the experience, Chad managed one word: "Wow . . ."

It was Ian. It was his music and more. It was glory. It was the sound the heavenly host made with nothing more than the noneffort of opening their mouths. It was all that, and, Chad knew, with a short-form video running in heavy rotation on MTV it would ship at nearly four million units in its first pressing.

"W-where did you g-get—"

"I got it."

"WHERE DID YOU—"

"I got it, okay?"

Chad's bullshit cool was burned up, which is what happens to bullshit cool when things get complicated. It was Paris, as much as anybody, who was handling business now.

"I got the tape. That's all you need to know."

"Yeah, all right, fine. You got it." More sweat from Chad. It ran faster over his face, cut deeper. He talked things up as sweet as he could. We're all friends here, his tone said. So let's just be reasonable, and don't nobody panic.

His thoughts got sharp with himself: Especially you, Bayless. Don't panic!

As nonpanicky as possible: "And . . . and I'm glad that you called me, Paris. It's a good thing that you called. Now, why don't you just bring the tape in here to my office and give it to me and maybe . . . How about for being such a good guy we can get you a few CDs. Would you like that, Paris? Would you like some CDs?" Keep it together, Chad baby. Keep it all together. "Just a way of saying thank you. Thank you for being on the ball."

Paris was a man without a plan. The tape he'd stumbled into possessing, and having sense enough to call the agent of the dead guy he'd gotten it from is where what little smarts he had quit him. From there forward Paris was doing just-in-time manufacturing of ideas only milliseconds before they spilled from his mouth.

"I want . . . I want a million dollars." That was a good number, right? Nice and round and big.

"Excuse me?"

"For the tape. I want a million dollars."

"You're out of your mind."

"It's worth that much."

"A million doll—"

"It's worth more than that." And it probably was. He should've done his strategizing before he dialed up Chad, Paris thought. He should've asked for more dough.

"So what how much it's worth? You think I've got a bucket of cash sitting around here?"

Maybe. Maybe not. Didn't matter to Paris. "I want my money."

"I don't have a million dollars!" Chad banshee-screamed.

Paris just got high off of it—making some dude he didn't know crazy. It was power he was feeling. First taste's free.

Chad: "Do you know what you're asking? That's not possible, okay? A million dollars is not possible. Now, let's just be cool and talk."

"There's nothing to talk about."

"Where am I supposed to get that kind of money? You know so much, where?"

Paris didn't know where, but he knew Chad could get it. He read magazines, watched the infotainment shows. They were always going on about rock stars and record guys, and how they got this and that—drugs and chicks and bowls of M&Ms with all the yellow ones taken out. How they were always living fast and high and hard, money flowing like blood from a bullet-shot heart.

A million dollars?

That was change. That was the dough they used to tip the bathroom attendant or last night's whore.

A million dollars?

That was nothing for a tape from a freshly dead legend, and a good tape at that. Chad didn't know how easy he was getting let off.

Paris: "Where you get it from's not my problem. All I know is, I don't get the million, you don't get the tape. And cash, too. No check bullshit. Whaddaya say?"

Time was audible, it clicked heavy in its passing—seconds a metronome for Chad to build up his rhythm before he cut loose furious to the beat.

"What do I say? I say you're a little cocksucking son of a bitch, that's what I say. Think you can call me up and squeeze me for cash, is that what you think?"

The rage was real, but driven by impotence. A man slapping a woman 'cause he can't stay hard.

Slapping on: "You don't know who you're dealing with." Spittle flew from Chad's mouth and lodged in the receiver. "I'll cut your little son-of-a-bitch heart out and fuck you in the hole. So you listen to me, you shit. I'm going to get my tape. I'm going to get you, I'm going to get my tape, then I'm going to put my foot on your throat and twist. You hear that, you hear that sound? That's your neck snapping!"

Sucking hard on the pipe of control: "Guess you're going to need some time to think about this. I'll be in touch."

Paris hung up the phone. The world was a better place, looked better from his platform of mastery. From way up there Paris got a real nice view of the people-ants and duty-bugs, the very things both moments and a lifetime ago he used to be himself: an insignificant mite that scurried from dropping to dropping, surviving on the scraps left by the movers and the shakers, the doers and high livers, the people who see life and grab onto it until fingers strike bone. The people who get shit done.

A phone call.

Just one phone call.

And now Paris was one of them. Almost. Would be with the cash he was about to collect. Paris would be a million dollars' worth of somebody.

How do you like that? he said to Ian, said in a spiteful prayer that he willed out through time and space and dimension to wherever it was grungy white guys who had suicided themselves went. How do you like that? You're dead in a heap of crap, and I'm here. Here with your music that I never gave a damn about before, and it's going to do things for me. Put a wad in my pocket, make me a man. It's going to buy her back. Who's the loser now? Paris prayed.

Fuck you, was his amen.


The click, the dial tone: a train wreck in Chad's ear. Then there was nothing. Then fear and panic and more fumbling at the phone.

"Marcus, Jay, get in here!"

Fifteen, twenty-five seconds later the pair walked in, and it was the longest fifteen or twenty-five seconds Chad ever had to endure.

"What's up? You don't look so good," Marcus noted, smooth and understated, opposite Chad's sweats and shakes. So smooth he should have been doing a malt-liquor ad. "Can't let the job get to you like that."

Chad got up enough muscle control to flick the name tag to Jay. "Find this guy."

"Paris? Who is he?"

"He's a guy I want you to find, that's who he is."

"New discovery, that it?"

Jay's shrill questions and shriller voice weren't doing anything for Chad's sweating and shaking but making them worse.

"What he is, is a little cocksucker who stole a tape of Ian. It's my tape. I want my fucking tape!"

"And is that," Marcus asked "where we're supposed to find him? In the Yellow Pages under 'cocksucker'?"

Tightening and twisting, Chad was a guy being introduced to the wonderful world of palsy. "Jesus . . . Jesus, is it that hard? Is it that hard to see? You go to every 24/7 Mart in the city until you find a guy who works there named Paris. That's what you do."

"Every 24/7 Mart?" Jay stressing *every.*

"How many Parises work at 24/7 Marts?" Slipping into a delirium: "Simple . . . It's so very, very simple."

"And when we find this cat, then what?"

"Bring him to me. Just . . . get his ass here." Fists pressed to his temples, Chad tried to squelch the mounting agony. "Oh, God, you make me hurt."

Marcus and Jay took that as their command. They went for the door.

Chad, dire: "Marcus!"

Marcus turned to see Chad's weak, trembling, whiter-than-usual hand stretched toward him.

"Don't fail me, Marcus. Please don't fail me."


Marcus and Jay elevatored it down to the parking garage.

Jay, with an overdone shiver: "Well, someone woke up and took a creepy pill this morning."

A Mexican guy in a red vest brought around Marcus's Audi. An A4.

Better than a Beamer, thousands less. Marcus was smart like that. Chad's two lackeys got in the car and went 24/7 Mart–hunting.

Chad sat in his office, door locked, the upper half of his body splayed over his desk, head pressed to the wood so that his forehead began to hydroplane on the film of sweat that leaked from his pores. "I'm not well," he wept. "I'm not well."

"No, Chad, you're not," Angela responded.

Without announcement, without ado, Angela was, as she was so often, there for Chad exactly when he needed her with severity.

Angela was the most beautiful woman Chad could have ever envisioned. Angela was black. Not lightly black, or black by definition alone. She was black as an endless night, as dark as an abyss. So much so as to be nearly reflective, as if her skin repelled everything else that was not already of her.

Angela was the most physically perfect woman Chad could have ever envisioned. Her body without defect, evident even beneath the smart business suit and skirt—white contrasting her black—she wore. And she wore the suit tight. Tight enough to hug the muscles that contoured her frame. Arms that were defined. Breasts that stood, not sagged. Elliptical thighs and thick calves, those draped in stockings— white as the rest of her suit—which Chad knew ended just below her crotch, just below the heart of her womanness. And above the white stockings and under that white suit of hers? Chad was sure, Chad imagined at least, Angela wore matching bra and panties that were just as white and two times as sexy.

The thought of her made Chad weak.

Weaker.

Chad said to her: "Gotta get myself together, Angela. Will you . . . will you make me feel better?"

"Don't I always?" Her voice was a deep whisper. Strip away the sexiness and she almost sounded like a man just waking up.

"Why am I so sick?"

Her black hand to his chest. It rubbed it a little. It massaged it some. "It's your heart. It's harsh, cold, and full of disease."

Chad, pathetic: ". . . It's my heart. It's because I love you."

This made her laugh—the truth and Chad's inability to see it. "You don't love me. You love what I give you."

"It's you I love." His plea begged for belief.

Angela knew better. She spoke as Chad's conscience. "You love my touch. You love the way it makes you feel." Hands to his hair, her fingers worked his scalp. "You love it so much you would do anything to have it. You have lied, you have cheated, and you have stolen for it."

"For you. It was for you. . . ."

"How much have you embezzled from the company to pay for it?"

How much? Chad thought of all the Will of Instinct royalty checks he'd signed over to himself, and all the faked Will of Instinct advances he'd charged against the band to cover his sleight of hand so neither the band nor the agency knew they were being scammed. Never the big checks. Small amounts. Almost undetectable sums. A few hundred bucks here, another couple there. All lost in the millions that flood from a band like Will of Instinct. But skimmed regularly, month after month, one year into another, all together it added up to . . .

"A few hundred . . . thousand. . . . More."

"More than three hundred thousand dollars." The number amused her. "You do love me."

Angela pointed to Chad's desk.

Chad looked.

On the blotter, between the keys to his Beamer and a bottle of Evian Natural Spring Water from the French Alps, was a polished mirror, a stainless-steel razor, and a packet of fine powdered cocaine.

Just looking at the three, Chad was a man swept up in the rapids of pre-orgasm. Coke wasn't crystal-meth chic or marijuana timeless, but, like the first '64-and-a-half Mustang to roll off the line, for Chad it was pure classic.

To Angela, through heaved breaths: "I need you."

She was unimpressed by his desire. "You needed Ian. You needed him to put out a new record. You needed the money it would bring in to replace what you stole."

Her voice accused without compassion. A caliginous, all-seeing, all-knowing seraph.

The combo weight of fact and revelation crushed Chad, made his body buckle and his eyes water. "Oh, God. I was going to give it back." The words drooled out of his mouth. "I swear I was."

"And now you need the tape. Without the tape you're nothing, and then you're finished."

"No . . . no . . ."

Angela fingerpainted cocaine onto the mirror. "It's only a matter of time before they find out what you've done."

"You would still come to me." He salivated for the dope. "Even . . . even if I had nothing, wouldn't you still come to me?"

The razor. The cocaine got hacked up into neat little rowlets. "Oh, Chad. Let's not think of such terrible things."

"I'm sick." Tears filled his voice. "So sick."

"Here, baby. Let me make it all better."

Angela's fingers coiled Chad's hair, directed his head down to the mirror. Chad handled things from there. A healthy sniff. The coke married his physiology, renewed him with vigor, strength, confidence, and other imitations of vitality.

"I love you, Angela."

"Love me all you want . . . as long as you pay cash."

*f*rom Ogden Street, in the traditionally Jewish Fairfax district, you could see Television City—the CBS complex where CBS taped a lot of the CBS shows. You could quite literally see success and glamour and all the other trappings of showbiz.

That view, that angle of Television City, from Ogden, from his apartment, was as close as Paris ever came to any of them.

Until last night.

Until he gave a ride to a grungy white guy who turned out to be a big-ass rock star. Until he stole some music from the big-ass rock star. Until that big-ass rock star got his self dead. On and on, domino-effecting like that, until this very moment.

His apartment, the one he shared with Buddy, like every other apartment on the street and in the neighborhood, was a quadplex or whatever the hell you would call it. It's what would have made for a decent house, split up into what were four shitty units.

Inside. Paris went to the fridge and downed what was left of a flat A&W root beer he'd been nursing since the night before. It struck Paris that now, by default, A&W root beer was his celebratory drink. It was the libation that accompanied him from nothing to something. In the future, he thought on, whenever there were good times—and believe it, brother, there would be a boatload of those—they too would be washed down with A&W. And no trying to stretch each can. It started to go flat, it started to go warm . . . hell, if it was too far away to reach for—another can would get popped open just like *that*.

Yeah. It's good to be king.

And then Paris thought of *her*. Thought of her *again*. How could he not? In the end it all came back to her. The tape, the money, the things a million dollars can do . . . How would she react to that? Breath hot? Nipples hard?

The root beer can trembled. Paris's shaky hand made it tremble. Even now, even on the edge of everything he had ever wanted, she could still do that to him.

The bedroom. Paris dug under his bed—his futon with a busted wood frame—yanked out a duffel, put the DAT inside. Slid the bag back where it came from. Good as any place to hide it. No sense dragging the tape around town, and he had to go out.

He had to go see her.

Daymond hadn't so much as set one black foot outside his crib since he'd rolled in at all hours of the morning, and already he and his kingdom of drugs were worth sixteen thousand dollars more than the day before. People in LA wanted to get high that bad. But even the extra money swelling his pockets didn't do much to quash the mad he had on for whoever had stolt his shit and kilt his cuz. And it sure didn't do anything to keep him from getting all kinds of crazy with Kenny and Omar for not finding who had done the stealin' and the killin'.

"What da fuck, muthafucka?" Daymond screamed at his boys and the two new girls he'd swapped out for the other ones.

Playaz gotsta keep da pussy fresh.

Omar played with the gold ring on his little finger. Omar dug gold. He liked to own gold. All his rings, four on his fingers and one in each of his ears, were gold. His watch, a Movado, was heavy on the gold too. Dig his smile: a gold-capped tooth. His suit, that was also gold. Gold in color at least. Most people would say that Omar was being too flashy, that he was being too showy of a nigga. Far as Omar was concerned, muthafuckin' right he was being showy, but ain't no such thing as too. What was the alternative, to be like his partner, Kenny, who, even with all his ducats, still rolled in hooded sweatsuits with one pant leg pushed up past the calf? Omar shook his head to himself: you can take a nigga out of the ghetto, but he still ain't nothing but a nigga.

"You gotta explain dat shit ta me," Daymond went on. "How's some muthafuckin' white boy gonna roll up inta my place 'n' steal my shit?"

Omar: "Got lucky."

Daymond: "Sheiiit!"

"No way he could have knowed you was moving pure horse. Hell, I bet he don't even know how much the shit he got's worth."

"Fuck dat," Daymond spat. "I don't give a fuck how much it worth! You think I give a fuck 'bout money? You know how fuckin' much money means ta me?"

Hand to a desk drawer. A brick of cash got whipped out. Hundreds, with no more fanfare than if bricks of hundreds were sitting in every desk in America. Daymond tore the bills. Ripped 'em. Shredded 'em. Was it a thousand, two thousand, five . . . ? Wasn't nothing now but a fistful of paper he slung at Omar, at Kenny. Greenback ash that rained to their feet after an eruption.

"Dat's," Daymond, talking about the cash, said, "how fuckin' much money means ta me. What I give a fuck about is some punk playin' me."

"At least they got him," Omar pointed out.

"Ain't about gettin' muthafuckas. It about gettin' muthafuckas dead."

Kenny to Omar, wise-ass: "Told you."

Daymond didn't hear the crack, too busy strategizing on how to handle his business. "This other one, da one dat did da drivin'. You find him. You find his bitch ass and you find my shit."

Kenny: "Big city, man."

"You got da license off his car. Hunt the muthafucka down. Damn, bitch. Git off yo lazy nigga ass and do work."

Pep talks like that is what learnt Kenny to keep his mouth shut in the first place.

"Hell, fuck y'all. Git them Nix niggas, Ty 'n' Sunder. Set them two boys on—" A thought came to Daymond. "No. Damn that. You git Brice. You put Brice on this punk's ass."

Omar, Kenny—they both got looks that could only be shared by two guys who just had hot coals duct-taped to their gonads.

Kenny, making sure—making very sure. ". . . Brice?"

"Muthafucka, wha-did-I jus' say?"

Kenny got all quiet, as if someone might listen and hear and run and tattle. "Brice is crazy."

"No shit, Brice be crazy. Muthafucka plays me, you best believe I'm gonna introduce him to a world of pain. Now do it. The only thing I'm trying ta hear from you is that some punk-ass white boy is dead, 'n' Brice be the one that got him there."

Omar and Kenny left.

Once they were away from Daymond, away from the possibility of getting their asses chewed for talking back, Kenny was all: "This is messed up. I ain't tryin' to deal with Brice nohow. You do the talkin'."

"Poor bastard." Omar was lamenting the soon-to-be-dead driver in the steal-drugs-from-Daymond misadventure. "Won't even know what hit him."

"Oh, he'll know. Muthafucka's gonna have a long-ass time to think about it before he goes cold."

*B*uddy. Typhoon-hard he blasted into the apartment, his shock two-to-one mixed with panic.

"Paris!" he called out, having settled on the fact—during the long, frenzied, dreamscape run/walk home—that Paris could help him. Paris could fix things. Paris had the answer. He might not have been the poster boy for success through hard work, but Buddy had to give up that compared to himself Paris was long on genius. Paris had told him not to hang with Alf. Paris had told him Alf wasn't anything but trouble. Paris . . .

"Paris . . . !"

Nothing.

No response, and nothing to do but wander the small space rat-in-maze confused. The shock/panic mixture coursing through him readjusted in favor of panic.

No Paris, no help.

No help, no answers.

No answers, no way out. Sooner or later the cops were going to find the shot-up drug den. Sooner or later the cops were going to find the car and bullet-filled Alf. And it wasn't going to take them any Charlie Chan ching-chong reasoning to trace the car to Buddy. To Buddy, who still had the drugs clutched up tight in his very hand.

Buddy's body did a scared little spastic jig. What did cops throw at you for being involved in drug murders? How many years did you get? The thoughts in his head stole Buddy's equilibrium. What was happening could not be happening. Instead of a drug-money–fueled ascent in status to a place populated with girls and sex and wealth and more sex, his trajectory was carrying him north toward San Quentin, where his days would be spent as a fuck-toy passed among gang-bangers doing hard time or members of the White Aryan Resistance locked up for trying to overthrow the government from the comfort of their trailer parks. That vividly, Buddy saw his future.

He laughed a little to himself. At least he would be having sex. Yeah. Real funny.

"Paris!" he called out, and called out again. And again no one called back.

Work! That's where he had to be: the 24/7 Mart. Buddy had to go find him.

Wait!

Dump the drugs first, then go find him.

The bedroom. Under his bed.

No!

Paris's bed; he should hide them under there. You know, if the cops came, maybe they would . . . Buddy didn't know what they would do, but to his jacked-up mind dumping the drugs under Paris's bed instead of his own seemed like the brainstorm to end all brainstorms.

A duffel. Buddy tossed the brown-wrapped package in and slid the bag back under the bed.

Out the door. 24/7 Mart, here he comes.

Paris would know what to do. Paris would have the answer. Paris would make everything all right.

"We're looking for Paris."

"It's in France."

Third time Jay and Marcus had heard that. Almost the third time. One of the 24/7 Mart managers had quipped, "It's in Germany." Not for nothing was he managing a 24/7 Mart for a living.

Marcus, like he'd done twice previously, elaborated on the question. "We're looking for an employee named Paris."

"What the hell kind of name is Paris?" the manager cracked. "That some kinda pansy name?"

Jay bit at his lip.

"Does Paris," Marcus asked, "work here?"

"Sounds like a pansy name."

The manager was a white guy. White guys didn't like being managers of minimarts. White guys figured if they were managing something it ought to be IBM or Boeing, or at least—at the very least—they ought to be managing a McDonald's in some Orange County tract our-house-looks-like-your-house-looks-like-their-house suburb. Any white guy worth his salt knew minimarts existed to be managed by Middle Easterners, Koreans, the occasional Hispanic, and the even more occasional black. So a white guy working where only color-skinneded people dared tread was not a happy cat.

This guy was not a happy cat.

"Sounds just like some kind of fucking pansy fruit name."

The day wasn't turning out to be any kind of a foot massage for Jay either. Jay came from a showbiz family. Sort of. His father did makeup at one of the local TV stations in San Francisco. His mother . . . Well, for some reason or another his mother had taken off when Jay was still very young. Jay's father had filled in both roles nicely, and Jay didn't much miss or remember his mom. What Jay did remember, even from a very early age, is that he loved Hollywood. He loved movies: the style, the glamour, the oozing Technicolor. Whether it was the spectacle of a big-budget Judy Garland musical, or the somber realism of one of

Barbra Streisand's later efforts, for Jay movies were nothing but special. What other manufactured thing could so touch people—make them laugh or cry or just bust out in song? Jay had come to Los Angeles, to Hollywood, to Tinseltown, wanting, hoping, dreaming of one day working in costume design or hair, or maybe of being a makeup artist just like his father. But, more than anything, he had come to Hollywood wanting, hoping, dreaming of nothing more in the world than to be a part of the wonderful, magical, glorious thing that was movies. The first job he got when he hit town was in the mailroom of an agency. He got moved up to a desk, then he got moved over to be second assistant to Chad Bayless. Now here he was, not doing hair, not doing makeup, just wanting to get an answer about a guy named Paris and move on to the next 24/7 Mart manager dealing with how-the-hell-did-I-end-up-here life issues.

Jay said: "Is that a yes, or a no?"

"That's a fuck no. Ain't no Parises here."

Marcus, Jay made for the door.

The manager grumble-grumbled at their backs, "Waste my time. Didn't even buy shit," and went back to mopping up where the Smoothie machine had run over onto the tile floor.

"**B**H adjacent." "B" is for "Beverly," "H" is for "Hills." It's what LA landlords called their apartment buildings that were anywhere close to the "nine-oh-two-one-oh" vicinity. But all "BH adjacent" meant was you got to pay those Beverly Hills prices without the pleasure of actually living there.

Kaila's pad—*her pad*—was like that, Beverly Hills adjacent. A nice apartment. Nice size. More than she could afford by a little. Not by accident did she live that way, just above her means. It wasn't like she was trying to front, trying to live high for the sake of living high. Ask her about it and she'd tell you how it made her work harder, made her do the extras to get the cash to pay for what she had. Kaila was just that way. She was the kind of chick who could've had a lot of what she wanted on the easy, but what she wanted was to work for what she got.

Swall was the street where Kaila's just-more-than-she-could-afford place was, and Swall, Kaila's place, was where Paris found himself.

He rang the buzzer.

A beat.

"Hello?" Even the bad wiring and cheap, staticky speaker of the intercom couldn't thrash any of the sexy in Kaila's voice .

"It's Paris."

Another beat. A bunch of them. The buzzer buzzed and the lock on the door kicked back. Paris opened up and went in.

Upstairs. Third floor. Kaila's door.

And Paris remembered.

Kaila's face contorted with disgust. The door slamming shut. The words she tattooed on him: "You're a loser!"

But that was before. Before last night, and this morning, and an unbelievable hopscotch of luck and fate and chance. Paris was stepping to her different now. He was stepping to her with all the positive, reinvigorated juice of a dude who just had himself a full and complete million-dollar makeover. Ladies and gentlemen, cats and kittens, please welcome your all-new Paris.

Paris knocked at the door. It opened, and there was Kaila. As many times as he'd seen her, looked at her, viewed her, each time he had the same thought as the first: of all her attributes, her tits were the least of her. To say that little bit was to say a lot. She had great tits. Real and large. Not mutant-large, just large enough to fit with precision comfort into a man's wide and groping hand. Her two beautiful boobs swelled in an upward curve ending in full nipples that always looked erect. In tight clothes they looked like they could just about take your eye out. Still . . .

Her tits were the least of her.

She was a hell of a woman.

Particularly hellacious was her skin. Fine, rich, smooth skin that was even in tone and texture. The kind of skin only the child of a black man and an Asian woman could be born with, and that was the type of child she was.

She was a hell of a woman.

The rest of her just got better. Every miscegenetic mixed-race inch of her. Her eyes, of course. Sharp, narrow, intense black/Asian eyes. Her face: exotic in feature. Her body: shaped, cut, defined like Michelangelo and them had worked on her. Her hair: so rich a mane. So full, as if it too had been blessed with vital muscles as firm and toned as was the rest of her.

Kaila was one hell of a woman.

Paris felt himself shrinking, his newfound monied-up manhood withering in the chick's presence. She burned too bright for any faux self-confidence, for any puddle-deep machismo to long survive.

Kaila went back away from the door, back to whatever it was she was doing before Paris showed up—cleaning, or straightening, or something—seemingly having only enough free time to deliver a scornful look.

"What do you want?" she asked of him but said to a countertop she was wiping down.

Paris came in, closed the door to let her know he'd be hanging for a while. He got a noseful of plumeria. It always smelled like plumeria in Kaila's place. On the balcony was the small plumeria tree. On the mantel was her plumeria-scented candle. She burned plumeria incense and bathed in plumeria body oil. Plumeria wasn't the most popular scent in the world, so whenever Paris sniffed it he always thought of Kaila. Seemed like ever since their breakup he was smelling that shit more and more.

He said: "Hey, baby."

"Don't 'baby' me. What do you want?"

"I want to talk."

Eyes rolling. "Like there's anything else you know how to do."

"I got something."

"Right."

"I'm serious this time, baby."

"Yeah. You're serious. Just like you were serious last time when you were going to get some money together and shoot a movie. When you were going to manage those singers. When you——"

"This time it's different."

A tabletop stain seemed to have particularly caught Kaila's interest. She rubbed at it viciously with paper towels, a sponge, extra-strength Formula 409 cleaner. While doing all that she said: "Sure."

"It really——"

"You writing a script? You going to photograph models? What's the angle now? What are you *almost* going to do with your life?"

"I'm not running any game. It's a sure thing. A million dollars."

That got Paris Kaila's full attention. What Paris got he didn't want, because what Paris got was a lot of rage.

"Get out of here!" Words hot enough to singe his eyebrows.

"Listen to me, baby. There's——"

"I told you! DON'T YOU 'BABY' ME!"

"This time——"

"This time is like last time is like every other time, and it's not enough anymore. I'm sick of the talk, and the dreams, and the shallow plans. I need something real. At least more real than what you've got."

"Real like how? Playing the dead girl in B movies? First you fuck, then you die."

"It's something, Paris. Yeah, okay, not much—shitty parts in shitty movies, but I worked to get 'em. *Worked.* I can look at everything I have and say: I earned that. Do you even know how to spell 'work,' because if you don't I don't think you'd so much as take the effort to look it up."

Kaila took to sarcasm the way some took to martial arts. She could kill with it.

"Screw off. I do shit for myself. I got a job."

"You've got a job, or you're going through the motions of earning a living? And how long before you tell yourself you gave the workaday life a shot and split it altogether?"

How long? Thirty nights at the 24/7 Mart, and giving it up was an itch Paris was already feeling the need to scratch.

Hackin' away at Paris, Kaila kept on swinging. "This . . . million dollars. How many hours of an honest day's labor did it take to earn it? How much of your own sweat and blood and brainpower did you put into it?"

Paris's response was to stand there and rub at one leg with the other.

Kaila's head shook. Pure disgust. "Know what your problem is?"

"No. Why don't you tell me what my prob—"

"You've had things too easy. You always got everything handed to you. A nice little suburban life in Irvine. White picket fences and little red schoolhouses. Ozzie and Harriet up the street, the Beav living right next door, and Mommy and Daddy giving you everything you ever needed."

"Sorry I didn't run with a gang or score crack. Would you like me better then?"

"I'd like you better if you were hungry. I'd like you better if you had enough fire inside you to go after something instead of hoping things'll come your way. Hell, Paris, look at you; look at your life. When it was time to go out on your own you made the drive to LA because it's close. You want to be in showbiz because the lifestyle's carefree. And when you're low on cash, when you don't have ends for rent or food, what's the first call you make?"

Paris opened his mouth.

Kaila jumped him with: "After you've hit me up for dough, what's the next call?"

For a sec Paris's mouth hung as it was, open, then closed without saying word one in his defense. He knew the truth of things. He knew the call he'd make. Ten digits, starting with the 714 area code.

"Christ, Paris, you're too old to be a slacker and too young to be a bum. You've never been able to follow through on anything, and now you've got nothing to show for your nontrouble."

Hard blows well landed. Every one of them. They should have taken Paris out of the game. They would have, except he didn't have nothing. He had something. He had a tape worth one million dollars, and now he was going to get the only other thing he ever needed. Her.

"Baby . . . baby, don't you see? It's for real this time; nothing halfway about it." While he had the opening, Paris took Kaila by the shoulders, held her. Her deltoids, strong like the rest of her, bulged in his hands. "This time I'm following through. And once I'm paid off you don't have to worry about going to auditions with a hundred other girls for a couple of lousy lines in something that's going straight to Viewmaster. A million dollars. Spread that around right and there's a whole lot you don't have to worry about anymore."

"Paris—"

"I'm going to do it this time, baby. And I'm going to do it for you. For us."

A dreamer, a nickel-and-dimer . . . but there was something old-shoe comfortable about being back in Paris's hands.

Easy.

That's the way life had been with him, Kaila remembered—the year and a half they were together as guy and girl. Real easy. But that's the way life is when there's no worrying about a job or money. How could you worry when you didn't have either? Rent would get paid somehow. Food would get bought some way or another. And days would get spent riffing on better tomorrows. Tomorrows full up with fast cars and good restaurants and big-time vacations all paid for . . . in some manner. With a movie deal or a record contract or a new hit TV show that sooner or later Paris was going to take a swipe at writing. But until then, don't worry. Take shit as shit comes.

Take it easy.

And isn't that what had attracted her to him in the first place—him over all the other guys in the city who thought they deserved some of what she had—his unassuming manner and the pipe dreams he blew that she got high off of?

Yeah, Paris's hands felt real good to Kaila. So did the notion of taking it easy. Why not? She'd been busting her ass a good long while. Why not let a few things come her way? And she and Paris weren't all that bad together, were they? There was the fighting and the screaming and the "fuck you"s that got swapped between them, but that was nothing but hot love. Wouldn't most couples kill for a few seconds of heat between them?

Jesus, did Paris's hands feel good to Kaila. And something else. Something more. Something that wasn't in his grip when he held her last. A little bit of authority. A little bit of sway. Was that a little bit of money she was feeling?

For a second things were the way they used to be, old pictures and well-worn memories: Paris holding Kaila. Kaila smiling. The two of them together and good.

For a second things were that way.

Time has a way of passing.

Kaila felt herself slipping.

Worse.

She felt herself falling.

Worse.

She felt the trapdoor of a gallows opening beneath her feet just prior to the quick drop and the existence-ending snap that waited at the end of a short rope. The rope was Paris, and he was giving Kaila just enough of him to hang herself with.

Un-uh. Not again.

Kaila had done her anti-Paris detox and her post-Paris rehab. She had done the revisions on the history of her and her man. The fights they had were just fights, not hot love. The "fuck you"s were for real. The easy was something she wanted no part of.

So, after that, after surviving all that, how could she for even one fraction of one moment ever fall for this man's half-baked, half-assed, half-planned, full-on bullshit again?

She couldn't. "Get out!" No way. Nohow.

"Kaila—"

"I'm through with it, Paris. I'm through with you. Get it straight:

it's over. Whatever used to be between us, used to be. So go on. Get your big money. . . . Then buy yourself a life."

What Paris wanted to buy, what he wanted, was Kaila. He wanted her. He loved her. He didn't have her. He couldn't have her. Not now. Not ever again. She was HIV-positively serious: they were through.

So Paris left. One last whiff of plumeria, then he was straight gone.

Should've hurt like hell, him getting kicked to the curb one more time: Kaila with her screaming and her door-slamming given away as a forget-me-not reminding him, again, he was a loser, nothing but a loser, and a loser was all he'd ever be. If even. And the pain of separation, the knowledge of the finality of things, that should've been just about unbearable.

Should've been.

It wasn't.

This time, different than last time, Paris didn't hear the door slam or any of Kaila's shrieked assessments on his state of being. This time, different than last time, he didn't hang by the door crying and weeping and ringing the bell, pleading his case for amnesty and forgiveness through an inch of wood. This time, different than last time, although he'd lost his woman, Paris had a bed fluffed a million dollars high to soften the fall.

This time, different than last time, he didn't feel a thing.

*C*oncerning 24/7 Marts: Marcus and Jay were coming to find out they had a comforting sameness about them. Go in one and you knew where, in all of them, to find the frozen burritos, which were across from the hot-dog fixin's stand, which was not more than arm's length from the Big Guzzle cups that you could carry to the counter, where you could grab a fistful of Slim Jims on the way out. Seen one, seen 'em all. Marcus and Jay had seen six. The 24/7 Mart they were walking into made for seven.

One guy working the counter. Marcus beelined for him.

"Excuse me, we're looking for the manager."

The guy behind the counter, nervous: "Would this have anything to do with food poisoning?"

Not hardly the reply Marcus had expected. "No."

The guy behind the counter was suddenly all smiles. "I am the manager. Mr. Bashir. How may I help you?"

"We're trying to find someone, a 24/7 Mart employee." Tired of Paris jokes, Marcus had modified his preamble. "You have anyone working here named Paris?"

"Paris? Has he done something? Are you the police?"

Jay: "We—"

Tasting pay dirt, Marcus cut his partner off before he could give anything away. "We're not at liberty to go into details. All we can tell you is that we're agents."

"Agents . . ." Bashir looked the guys over: the suits, the sunglasses. He got hip. "Oh, my goodness. You are with the FBI."

Marcus did a quick calculation. Nervous foreign guy thinking he and Jay worked for the gov. That could make for a very nice way to hack through a good quantity of bullshit.

"Yes," Marcus said.

Jay, a "Huh?" beat, then following Marcus's lead: "Yes. Surprise."

"I am only too happy to be of service to representatives of my government." Bashir couldn't flag-wave hard enough. "Where else but in this great land of freedom and opportunity could an immigrant such as myself one day be given responsibility for all this?" Bashir spread his arms wide, accidentally knocking over the Chiclets/Certs/Tic Tac display.

"About Paris. Do you remember seeing him with a young man, early twenties? White guy?"

"A white fellow . . . ?"

"Long blond hair, deep-blue eyes." Jay got intensely descriptive. "He had a sort of sinewy quality about him. Not a good dresser. Never a good dresser."

"Yes, yes, yes. I remember such a man. In the parking lot. I believe that he left with Paris. He looked so sickly, the young man did, but all white people look sickly to me. Such pale skin. Like—"

"His last name?" Marcus asked.

"—the dead. Yes, it is like the skin of the dead."

Marcus asked again, stiffer: "His last name, this Paris cat—what's his last name?"

"Scott. Paris Scott. But I do not . . ."

Outside, reaching for the door handle of the 24/7 Mart, Buddy. He dead-stopped, door part open, when he saw Bashir and the two suited, sunglassed guys he was talking with.

Bashir pointed a finger at Buddy. "There. That young man. That is the roommate of Paris." To Buddy: "Come here, Buddy. These men are from the FBI."

FBI? That's all he needed to hear.

Buddy moved. Bolted. He had no idea where he was going, but he was going to get there fast as he could, fast like a rocket flying on a solid fuel of terror.

Marcus, Jay, out of the mart and giving chase. But their hearts weren't pumping fear-laced adrenaline. Their legs weren't churning with a "save me" frenzy. They didn't get close to Buddy. The LA heat stopped them from trying.

Jay turned to Marcus huffing, but not very much more than his partner. "What," he asked, "do you suppose got into him?"

.   .   .

Displaying athletic abilities he hadn't previously known he possessed, Buddy made the distance from the 24/7 Mart back to his—his and Paris's—place at a dead run. Red lights got crossed against. The old Jews coming out of Cantor's got shoved aside. Buddy wasn't slowing down for nothing. Buddy wasn't letting the feds get the jump on him. He had to get back to the apartment. If he could get back to the apartment he could . . . He could what? Something, right? He could do something. Jesus Christ, there must be something he could do.

Almost there. Almost to the temporary sanctuary of home.

One more look behind. One more look to make sure the G-men weren't—

From the corner of his eye Buddy caught motion. Caught it too late to do anything about it. He hit something, tumbled. He heard a squeal and a grunt as he went down. That got followed up by the double sensation of smacking both pavement and flesh. Somebody else's flesh.

A cop!

No. Not a cop. A girl. Then Buddy thought again. Maybe it was a chick cop. Except she wasn't in uniform, she wasn't sporting a gun or a badge. Just a girl, so Buddy struggled up to get back into the race for his front door.

The girl: "Oh, like hell."

Hands snatched out, clawed Buddy's leg.

"Let go of me!"

"Fuck that! You're not going anywhere!"

"Let go!" Buddy tried to kick her away, but the chick had him bear-trap caught.

"You think you can put me on my ass and keep running? You could've killed me."

"Please . . . Please . . ." The FBI, the police, drug-lord hit men, Osama Bin Laden, and probably Mossad—they were all at that very moment converging on Buddy's position. Buddy couldn't see them, but his new seventh sense of paranoiac precognition told him they were ready to swoop down, sink their talons into him, then whisk Buddy away to a hell selected especially for him.

"I'm hurt," the girl ranted, "and I'm going to sue your ass. I'm a dancer. I've got to dance to eat. I can't dance, I'm going to sue you. Hell with that, I'm going to sue you anyway."

This was all too, too much for Buddy. Same as an engine running hot, he started to break down. "Just let me go. . . . Please let me go. . . ." He sank to the concrete, made a nice little puddle of himself. He cried.

"Hey . . . I'm not going to sue you." The girl's grip went slack. "I was just, you know, talking. Come on, man."

Buddy was scared and confused and hopeless and defeated, and all that came out in tears and snot bubbles. "They're going to kill me!"

". . . What?" The girl's head whipped side to side looking for street punks or stalkers or gang-bangers or any of the other oddballs, wackos, and creeps people in LA mean when they yell out someone's going to kill them. She didn't see anyone, anyone in particular, other than the elderly Jews and failed starlets who roamed the Fairfax district, and who were currently gawking at a young woman and the crying man laying next to her on the sidewalk.

The girl: "Who's going to kill you?"

Buddy didn't catch that. Buddy was in his own freak zone. "I didn't do it. I didn't have nothing to do with it."

"Wait. Slow down. You di—"

"It was Alfonso. They can't kill me for that."

"Kill you for what? You want me to call the police?"

That Buddy heard. "No cops!"

"But they—"

"NO COPS!"

Having had things made clear for her, the girl backed off and backed off quick. "Okay, okay. No cops."

Managing up to his feet, leaning in the direction of his apartment: ". . . Take me inside."

The girl gave a couple of nervous looks around like she was scoping again for stalkers or bangers or visible wackos. None yet. "Yeah. Maybe that's a good idea." Scooping up Buddy, she helped him toward the door.

Buddy was still panicked and frightened and all that, but not so much any of those that he couldn't take a moment to dig this girl who had her arms wrapped around him. Blond hair in a pageboy, a face clean of defect. Displayed beneath a jean vest, white T-shirt, tight black biker shorts, and construction boots was a tan, toned, fat-free, and fine body. The physique, the outfit—this chick was almost to the point of being a dyke, but her sexiness brought her way, way back from the edge of that cliff. She was hot. Molten ready-to-pour temptation. Like Miss Ann-Margret in *Viva Las Vegas*, or Miss Ann-Margret in *Murderers' Row*, or Miss Ann-Margret on any day she ever drew a breath.

Too bad. Too bad that she was so well built and so good-looking, because Buddy's panic and terror were still just enough that his survival instinct had crushed his sex drive. Wouldn't you know, the one time he'd finally gotten a ripe one back to his place he'd have drug dealers and cops both trying to light a fire under his ass.

Once inside, the girl locked the door, pulled the shades. Maybe Buddy's paranoia was catching. She took a quick peek in the bedroom, the bathroom. They were alone.

Buddy slumped at the wall where the girl had dumped him, stared off in a daze.

"Want some music?" the girl asked. "How about I turn some music on. That make you feel better?"

Buddy kept his dazed stare going.

A beat-up Sony. Boom box with a tape thing. Except that one of the little speakers was fried, it was stereo. The girl station-surfed. A few were playing tributes to Ian Jermaine, lovesick chicks calling in talking about how some obscure song he'd written in the middle of a drug haze deeply and profoundly touched, affected, and reflected their all-of-nineteen-year-old lives. The girl skipped over all that and some Country and some Speed Metal, lots of Mexican stuff, a sort of old Yolly Maxwell song, and landed on "That's the Way of the World." Earth, Wind and Fire.

The girl asked: "Is this cool?"

Buddy had that dazed stare down cold.

The girl went to him, took his hand in hers. The fingers that had clamped his leg hard now gently, gently petted his digits.

She said: "Look at you. You're shaking like a leaf. It can't be that bad."

"You don't know." Going weak, Buddy slid along the wall.

The girl held on to him, held him up. "Tell me. Tell me everything."

"It wasn't even my . . . It was Alf."

"Alf?"

"Alfonso. It was his idea."

"Who's Alfonso?"

"He's my friend. Was my friend. H-he's dead."

"Oh, God . . ."

The girl's arms went full around Buddy. He fell into her, and if not for her he would've kept falling until he hit ground. She was his strength and substance. He was her puppet. She rocked him. First like a baby, then to the groove of one of the legendary R&B acts of the seventies. With great imperception the rocking turned to swaying.

"Alf said he knew about a guy. Just some addict, he moves drugs—"

An echo cooed: "Drugs."

The swaying eased into a hint of dancing.

"And Alf said it'd be the easiest thing in the world—go in there and grab some from him."

"Steal the drugs."

The girl pulled her hands in and pressed herself to Buddy. Their lower sections met, ground together. The subtle slow dance became not so subtle. Not so slow.

"We cut it up," Buddy mind-drifted on, "we sell it ourselves. Money. I just wanted to make a little money."

"We all want something."

"I wanted . . . I wanted to be somebody." More tears and snot from Buddy as he drooled some of that oh-my-fucked-up-life babble that, right then, maybe one thousand other people in LA were cutting loose with. "Jesus, I just . . . if I had money I could've . . . All I wanted—"

"We all want something," the girl said again.

"I wanted people to like me, you know? I . . . Fuck . . . You get some money, and people . . . You know?"

The girl stopped dancing for a sec. She took Buddy's face in her hands. Something about her became real sad.

She said: "I do know. I know how it is. You want someone to care about you. You want them to know that you're . . . that you luhhh . . . lov . . ." She had trouble with that word. "But they don't know and they don't care, and you end up where you end up. You end up *what* you end up." To Buddy the girl asked in a way that made it seem she very badly wanted to know and with extreme desire understand: "If love is so good, how come good love is so hard to find?"

Buddy was too busy twisting on a spicate o' fear, too preoccupied with survival to get what the girl was rapping about. Didn't matter. She was done rapping about it.

"Hey," she said, putting her recent thoughts behind her, being stoic about them. "If you can't be with the one you love . . ." The girl danced Buddy to a wall. "The drugs . . . ?"

"I didn't want to deal no drugs. I didn't want nothing to do with them. I just wanted this one time to make this one score. I swear to God I just wanted it this one time."

"I understand. I really do." The girl eased Buddy down, let him collapse in a heap on the floor. His lap got straddled by her legs.

"There was someone else there. Couple of guys, I think. There was . . . They shot Alf. They k-killed Alfonso. There was someone else. . . ." Flashback. Gunshots. Muzzle sparks. Bullet wounds and spraying blood.

The blood.

Visible or not, the blood was still all over Buddy. It drenched him, soaked him through and through. Probably never could he clean it off.

Time to freak out: "Oh, God! Oh, Jesus! He's dead!"

Holding him tight, riding him, the girl fought to keep Buddy from going epileptic. "Come on. Don't do that."

"Jesus Christ, he's dead!"

"You've got to hold it together."

Her coaching was wasted. Buddy freaked on. "They're going to find me! They're going to find me and kill me too! I know they are!"

"Shh, shh, shh. Just relax. Keep it together." Sweet words. Warm breath. They tag-teamed to slow up Buddy's heart some, to coax him back from beyond. "That's it. You okay? You going to be okay?"

"I . . . I think . . ."

"You're going to be fine." Her fingers stroked and curled Buddy's hair. "Everything's going to be fine."

Weird, but it did seem that way. In this girl's strong/gentle arms it seemed like somehow all the jacked-up craziness he'd been fighting was going to calm down, ease up, and just maybe be survivable somehow. Somehow everything was going to be okay.

Buddy was saved. This blond bombshell of a saint, Mother Teresa reincarnated as a piece of ass, had stepped off the cold, cruel LA sidewalks and saved him. He said a prayer, good and quick, for her sake, that while she was in the process of doing her redemption bit he wouldn't drag her down into a bog of iniquity with him.

Saint Blondie took a deep breath—her chest rising and falling against Buddy's—as she did a change-up of gears, shifting to an uncomfortable subject. "Now, there's just one thing more you need to tell me."

Anything for you, Saint Blondie, Buddy thought. Anything for you.

"Where are my boss's drugs?"

Beat.

"Wha . . . ?"

"Daymond's drugs—where are they?"

Even after her asking twice it took a second for two tons of obviousness to bash its way into Buddy's thick skull. This girl that he happened to run into accidentally outside his apartment wasn't just some girl, and he hadn't just happened to run into her accidentally. The girl occupying his lap was an eight-ball chick, a gangsta bitch, and it was 20/20-hindsight painfully obvious she was getting paid by the guy he and Alf had tried to rip off, the guy who most likely wanted Buddy and wanted Buddy dead.

Quick, Buddy tried to jerk himself up, over, out from under—any direction away from the girl. Her body full on his legs, all he could do was fish-on-dock flop around.

From the small of her back, hidden by the vest, the girl whipped a nickel-plated .38, which put a stop to the discussion about anybody going anywhere.

"Sit the fuck still before I open you up like a box of crackers!" Any sweetness and light the fallen angel might've had got tossed out to make room for a stone-cold stare.

A stare Buddy responded to with whimpers.

"And quit crying." Mocking: "Oooh, she's going to shoot me, she's going to shoot me."

That didn't help Buddy to whimper any less.

With her free hand the girl took out a pack of Camels, Wides, slipped one between her full lips, Zippoed it lit.

"What the hell you think's going to happen when you go around stealing people's drugs?" The cig bobbed up and down as the girl spoke. "You want to play a big boys' game, you got to play by the big boys' rules. Now, just shut up and take what's coming to you. But first I got a couple of questions."

As fast as he could get it out: "I don't have the drugs."

No hesitation. The chick pulled the cigarette from her mouth and ground the hot end into Buddy's cheek. Smaller around than a dime it was, but the tip of the cigarette delivered a pain greater, deeper, and longer-lasting than he ever could have imagined any kind of known pain to be, and the smell of burning flesh, the sizzle that went with it, made the hurt come at Buddy in Sensurround. He screamed, he struggled, but with the girl planted on him he had nowhere to go and no other options but to sit there and feel the burn.

Finally, the girl let the burning stop. She pulled back the cigarette, put it to her lips, and sucked some of the smoke down into her lungs.

She said: "You can't answer the questions before I ask them. It's like *Jeopardy:* even if you're one of them smart Asian fuckers and you know the answer, you gotta wait until Alex is done asking the question, you dig?"

A mumble lost among sobs: ". . . Bitch."

"Close. Brice. 'Kay. Question number one. Think you might be familiar with it. Where are my boss's drugs?"

"I don't have the drugs," Buddy said, his thought for the moment being not having the drugs might equal getting to live.

The cigarette was back out of Brice's mouth and jammed against Buddy's face. It was accompanied by the requisite screaming and thrashing. A little bit later, done with burning Buddy for the minute,

Brice took herself another long drag of the cig, not caring that it was more than getting to be severely mangled.

"Wrong answer. Look, they found your bud's body, your car. You two boys were a couple of dumbasses, and from where I sit"—she bounced on Buddy's lap—"you're not getting any smarter. Now, here's the situation: I'm a single girl with a lot of time on my hands, a whole pack of cigarettes, and I only have eyes for you. So let's get down to some serious Q&A."

Of its own accord, per a long-disremembered survival instinct, Buddy's bowels slackened. Fecal matter flowed free from his colon, squishing out beneath him and atomizing between his ass cheeks and the floor into a stench. It was the smell of fear. Brice inhaled it deeply.

You could call it a break room. It was really just an extra storage room with empties waiting to be recycled, a mop, a bucket, a broom, and other cleaning supplies used to sop up what got spilled on the 24/7 Mart floor, and a misplaced, forgotten case of Hostess products that were still as fresh as the day they were delivered four years and three months ago. So it was really an extra storage room, but Mr. Bashir had put a chair, a radio, and a couple of small lockers in there and called it a break room for his employees, and that was more than most 24/7 Mart managers had ever done for the people who clock-punched for them.

Mr. Bashir opened one of those little lockers, the one Paris used, and stood back while Marcus and Jay pawed through it. Sunglasses, a pair of socks, deodorant, a toothbrush . . .

Either, Marcus figured, this Paris used the room to dress in, or he was prepared in case he turned out to be the one convenience-store counter guy in America who ever got lucky on the job. Besides all that stuff there were some other bits of uselessness, but there was no tape. No songs by the late Ian Jermaine.

But there was a picture. A guy and a beautiful half-black, half-Asian woman standing on the edge of desert/edge of city—arm in arm—before a gold-trimmed sign with blue and red letters over white backing. A famous sign. A sign Marcus had seen before. The sign said: "WELCOME TO FABULOUS LAS VEGAS NEVADA."

Marcus showed the picture to Bashir. "This him?"

"Yes, yes. That is Paris." Feeling guilty: "I really should not be allowing you to look through his personal belongings."

Jay piped up excitedly, getting into his little cop act. "I can assure you your assistance is noted and appreciated by the United States government."

Marcus to Jay: "Shut up." Marcus to Bashir: "Can you give us his address?"

"I . . . I really don't know." Bashir was tussling with some serious inner conflict: good citizen vs. good 24/7 Mart manager. "What is it exactly you say Paris has done?"

"That's not something you really need to know." Marcus was dagger-sharp.

"But he is my employee. And a good one. If you say he has done wrong, why is it you cannot tell me what he has done wrong?"

"Mr. . . . Bashir, right? Do you know what being an accessory to a crime means?"

"I . . . I—"

"Do you know what obstruction of justice is?"

"Obstruc—"

"It's kind of a tongue twister, but fifteen to twenty-five'll give you plenty of time to practice it."

Sweating. Goosy. Good citizen vs. good 24/7 Mart manager vs. hard time. "But . . . I don't really—"

Jay just stood and listened and watched Marcus play hardball. It was exciting. Jay felt himself get excited.

"By the way," Marcus wondered out loud, "your immigration papers—are they all in order?"

$B$uddy's exposed flesh had become canvas for a particular kind of métier. Brice's specialty. Call it: making a guy hurt every way you know how. And, shirt ripped open, there was plenty of flesh for Brice to get creative with.

Most of Buddy's fine collection of wounds were of the cigarette-burn variety in an assortment of severity: the not so bad, the very bad, the horribly ulcerated. The ulcerated ones were Brice's best work: deep depressions, the edges of the burns white and elevated like the rim of a volcano, this surrounded by cherry-red and swollen skin. Those burns that had been festering a bit—and they'd a bit to fester, Brice closing in on one very long hour and eighteen minutes of fucking Buddy up—were filling with a creamy yellow pus that bubbled up and seeped at the slightest pressure. The pressure Brice had applied to most of them was more than slight. Buddy was bathed in an oily sheen that was continually manufactured and pumped from just beneath his skin.

The others, the fresh burns, were red and black, and the only thing that ran from them was blood.

The rest of Buddy was simply decorated with the usual assortment of bruises and cuts and lacerations that are normally incurred during any standard torture session. The one real unique welt was the "Tim" from "Timberland" imprinted across Buddy's back where Brice had stomped him with her booted foot.

Buddy was starting to remember that, the getting stomped. Buddy was starting to remember a lot of the last hour and eighteen minutes. He was back now, having gone away for a little while during Brice's festivities. Unfortunately, not far enough away that he couldn't feel every burn, every slap, every brass-knuckle punch Brice had given him. He unstupored to find himself alone in the living room. He wasn't alone in the house. From the kitchen came the sounds of plates, utensils, pots, and pans being tossed around. Brice was looking for the drugs. From the way the living room had been torn up, or from what he could see of it through his eye that wasn't filled with blood and swollen closed, it was obvious to Buddy she'd already whirlwinded through there during his absence.

But if she was still looking, still searching, that meant she hadn't yet been in the bedroom, hadn't yet taken a gander in the duffel under Paris's bed. That meant Buddy hadn't told her. Despite the pain and the passing out, Buddy hadn't told Brice where, in the very next room, he'd hidden the drugs.

Buddy had to snicker at that some.

Everybody had always said that even on a sunny day at high noon he was never anything but a scared little bitch. Alfonso had told him that. Alf had told him that so many times Buddy got it in his head he had to go help steal some smack just to prove who was what.

Alf was dead. Alf was dead, and here Buddy was still somewhat alive.

More than that.

Cigarette after cigarette, pack after pack, burn after deep sizzling burn, Buddy hadn't given up anything to Brice. Not a word. Screams, sure, lots of those, but not a word.

Who's the bitch now? Buddy taunted at Alf in hell and at Brice in the kitchen. Tried to taunt, but the blaring radio that had kept his cries of agony from being heard also prevented Brice from hearing his little voice, which barely made it past swollen, blistered lips hanging from a bloody, bloated, repeatedly kicked face.

Who's the bitch n . . .

The door.

Buddy caught a one-eyed glance of it and his train of thought jumped to another track.

The door. Right there across the room—the door to the apartment that led outside where there were people. People who could save and rescue Buddy and help him wake from this dark dream he was living.

The door. Brice was in the kitchen and the door was waiting. All Buddy had to do was walk to it, open it, and keep walking on through to all those glorious, ready-to-aid-their-badly-beaten-and-busted-fellowman Angelenos.

Except he couldn't walk.

Brice had done something to his legs. Something Buddy didn't want to look down to see exactly what because he was pretty sure it would just make them hurt worse.

But he could still crawl. Oh, yeah. Crawling was something he could do with newborn proficiency. So Buddy crawled for the door, only it wasn't quite a crawl but something much more feeble. It was a lot like a sea lion trying to drag itself across an acre of broken but not very ground glass. Hands crept out, then pulled the body forward. Grunts and groans and snarls went with every millimeter covered.

Still in the kitchen looking for those drugs, Brice didn't notice the crawling Buddy. And the radio that had kept Buddy from being helped now kept him from being found out.

Hands crept out, then pulled the body forward.

Right, I'll just get to the door and everything'll be okay, Buddy's mind propagandized itself. Outside'll be people. Outside'll be Good Samaritans and police and maybe a TAC squad to take this bitch down. Outside everything is beautiful and wonderful and there are no more cigarettes out there. Please, God, don't let there be any more cigarettes out there. Don't let there be any more cigarettes anywhere in the entire world.

Hands crept out, then pulled the body forward. Three millimeters down. A mile to go.

He could do it. He could make it. He could, if Brice just stayed in the kitchen another hour or so. Just another hour . . .

The song on the radio faded, mixed into a fresh one. Seventies guitar licks led it off.

Before the song made it through the first few bars, from the kitchen, Brice squealed. Into the living room she came flying.

Buddy went still, like maybe being still would somehow make himself and his welts and pus sacs that he was moving for the door blend in with the rest of the room: nothing unusual here, Brice, just a guy dying.

Only he knew it wouldn't.

Only he knew she would see him.

Only she didn't.

The only thing Brice did do was go to the busted Sony. Crank it. Bachman-Turner Overdrive's "Hey You" slammed off the walls.

Brice, little-girl excited: "I love this song!"

And she danced. Right there in the middle of the floor, between using some guy as an ashtray and scouring his pad for drugs, Brice did a go-go bump and grind that was only missing the thigh-high Nancy Sinatras with zippers up the calves. Brice had a way of shaking her groove thing that was serious with its hypnotic self. The whole section of her that circumferenced ass and muff was a combo aphrodisiac/Venus flytrap. Most likely as many men had been killed by that as by her cigs.

Her head whipped.

Her body flailed to the licks.

Her tits jiggled just enough to indicate their realness without giving up too much firmness.

The whole package was a sight to see, if there'd been anyone there to see it. There wasn't except for Buddy, and Buddy—while Brice was busy giving it up for tunes from fat Canadian rockers—was making double time for the door. Two millimeters a drag now instead of one.

Hands crept out, then pulled the body forward. So very much pain.

Brice lifted her arms, twisted side to side. Her navel was exposed. A little platinum ring pierced there.

Hands crept out. . . . They bumped wood. The door! The most beautiful door in the entire history of the human race. Hand up now instead of out. One arm was all Buddy could manage the strength to operate. The hand reached, groped, fumbled at the knob. Its weakness and the blood that covered the palm made grasping an event. It reached, groped, fumbled more. Fingertips barely took hold of brass.

In time to the music Brice moved across the room. Her hands took Buddy by the ankles. One hard yank pulled him clear of the door.

His head bounced off the floor. One ear took the thud. The other heard from Brice: "Silly rabbit, Trix are for kids."

She knew. The whole time she was dancing and gyrating and carrying on, she was hep to Buddy's grand and elaborate crawling-escape plan. She let him drag himself across the room just for the subsequent pleasure of jumping in and stubbing out what little bit of hope he had left, the same as she'd stubbed out her cigarettes on his body. She was just toying with him, playing with him. It was like . . .

Oh, yeah, Buddy reminded himself. It was like she was torturing him.

Brice towered over Buddy. He looked up her legs past her privates and stomach and tits to her face—her face, which was, to Buddy's fucked-up senses, so very, very far away but so easy to read: "Playtime's over."

"Look," the face said out loud, "we've had some laughs, right? Played a few songs, smoked some smokes. But you've turned out to be kind of a boring date, and I've got business to take care of. So why don't you tell me where the drugs are, or I'm going to have to start rubbing salt in your wounds. And I do mean that."

"Well, this is it, then, isn't it?" Buddy thought. "I'm just about dead, aren't I?"

He should have listened to Paris, he admonished himself. Yeah, Paris had never amounted to much, just a guy working the counter of a 24/7 Mart, but he'd been right. Right about Alf, right about the trouble you can get into ripping off the property of urban drug lords. That Paris was a bright guy. Scrappy, for all his faults. And Buddy was sure now of what he'd only somewhat believed before: Paris could find a way out of this fix. Paris would know what to do. If he could just talk to Paris.

Paris . . .

Brice saw what was left of Buddy's lips flutter. She went down on a knee, put the side of her head to his mouth.

"Paris? What about Paris?" she asked.

His answer rode a slight voice up to her ear.

"Paris is your roommate? What the hell kind of name is Paris? Where is this guy?"

The voice was diminished beyond a whisper.

"Which 24/7 Mart?"

And then the slight voice was almost gone.

"I guess I'm going to have to have a little talk with your man Paris. Well, Buddy-boy. Looks like we're all done with each other. Now, this is what I want you to do. I want you to lay there with your eyes closed.

That's all, just lay there. And don't open your eyes, or you'll ruin the surprise."

Buddy closed his eyes. Closed his one eye that wasn't swollen shut. As crazy as everything was, the world got even scarier in the self-imposed dark. Buddy began to mumble.

The radio went off, and the scary world got scarier still.

Buddy mumbled more, louder. "Please don't kill me. . . . Please. Please don't."

"Eyes closed. Don't spoil the surprise."

Just the sounds of Timberlands walking over the wood floor, then nothing. Only quiet.

Terror reached fever pitch.

"Don't. Don't kill me. Oh, God . . ."

Only the quiet.

Only the quiet.

Buddy kept his eyes closed. Was it five minutes? Twenty? Fifteen seconds? It was impossible to tell, except that it felt like forever, and, struggle as he might, that was as long as he could lie in the dark and quiet.

Buddy, eyes open.

Above him, Brice, gun in hand.

Brice said: "Surprise."

The gun said: Bang.


Marcus worked his Audi through traffic toward the Fairfax district. Jay sat next to him, just about glowing.

"That was so . . ." Jay was so excited the only word he could think of to describe their little adventure thus far was "exciting. That was *sooo* . . . I've never done anything like it. Letting him think we're federal agents."

"It's just bullshit. That's what we do for a living. We bullshit the artists, bullshit the label, then we sell the bullshit to the public. That 24/7 Mart guy? Just bullshitting someone else for a change."

"And you. You were so cool." Jay couldn't help looking Marcus up and down. "So tough."

Marcus just drove.

Jay watched him drive. Watched him very intently.

Marcus felt himself getting watched. "What? What are you look-ing at?"

"Nothing. I . . . Nothing."

Catching an address as they rolled, same as the one Mr. Bashir had sweated over to them back at the 24/7 Mart, Marcus nodded at an apartment house, said: "Here it is."

He angled for the curb, parked the Audi. Up and out, Jay was at his side as Marcus went for the door.

Marcus said: "Man, I don't need this. Running all over town look-ing for some music. I signed up to be an agent, not captain of the Tape Retrieval Unit."

Jay didn't say anything to that. Jay was too busy giving Marcus the heavy stare again.

"What the hell are you looking at?"

Quick, sheepish, Jay looked away, rang the doorbell.


Brice had her piece ready before the bell even stopped sounding. She was pretty sure it wasn't cops. Cops don't ring bells. Cops bust down doors. And this was LA. LA cops are just as happy to shoot through a door as expend energy slamming their fat asses against it.

Most likely, Brice figured, it was a neighbor who'd heard her put a bullet in Buddy. She probably shouldn't have shot him. A bludgeoning or strangulation is quieter, not to mention just taking a kitchen knife to a guy. Although, don't get the job done fast enough, and knifed-up people can get crazy with their screaming. It's surprising how many jabs with a sharp object the human body can take.

Brice knew. Brice had counted.

So she'd shot Buddy, and what's done is done. And if one of his neighbors wasn't street-smart enough to keep to himself when he hears a gunshot, well, this was one of those jobs where sometimes you just had to do a couple of extra things gratis.

The doorbell rang again.

Brice went to answer it.

.   .   .

Jay kept ringing the doorbell. It gave him something to do. Something besides looking at Marcus one more time.

Jay said: "I don't think anyone's here."

Marcus eyed the duplex. It looked nothing but quiet. Heading around the side of the building: "I'll check a window."


Brice pressed herself against the door, put an eye to the peephole. There was Jay, his jowly face fish-eye distorted. Didn't look like a neighbor. That suit. Salesman? Jehovah's Witness? Far as Brice was concerned, what he was, was a sack of flesh waiting to become unalive. Brice put her hand to the knob, ready to fling the door open, ready to yank Jay inside. Ready to lay out another body next to Buddy's.

The window. It rattled and pulled against its lock.

Fat-Faced Suit Guy wasn't alone. Blinds drawn, she couldn't see if it was another fatty, or whether guy #2 had a look all his own. Brice shook her head. Killing a guy is one thing. Killing an extra somebody who stumbled along is another. But three bodies in ten minutes? All of a sudden she's Chuck Manson.

Again the bell rang. And again.

Brice wanted to pop Fat-Faced Suit Guy just for being annoying.

Fuck it, she thought. Standing around plugging strangers didn't get her any closer to Daymond's drugs.

Back of the apartment: another window that opened on an alley. Brice made for it, stepping over the pile of Buddy as she went.


Marcus came around from the side of the house.

Jay kept ringing the bell. "No one's answering."

"Window's locked, shades are drawn."

"Maybe he's hiding." He rang the bell again.

"Hiding from who? How's he going to know we're looking for him?"

"Well . . . so what do we do? Wait?"

"You can wait if you want. I haven't even had breakfast yet." Marcus was already heading for the Audi.

Like a little puppy dog, Jay trailed right behind.

P aris blew quick into the 24/7 Mart like a guy who had places to be. Like a guy who was late for an appointment to collect a million cash.

He talked just as fast. "Mr. Bashir, I hate to tell you this—actually, I don't hate to tell you—but I'm quitting. And that's nothing against you, 'cause you've always been do-right by me, but it's time for me to get up out of here."

Bashir was filled with nothing but lamentation. "Are things that badly for you?"

"They're not bad at all. It's all good."

Bashir took that same as a knife to the heart. "Oh, my boy. There is no need to hide the truth from me. I know what it is like to be hunted."

One word out of Bashir's little roll jumped up and slapped Paris. "What? What do you—"

"In my country, killing certain animals just to put food on one's table is enough to put a price on a man's head."

"Wait, wait. What do you mean, hunted?"

"They came here looking for you."

"They? Who, they?"

"Two men. A black man such as yourself, and another who was white. Such angry men."

"But who—"

"They did not say. Not really. They were . . . I don't know. They were . . ."

"Agents?"

"Yes. That is what they said they were. They said they were agents."

Beneath Paris's blackness he was white with panic. His head snapped side to side doing a swift visual recon for any sign of the two guys sent after him. "Where are they?"

"I do not know. I . . . Threats were made, Paris. There was nothing I was able to do."

"Where are they!?"

"I was compelled to tell them your address."

"Jesus! The tape!"

"I am sorry. They forced me to tell them where you lived. You understand, do you not? Such evil, cruel men. I do not know to what lengths they would go in order to locate you."

Paris blew quick out of the 24/7 Mart like a guy who had some-place to be. Like a guy who was about to have a million dollars yanked out of his pocket.

"Beware them!" Bashir yelled at the swinging door. "Beware them!"


It was strange.

Paris and Buddy had never been much more than roommates. Never been much more than two guys who split the rent. Buddy's ini-tial relation to Paris was that he was a friend of Paris's old roommate, who had gone back to Wisconsin when he was good and fed-the-fuck-up with LA, letting Buddy move into the space.

It was strange.

Buddy and Paris shared a roof, but little if anything beyond that. They didn't share off-hours together, or interests, and they very sure didn't share much of themselves. It was just two guys who occasionally occupied the same space at the same time. Paris couldn't tell you with certainty what Buddy did to earn his keep, or what he wanted to do if they had been grace-of-God lucky enough to live in a world where people actually got to do what made them happy in life. Paris didn't know, except for Alfonso, any of Buddy's friends. If the rest of Buddy's friends were like Alf, then Paris didn't care to know them. What his favorite food was, the name of the last girl he'd laid, anything that passed for a hobby—none of that did Paris know concerning his roommate.

It was strange, then, that the body of this guy who was a foreigner to him, Paris should be cuddling so tightly on the floor of their apart-ment. Paris didn't remember dropping down and wrapping up the carcass in his arms. Racing the Gremlin from the 24/7 Mart to the apartment, he recalled. He could remember opening the door, too.

Then there was a haze: The place a mess. The stink of gunpowder. Buddy, who looked like he was sleeping. Except for the purple-and-black defect smashed into the center of his forehead, some cuts, and a whole lot of burns, he looked like he was sleeping.

That was it. Right then, that was when Paris ran to the body, took it in his arms, started bawling for the poor slob who'd never amounted to anything and now never would.

That Paris could find it in himself to cry for a person known, yet unknown—that was the most strange of all.

And while he was crying, while he was rocking his dead roomie, Paris started remembering some other things. He remembered Mr. Bashir yelling after him as he ran from the 24/7 Mart. Evil, cruel men, he had said. Beware them, he had screamed.

And something else came back to Paris. The agent. That Bayless guy: "Cut your heart out . . . put my foot on your throat . . . Hear that sound? That's your neck snapping."

Just a lot of talk. Just hot air from a pissed-off suit. That's what Paris had thought at the time. With a fresh-dead body in his arms, Paris had to think again. Maybe they weren't just words. Maybe this Bayless guy wasn't just talk. He was an agent, wasn't he? What was the word on the street about Hollywood agents, the word Paris's actor and singer and writer friends passed on to him? The word was, agents were scum of the earth. Rattlesnakes in a preschool were more innocuous. In this part of the world, when you said "agent" the associated phrases were: rough bastards, back-stabbing assholes, vindictive motherfuckers who'd slit your throat, then sell your blood to cover their expenses. That's if they didn't just drink it.

Very quickly Paris got to thinking there was more to that talk than just euphemisms and exaggerations. Very fast he got to wondering, what was to keep agents from truly stabbing backs and slitting throats? People killed for pocket change, Air Jordans. They killed 'cause they got the wrong look from the wrong guy while stuck in traffic on the 405. So, for the last of Ian, for a tape that was worth how many tens or hundreds of millions, what would somebody—what would a Hollywood agent—do for that?

Shifting Buddy in his arms, the trapdoor-like flap where the bullet had pushed his brains from his skull squished against Paris's forearm. He began to think on what he should—

They're still here!

Finally and suddenly, the idea that whoever did the killing might still be around to do more came to Paris. He scrambled to his feet, dropping Buddy's carcass. Its thought-free head smacked against the wood, knocking more brains onto the floor like catsup whacked from a bottle.

Paris listened hard, strained to hear the unseen killer over his thud-thud-thudding heart. He thought he should go for the door, get out of the apartment, but his body, weighted with fear, disobeyed him. So he stood, frozen, a perfect target. A while passed, but the invisible killer never came from one of the other rooms to put a bullet in Paris. After a while more, Paris finally realized the invisible killer in the apartment wasn't in the apartment. He was safe.

And just then Paris came up with a new thought: He'll come back! Him, them. They—the army of foot soldiers who marched up and down Wilshire Boulevard Bayless had sent to repo the tape by any means necessary—it was just a matter of time before they once again came for Paris.

Paris went fast to the bedroom. Arm under the bed, he grabbed out the duffel. The tape was still as good as a check waiting to get cashed. If the killer—killers—hadn't found it. Paris felt a lot of air as he fumbled a hand around the inside of the bag. A lot of air and . . . What the hell is that? A package wrapped in brown paper? Where the fuck's the . . .

The tape! Still there. Paris tossed the tape back into the duffel bag, and with it went some jeans, some T-shirts, some hope, and a little possibility, because that's all he was riding on now: second chances.

Closing it up, Paris threw the duffel over his shoulder and moved lickety-split for the door.

He stopped.

The faceless assassins could be watching the door. Worse, they could be on their way in as he was on his way out. Paris didn't much want to die by virtue of a fluke in timing. A back window, that was the way to go. Paris turned and moved fast for the new exit.

He stopped.

He went back to the living room. Back to Buddy's body.

"I'm sorry, man," he said to his ex-roommate. "This . . . this is all my fault. It's my fault and . . . and I'm going to put it to them," Paris swore. "I'm going to screw that bastard Bayless. I'm going to . . ." Paris's revenge-fueled bravado was doused by a quick wave of fear. The more time he spent apologizing and vowing to dead Buddy, the more chance there was he would end up like dead Buddy.

His *mea culpa* aborted, Paris shot out the bedroom window without looking back.

The Ralphs, south on La Brea, north of Third. It was just far enough away from the Fairfax district that Paris felt safe pulling over the Gremlin, dropping change in a slot, and dialing some numbers without being picked up by the watchful eyes of the hit squad sent to eradicate him by—

"Chad Bayless's office," the skirt on the other end of the phone said.

"Put him on."

"I'm sorry," the secretary came back with. "Your name is . . . ?"

"Put him on the phone."

"I'll need your—"

"You put him on this fucking second!" Paris jammed his words into the woman's ear. "Put him on the fucking phone!"

Paris's anger was wasted on Jen. Eight months on the job and she was well used to the vitriol spat at her by stars and stars' managers and hotshot record producers concerning life-and-death situations like a limo being late, the wrong hors d'oeuvres being served at after-concert parties. Worse yet, the wrong whores being sent to a hotel room? Oh, the kind of screams that came with that. So one more person calling, ripping her a new ass to put fucking Chad on the fucking phone that fucking instant . . . ?

Whip a dog long enough, it learns to take it. Jen buzzed her boss.

Chad's coked-up brain collected itself enough to manage a hand over to the phone.

"Chad, there's a guy calling. He sounds very upset."

Chad's hearing was slurred. He had to fight to understand the woman in the next room.

She went on: "He wouldn't give his name, but I think it's the same guy who called this morning."

To himself: "They must have found him." Chad snatched up the phone, high now not only on the drugs but also on his ability to send his minions marching into the sprawl of LA and have them return mission accomplished. You know what they called guys who could do that in this town? Chad asked of himself.

Honchos, he answered.

Yeah, that's what he was. He felt warm where he'd just hung a medal on his own chest.

Into the phone: "Hey, you little prick. You like the way my boys play?"

Paris didn't know what he'd expected from Bayless. Anger, maybe. Maybe rage. But this—glee? You read about guys who killed and were happy for it. Guys who killed for the kick of killing. Media-tagged catchy-named guys. The Night Stalker. The Highway Killer. The Hillside Strangler. They were drifters, wanderers—degenerates you'd figure to find trying to hitch rides where the 10 met the 15, hair buzz-cut three-state-killing-spree short, ready to get down to the serious business of hacking up young boys and prostitutes. Where you wouldn't figure to find happy psychos is in the business district of Beverly Hills.

Or maybe not.

Maybe that's exactly where you find them. Maybe Hollywood, USA, was a breeding ground for nut jobs.

Maybe Paris just didn't know the business of show that good. "Why did you do this?" Paris asked, and asked again: "Why?"

"Because it's my tape, that's why. Because you think you can fuck with me, and you need to get learned. You're nothing, you know that? You're a goddamn bug under my shoe."

The heat, the noise of the city, the whole environment of Los Angeles pressed on Paris, tried to squeeze the life from him. It had worked its slow kill on him every day of every year since he'd taken that hour drive up to LA, moved up to the city to be something besides just a kid from Irvine.

Years later.

Paris wasn't a kid anymore. That's all about him that had changed, and the toll the city of his dreams had taken on him was just now reaching critical mass, just now readying a death blow.

"You sick son of a bitch!"

People in the parking lot turned, stared at Paris. It was a hell of a yell he put together that Angelenos should bother to notice him.

He yelled on: "I'm going to the cops! I'm telling them everything!"

Cops.

That one word barb-wire caught in Chad's ear and tore loose a flood of bad thoughts: Investigation. Embezzlement. Drug buys.

Cops?

Jesus Christ, what the hell did Marcus and Jay do to the kid? He just told them to get the tape back, that's all. Just get back the tape. Maybe he said it a little harsh, but that was just a way of expressing the seriousness of the situation. He didn't mean for them to . . .

Had he told them to hurt the kid? The cocaine made things so very hard to remember. He didn't say hurt the kid, did he? He didn't tell them to get the tape back even if they had to . . .

Chad went girlie with himself. The honcho medal slid right off his chest. "Wha . . . Wait—"

"The police, asshole! What did you think, you could get away with this?"

"You don't . . . There doesn't have to be any police involved."

"It's a little too fucking late for that! I swear to God I'm putting you away! You're never going to see this tape!"

"Listen to me—"

"Never!"

"You listen to me!" Chad came back strong, words blowing over Paris like they were riding a steamroller. "You stole that tape. You're the one who stole it, and you're the one who tried to extort money. Who do you think the cops are going to believe, me or a piece of street trash like you? Go on," Chad bluffed. "Go call the police. Money talks, and

I've got enough to scream for days. You're fucked, you little bastard. Good as dead. I'm coming for you. I'm coming for you, and I'm going to ki—"

Chad's voice was cut off, dichotomized by Paris slamming the phone down into the cradle. All strength trickled from Paris, so that he didn't as much hold on to the phone as use it to hold himself up. Then came the question-asking as Paris cross-examined himself like a two-yard-an-hour shyster who was getting all indignant for the cameras on CourTV: How? How does a guy end up where he is? How does a guy get to a place where some Hollywood suit he didn't even know a full day before was now making hunting him down job one, top priority, with no skimping on expenses?

And he would come after him, Paris thought. From where Paris saw things, Chad's thugs had already drawn a bead on him once, barely missing, and leaving a body in their wake as a consolation prize. That was just for warm-ups.

How? How does a guy who's wanted dead stay alive?

His hand on the phone. The keypad just beneath it.

Ten digits, starting out with the 714 area code. Orange County. Irvine. That's how a guy gets out of things. That's how Paris had gotten out of things in the past. That's how he had helped himself when rent was due but nowhere to be found. When the insurance company was coming around looking for payments to keep the Gremlin covered.

Ten digits, starting out with the 714 area code. Orange County. Irvine. Mom and Dad.

It wasn't like Paris wanted to call them every time cash was short or a loan needed to be cosigned or a car was stuck in impound until tickets were paid. It wasn't like Paris hadn't tried to make it on his own. He'd tried as best he knew how to get over with some bit of slickness that had to do with music or videos or singing or acting, none of which—admittedly—he had worked at very hard or done very well. But regardless of talent or brains, you were supposed to come out to LA and surf a slithery and smooth and superficial wave to a state of perfunctory idol worship, big money, and loose women. Everything about this town told you that was the way it was supposed to be, from the movies it made to the daily propaganda it spewed on *Entertainment Tonight*.

That was the problem: this town itself. This fucking town, seemingly fertile for accomplishment yet inimical to success. Hollywood and her tramp sisters fame and fortune were nothing but a bunch of whore seducers. With a smile and a wink and a wiggle of the ass they shanghaied you over to some dark corner where their brothers, the twin goons despair and defeat, waited to come at you bearing all the pleasantries of a back-alley abortion. That's when you got what the town really had waiting for you: the pounding of a lifetime just for thinking you could get a little of what the city had to offer. In Hollywood, in the land of entertainment, beating the little guy into bloody submission *was* entertainment, and the body cooling back at the apartment made Paris think Chad was an impresario.

Ten digits, starting out with the 714 area code. Mom and Dad would make everything all right. Didn't they always? Paris wanted to know of himself. When you were the only black kid on the block, when the white kids called you jig and coon in the same breath they called the kid with glasses four-eyes and the fat kid lard-ass, didn't Mom and Dad do something or other and make everything okay? When you were in high school—going on a junior, mind you—weighing in at 135 pounds, and there were freshmen who wanted to kick the living shit out of you, didn't Mom and Dad come to the rescue? There had always been a stopgap, a safety net. There had always been a fallback. There had always been them, and as long as there had been *them*, Paris never once was required to do the extra little bit of whatever it takes to sneak across the border separating the no ones from the someones. It had been that way through grade school and through high school and through college and through life and . . .

And—the high-priced shyster stepped in, took over, made an angry accusation for summation—and maybe, if you hadn't gone running to Mommy and Daddy (Mommy and Daddy—that hurt) for help back then, you wouldn't be running to them for help every time the sky gets partly cloudy or a dog shits on your doorstep. Maybe, if you hadn't cowered behind them like some Charles Atlas sissy fag dodging the sand flying at his face then, you wouldn't be standing in a parking lot talking to yourself now. And maybe it's all just like Kaila had pointed out so simply and precisely. Maybe, Paris Scott, you are nothing but a loser.

Paris thought about all that for a sec.

Then he thought about the alternative.

Maybe he had been a loser. . . . Okay, not much doubting that, but maybe there was still time for redemption. If he could somehow get out of this—get out of this stolen-property/suicide/murder turmoil— and do it on his own without dialing those ten digits, didn't that amount to something? Something more, at least, than trying to book acts into Sunset Boulevard clubs for 10 percent of nothing, or whatever other entry-level Hollywood bullshit he'd spent the last bunch of years trying to perpetrate. If he could extricate himself from all this death, chaos, mayhem, and money lust, then just let Kaila try and call him a loser.

Just let her.

Paris took his hand from the phone. He spent about half a second coming up with an obvious, front-of-the-shelf plan: Put as much space as he could between himself and Hollywood and the people in Hollywood who wanted him dead. Get out of town, get some money, then get more out of town. The tape, the last of Ian, had to be converted from commodity to cash. Quick cash. It could be done, but it would take some illegal, below-the-table double dealing: the exchange of stolen goods for loose money without the bothersome question-asking of the right-minded. There was only one place on earth—one other place— Paris knew of where that kind of behavior was not only accepted but encouraged. Fortunately, it was just a four-hour drive away.

Paris made for the Gremlin.

**M**r. Bashir was working the counter when Brice walked in. Other than the old Russian woman who had survived Zagrodski and a Mexican who had survived a dash across the border, the 24/7 Mart was empty. Had the USC marching band been in the middle of a bare-naked fuckfest next to the Tast-E-Freeze, Brice still would've got the notice from Bashir. As it was, she received his full and complete attention.

"You the manager?" Brice asked.

"Yes, ma'am." Bashir smiled big and broad, like a guy who made his living from a service job and knew that smiling at the customer is what got you paid. The fact that the customer looked as fine as Brice did didn't hurt his smile in the least. "What is it I may help you with?"

"I'm looking for someone. Paris. He around?"

"Oh, God in heaven." Small shakes from Bashir's head. "Not again. What is it that he has done this time?"

"He's been a bad boy. A very bad boy." Brice wore a little sneer whose edge carried a sharp-force impact.

"I do not understand what has happened to him. Paris has been such a fine employee."

"Yeah, well, you have to be careful. People are a strange animal. Never know which way they're going to jump from one minute to the next. Know what I'm saying?"

"I most certainly do. There was a time when a man I once called a friend borrowed from me a—"

Not caring anything for Bashir's story: "Know where I can find m' man Paris?"

"I don't . . . I am not . . ." Mr. Bashir hemmed and hawed, having already given up more information on an employee than an employer should have to in a string of months, let alone one day.

"You know something? You're not a bad-looking guy."

Brice couldn't have been any more offhanded with the remark. Still, any kind of come-on from her didn't much help Bashir get over his stammering. She leaned to him across the counter. Not a drop of perfume on her body and still she smelled good.

"You know that? Huh? You're not bad-looking."

"I . . . thank you."

Brice got with a curious look. "Where you from, India?"

"Pakistan."

"Pakistan. Yeah. I've never been with a Pakistan guy before."

Brice floated her way through the partition, floated herself right up to Bashir, who backed from her all-consuming presence only to run up against the far side of the counter. With nowhere to go, Mr. Bashir's body went flush against Brice.

"What do you Pakistan guys got?" she asked. To answer her own question, Brice's hand snaked down to Bashir's groin.

Mr. Bashir was uncomfortable, to say the least, about having a strange woman fondle his privates behind the counter while an old Russian woman and a Mexican did their shopping. Never-minding that, Bashir went steel-rail hard.

"Miss, please—"

"Come on, we're all big kids."

Brice's hand found Bashir's zipper. Bashir's zipper went down. Brice's hand went in. Brice got herself a gripful of meat, pleasantly surprised by the quantity.

"Yeah, I think I like Pakistan guys."

Mr. Bashir's eyes closed. His head tilted back at the end of a shiver that ran his spine.

Brice, close, lips to Bashir's ear: "I have to find Paris."

"I . . ." The little waves of excitement that sparked and popped in Bashir's body made concentrating, talking, as easy as climbing a mountain. ". . . I do not know where he is. I think th-that perhaps he is in hiding."

"Oh, that's no good. You suppose he might call you?"

"I . . . I . . ."

Brice's hand squeezed and stroked. "If he does, would you call me?"

"Yeeeeee . . ."

"Hmmmm?"

Squeeze. Stroke.

Orgasmic: "Yehhhhssssss."

"Man, you're so good." Brice's tongue lapped Bashir's ear.

From the counter she took a Sharpie, put it to Bashir's chest and wrote a phone number.

She said: "Call me."

Done, Brice withdrew her hand and slipped from the mart, brushing past the old Russian woman, who approached the counter with a carton of milk.

With his customer-comes-first smile, Mr. Bashir said: "Yes, Mrs. Litvak. Will that be all?" He said it normal. Normal like a guy who didn't have a chick's number tattooed on him, or his cock flapping from his zipper hole.

**I** think . . . Oh, God. I think I s-scared him away."

Across the distance, over the digital PCS, through his cell phone on a crystal-clear connection, Marcus could feel the wet of Chad's tear-soaked words.

"What did you tell him?" Marcus asked.

"I told him I was going to find him and kill him."

"Yeah, well, threat of death is the kind of thing that tends to scare people off."

"I'm sorry. I didn't mean to scare him."

Chad went into a near-full-on breakdown. With every sob, Marcus heard the spray of mucus from Chad's nose. It made Marcus regret the sarcasm he'd thrown out a moment prior.

"Okay, man. Just be cool. We're going to find the tape, all right? We'll find it."

Marcus closed up his phone, stared at it, shook his head, then tossed the phone on the dashboard. "Damn, that boy is tore up."

Jay: "What happened?"

"He scared off the kid. Told him we were going to come looking for him—we were going to kill him."

Jay went playfully buoyant. "Oooh, I'm a killer."

"Now he's gone underground and we've got to find him before Chad pops a vein."

"Sure. Eight million people in LA, and we've got to find this one guy. We ought to be home in time for *Ellen* on Lifetime."

"He's not in the city."

"Oh, then we just have to search the entire state. What's another half hour of work?"

Marcus slipped out a picture from the inside pocket of his jacket. The picture of Paris and the girl next to the Vegas sign. He handed it over to Jay.

Jay asked: "What?"

"Look at the picture."

Jay looked. "Vegas?"

"That's where he's heading."

"You think?"

"If somebody was going to rock your world, what would you do? Where would you hide but someplace you felt safe. Look at him."

Second time. Jay looked at Paris snapshotted for eternity at the very south end of The Strip.

Marcus gave running commentary. "Look at him smiling and all happy. He feels good there. He feels safe. Vegas."

"But he doesn't really think we're going to hurt him."

Flipping up his hands in a noncommittal gesture: "Hey, I don't know what he thinks. Not for sure. But I can put myself in his place. I can crawl around in his head: I'm a frightened street punk. I've got something I shouldn't have. I've got some asshole on the phone talking about how he's going to have my hide. Yeah, I tell you what I do: I get the fuck out of Dodge, sell whatever contraband I was carrying, then go underground for a long time. We intercept him in Las Vegas, or not at all."

Marcus had explained things clear and reasoned, like at some point, somehow, Paris had let the assistant in on exactly what his plans for squeezing out of a jam were. And Jay had listened to Marcus in pure rapture, not as if his partner was breaking down the psychology of a terrified mind on the run, but like he was watching Jesus himself doing water/wine tricks at a sold-out show.

"Wow. It is so amazing you can figure that out. All you did was look at a picture, and you just . . . you . . ." That old, flushed feeling was coming back to Jay. "You knew everything."

Marcus shrugged. "Nothing special about it." While he talked he thought: At this time of day, what's the best way to get to the 10? "You use your head. You use your gut. Listen to what they've got to say. They'll tell you how to handle things. You know what it's about?"

"What what's about?"

In the middle of a preach, Marcus missed Jay's question to his question and just went on sermonizing. "It's about how you approach a situation. It's about attitude."

"What do you mean?"

"Bridgeport."

". . . That a shoe?"

"Part of Chicago. Ethnic. Ethnic meaning Irish and Polish and Italian and anything else that isn't black. That's the way it's always been, and that's the way you best believe they're trying to keep it. Those Irish and Italians and whatnot are serious black-people haters. Make the Klan look like Girl Scouts doing laundry, you know what I mean?"

People who hated people for no good reason except just because. People who hated people who were different. "Yeah," Jay said. "I know what you mean."

"One time when I was a kid, in my teens, I was walking along Lakeshore Drive. . . . I'm from Chicago, did you know that?"

"No."

"So I'm walking along Lakeshore Drive, the Gold Coast, at night, and this cop rolls up next to me, asks me what I'm doing in this part of town at night. *This part of town*. Like that part of town couldn't be my part of town, which it was. My parents did okay. We had a place near the lake. Not too much. Same as most middle-class families. But the cop didn't see that, didn't know that, didn't want to hear anything about that. All the cop cared about was a black kid walking at night in this part of town."

Prejudice. Bigotry. "Go on," Jay prompted, hoping the story would end with the cop's comeuppance.

"So I tell the cop, This is where I live and I have every right to walk where I want.

"Now, I can tell he doesn't care for my way of talking to him at all, and I don't care that he doesn't care. So the cop tells me to get in the squad, talking about he's going to give me a ride home and how I had better live where I say I do. I get in and he drives. Only he doesn't take me home. He takes me to Bridgeport. Irish, Polish, Italian, black-people-hating Bridgeport.

"The cop opens the door and kicks me out. The cop's all smug with himself. Says something smart, like I should see if I have every right to walk where I want now, then drives off. Just leaves me there. A black kid. Middle of the night. Bridgeport."

"Jesus." Jay campfire-ghost-story hung on every word. "Did you . . . What happened?"

"I started walking. I knew that was the only way I was going to get home."

"But weren't you afraid you were going to get roughed up?"

"Hell, I knew I was going to get beat. Probably, if I was lucky, to an inch of my life and no more. Couldn't run, couldn't hide. Nothing I could do to stop it. So I got it in my head, If I'm going to get beat, then I'm going to give some beating back too. I'm going to give back as much as I can. I started thinking, if somebody messes with me, well, then, I'm going to kill them. Not hurt, kill. And I wore that on my face, tacked it up like a neon sign: Start something, you die.

"I hadn't made as much as a mile when I came on three white guys about my age and twice my size. I didn't know if they were Poles, or Italians, or what, but I could tell they were drunk. Of course they were drunk. You live in Bridgeport, what else is there to do with your life but drink and beat your wife, and these three were too young to be married. The three of them, they eyed me fast and made my way, ready to do some pounding."

By itself, of its own free will, Jay's hand rubbed back and forth on his leg, working its way from outer thigh to inner.

"So, so then what?"

"Then nothing. They saw my look. They read the sign: Start something, you die. They saw I meant it. They could smell kill-or-be-killed drifting off of me. Sure, I couldn't take all three of them. One might have gotten away with a nick, another one some bruises and cuts, but one of them was going to die, and none of them wanted to be that guy.

"They believed it. I made them believe it. And those three white boys went back to their corner, went back to their drinking, were probably still drinking when I finally got home a few hours later." Straight down Fairfax, Marcus figured. That was the best way to catch the 10. As coda to the tale he offered: "Probably still there drinking their lives away now."

Story over, Jay became self-aware and jerked his hand away from himself. He covered the awkward motion with: "That is so amazing. You are . . . you're just amazing. Could you have . . . could you have really killed one of those guys?"

"It doesn't matter if I could have or couldn't have. Attitude is what I'm talking about. I believed I could have, and they believed it. Attitude.

"See, that's the problem with guys like Chad. He wants to play like he's a big man, fakes it with silk suits and fancy cars, but he's had everything handed to him. Nothing but softballs all his life. All of a sudden a situation comes around and he doesn't know what to do; he can't pull together the frame of mind to handle things. He's got no—"

"He's got no attitude."

Marcus nodded.

Jay beamed, the teacher's pet.

"That's why black people are better than white people. Black people have to work twice as long and twice as hard to get half as much. They didn't know somebody who knew somebody at some fraternity back in Ivy Leagueville. They didn't get the right introduction to the right guy at the right country club. All they did was work their ass off. So, when you see a brother or a sister who's making it, you know they put in more to get there than the white guy sitting next to them. No offense."

"No. No."

Marcus's head shook in bemusement. "You always hear black people complaining: I can't make it. White people have everything. They got the power. If only I was white . . ." A laugh now. "I'm glad I'm not white. I'm glad I'm different. I'm glad I have to fight for every scrap I can gather up. That doesn't hurt me. That just makes me stronger."

"I know what you mean."

Marcus looked at Jay, curious. Pretty much the first time he'd looked at Jay since the allocution had begun. "What do you know? I mean, I'm cool with you and everything. As white people go, you're one of the good ones. But what do you know about being different?"

Jay hadn't meant to say anything just previously, and didn't know what to say now. Words tumbled awkwardly like misshapen cubes in his mouth. "I . . . well, I . . ."

"Come on." Marcus twisted the key in the ignition, bringing the Audi's engine to life. "We've got to hit Vegas."

*B*arstow was on the way to Las Vegas from Los Angeles. Barstow was on the way from Las Vegas to Los Angeles. Both cities—LA and LV—had something to offer. Not much and not much good, but something. Something more than the dirt and arid-weather vegetation that surrounded Barstow. But for some reason, over both just about equidistant places, people chose to live in Barstow.

Maybe they chose to.

More likely they were heading to one location or the other, broke down in Barstow, and decided to stay there. Like how a bug that gets stuck decides to stay in a roach motel.

Lot of gas stations in Barstow. Fast-food places did well too. The faster the better, as most people couldn't wait to be at either end of I-15. There were a few sit-down places, places where the person who took your food order wasn't talking at you through the busted speaker of a clown head. Not many. A few.

And there was The Trading Post. The Trading Post got built back in the forties, when just about the only thing to Barstow *was* The Trading Post. It did very well. People stopped at The Trading Post because if they didn't stop at The Trading Post and load up on gas, extra water, and food there was a good chance they would break down just south, toward LA, or north, toward Vegas, and once they broke down there was an equally good chance they would not be found and would end up baking to death in the desert sun. Anyway, that's what the people who ran The Trading Post would tell you. A little piece of info that did wonders for business.

So the Post prospered over the years, with people buying over-priced gas and food and souvenirs and tchotchkes and knickknacks and postcards (Greetings from Barstow). The rest of the city, what little bit of city there was, grew around The Trading Post. By this day and age there were other places to buy gas and food, or get tchotchkes, knick-knacks, and purchase postcards (Greetings from *Downtown* Barstow), but there was only one place where you could do all those things.

The Trading Post.

Paris eased the Gremlin next to one of The Trading Post's pumps. By *that much* he'd undazed enough along the drive to realize he needed to fill up. Once he started pumping he dazed up again.

Nearby, close to the bin where the complimentary squeegee sat in dirty water, a crazy guy sang "Raindrops Keep Falling on My Head" into a plastic cup. He either didn't know or was too insane to remember the words, so he spiced up the lyrics with a few non sequiturs. Nutty as he was, he didn't rate so much as a look from Paris. After you've cradled the dead, guys singing into cups amount to little.

Paris just kept up his from-here-to-eternity blank-eyed stare, and it was only the overspill of gas onto his feet that jerked him from visions of shot-up bodies and screaming telephones and a million dollars going from cash to ash, back to real time. Barely at that. As he walked from the Gremlin inside the log-cabin building—aluminum covering drywall—to pay up, he zombied out again.

Inside. Something grabbed at Paris's nose. The greased-up smell of food cooking on a grill. It made Paris remember he was hungry.

Past the gift shop, past the Western Union counter was a restaurant. Katie's Kountry Kitchen, the sign said. Chairs and tables of polished oak that were supposed to make the joint look rustic. They made it look like somebody was too cheap to spend a little money and update the decor to one of any number of styles that had become popular in the post-Kennedy era.

Paris wandered to the restaurant, slid into a booth, the vinyl seat and backing squealing under him. After a while a waitress came around; twenty-five at most, dark hair that was long, dark eyes, and brown skin. She could have been a lot of things, but in this part of the world she was most likely Mexican. The name on her tag: Nena.

Nena asked: "Need a menu?"

". . . I filled up on number . . . four, I think." The visions that had plagued Paris since he'd hit the road were diminishing none. If anything, his weakness from hunger just made them all the more vivid and made it all the more impossible to concentrate. "Can I—"

"I'll put it on your bill. You want that menu?" Nena was cute. Not quite beautiful, but very, very cute. Her waitress outfit—even though it was just brown polyester and white trim with a zippered front that bifurcated her tits, and matching skirt that showed off her decent legs—just made her look the cuter. Something about a girl in uniform . . .

Still, in his condition, a third eye wouldn't have gotten her the notice from Paris.

She said, putting on the table the menu Paris hadn't gotten himself together enough to ask for: "Do you want to hear the specials?"

Taking up most of the space behind the grill was Vic, a bull of a guy. Crew-cut hair, biceps big enough to have "Semper Fi" tattooed across them in forty-eight-point type, no matter that he was pushing sixty. He chomped at a cigar while he cooked with no regard to health codes. His white T-shirt—his T-shirt that was once white—looked to have been some kind of souvenir item: stains of the foods of The Trading Post past to present.

Vic had the tracheotomy voice to go with his size and look and cigar habit. He sent it growling after Nena.

"Nena! Order up! Let's go!"

"I'll, uh, give you a couple of minutes," she said. Nena backed away, watching Paris watch empty space.

Daymond was on the phone. Daymond was angry. Angrier than he normally was as an angry young black man.

"I didn't sent you out on no goddamn field trip!" he screamed. "I sent you out ta do a goddamn job! Don't tell me you can't find a muthafucka. I ain't trying ta hear you can't find a muthafucka."

Brice was on her cell phone. Brice didn't care Daymond was angry.

"You really need to do something about your language." Brice was driving her Lincoln Navigator. Like most everybody else who bought a sport-ute, she didn't need the four-wheel drive or the ground clearance. What she dug was the way the vehicle rode high, let her look down at all the rest of the traffic. Brice got off on looking down at people.

At Santa Monica and Highland the light went red. Brice slowed, stopped, but kept talking to Daymond. "You normally talk like that— 'goddamn,' 'motherfucker'—or is all the foul language just . . . I don't know, some kind of cool, urban affectation?"

"Urban . . ." Daymond didn't even make an attempt at the second word. "Fuck you! You like dat language? Fuck you! Now, why don't you do yo job?"

Brice went very cold. The picket-fence transmission did nothing to diminish the chill in her voice. "Don't tell me about my job. I do it, I do it very well, and don't you ever doubt it."

Daymond got nervous. Just the sound of Brice's ice made him that way.

On a couch, across from Daymond, one of the sundry and inter-changeable girls he kept coolin' watched him with a half-smile. She'd never seen him squirm—out of bed—before, and she was digging it.

Daymond, into the phone: "Aiite, damn, jus' be cool."

"I already killed one person," Brice shot back. "What do you want from my morning?"

"I want every muthafucka who had sumthin' ta do with my shit gettin' stolt opened wide da fuck up." Daymond postured hard, trying to wipe the grin off his girl's face without actually having to get up and go slap it off. "You got dat? I want people dead!"

Brice pushed herself back in the leather of the ute's seat. "God, you get me so hot when you talk like that."

"Wha . . . ?"

Cars behind her honked, the light long since having gone red to green. Brice didn't care. Brice shifted to park, put a hand between her legs.

To Daymond: "Say it again. Say you want me to kill somebody." She worked loose her fly. "Say you want me to open somebody up."

Across from Brice, sitting at a bus-stop bench: a young guy, twenties, with looks and a body. A guy who, same as a whole lot of other young guys, twenties, with looks and a body, most likely had come to LA with a whole lot of ideas about becoming an actor or a model, but, like a whole lot of other people with ideas in Hollywood, just ended up a guy sitting on a bus-stop bench. Brice gave him the eye and some smile to go with it. After having every other plan in his entire life go away and leave him alone, it didn't take much for the guy to notice the drop-dead blonde in the sport-ute giving him the come-on.

The guy got up off the bench and swaggered for the Navigator.

Over the cell phone, in her ear, Brice heard Daymond freaking out. "I ain't tellin' you shit, girl. You got problems, you know dat? You are serious crazy."

As she unlocked the door for Bus-Stop Guy, as she hung up: "Oh, Daymond. You don't know how tired I am of hearing people say that."

"Crazy bitch," Daymond spat at the dial tone.

Bus-Stop Guy climbed up into the Navigator. Puffing his chest, and with a weak delivery that explained why he failed as an actor: "Hey, babe. You want some of this?"

Brice's eyes made a circle in their sockets. "Just shut the door and fuck me."

Through an intense, concentrated effort that still required nearly one full hour of sustained application, Paris was somehow able to choke down half a plate of the food he'd been brought. Now, cold and shuffled all together, he couldn't even remember what he'd ordered, if he'd ordered anything. The girl, the waitress, may have just served him some whatever.

The girl, the waitress, Nena, came back around. If she'd been around before in the last hour a steel haze kept Paris from recalling.

She said: "How's everything?"

How's everything?

People Paris knew were dead. People Paris didn't know wanted him dead. People Paris had never seen might be eagerly waiting just beyond the door to slip a bullet past his skull and into his brain.

How's everything?

"Okay," Paris said.

"It's not much," Nena nodded at Paris's plate, "but since there's not much around here it makes the food pretty darn good. Least it makes it seem that way."

Paris made some kind of sound.

"You want any more fries or anything?"

"I'm all right."

At another table a woman who was in a hurry to get her bill so she could get back on the road to Las Vegas called at Nena, "Excuse me, miss . . ."

"How about some apple pie?" Ignoring the woman, Nena kept on with Paris. "You can't leave without trying a slice. Warm with ice cream, would you like that?"

Nena knew she'd never get over as sexy or a knockout. In a city like New York she'd get buried under the everyday lovelies walking the avenues, who were themselves table scraps scraped away by the even more stunning: the women who were beautiful for a living. But here, in Barstow, she figured at the least she was very okay in the looks department. Very okay enough to rate a grab to the ass from every long-hauler who thought getting frisky came with the price of a meal.

So, with that kind of history working for her, she wondered what it would take to earn as much as a solid glance from the distracted but pretty good-looking black guy she was serving.

Paris started to say: "I don't really—"

"Miss . . . !" the in-a-hurry woman cut him off.

From behind the grill Vic got into things. "Nena, you got customers, okay? Go do some work."

"Yeah, okay," she shouted back. "I heard you twice the first time." Finishing up his check, Nena tore it from her pad and let it drift down to Paris. "You, uh . . . you take care, all right?"

Paris didn't rejoin that.

As she moved over to In-a-Hurry Woman, Nena watched Paris take up the check and start for the counter. Watching him go was like watching possibility leaving, just like possibilities had cut out on her so many times previously.

Vic came around from the grill to the register. Vic seemed to run the show, and along with Nena was the only staff Katie's Kountry Kitchen had. The place could have used a little help—an extra waitress, someone who rang up while Vic cooked. But something about Vic said he was too cheap to hire out, that he'd rather pocket his dough than spread it around.

Vic took Paris's bill, totaled it.

Paris looked down at his thigh. There was a big fat once-red, now-brown blood/brain stain on his Levi's from when he'd cradled his former roommate. It was all that was left of Buddy, an unmissable blob that everyone had missed because it looked too much like a food spill, dried paint, or just a new wild design that "the kids" were wearing. Buddy was in death as he was in life: anonymous.

"Eight seventy-five," Vic said, and said angry, like with all the time Paris had wasted taking up space at the booth he should've managed to chow a few more dollars' worth of food. "Twenty-four fifteen with the gas."

Paris fumbled a hand to his back pocket and broke out his wallet. The haze he was living in split open and reality rushed in to fill the void. The wallet was empty. Paris didn't have any money. Quick, his hands patted himself down but came back to report what he already knew: You're broke.

"I don't have any money," Paris said to himself.

"Excuse me?"

"I don't have any money," Paris said again, this time for Vic to hear.

"You don't have any money? What is that, you don't have any money?"

Paris remembered throwing clothes into the duffel with the tape, busting ass out of LA. "I was in a hurry when I left. I don't have anything on me."

"You got a credit card? You got a check?"

"I don't have—"

"You don't have any fucking money. Yeah. You said. You fill up your car, you eat my food, then you get wise you don't have any dough."

"I was in a hurry. I thought—"

Vic wasn't even vaguely interested in what Paris thought. "You know something? I'm getting pretty sick of you people coming in here taking me for what I got, then trying to play me."

"I'm not trying to play you."

"Well, then, if you ain't playing with me you better come up with some cash." Vic's hands squeezed into fists. The flesh rubbing flesh made the same sound as twisting leather. "And you better come up with it quick."

The silent "or else" didn't need to be articulated.

Paris hardly knew anybody, and knew even fewer somebodies who would jump up and get happy at the chance to be involved where lending money was concerned. The glare from Vic that rained down steady on him wasn't helping Paris come up with any new ideas on who might be eager to help him out of a tight spot.

"I don't . . . There isn't anyone to get the money from."

Vic didn't say anything to that. Vic slid his hand behind the counter. It reappeared gripping a cut-down baseball bat. Chipped, battered. Stains of red. The thing looked well used. Very well used.

It was time. Paris had given it a shot, tried to tough it out on his own. But the wood of the bat twisting impatiently in Vic's hands explained to him real good how the situation was. It was time to make the call.

Under Vic's very watchful, scornful eyes, which seemed to do their staring with that hunk of wood, Paris crossed over to a phone, picked it up, dialed ten digits starting off with the 714 area code.


Somewhere in Irvine a phone rang. A man picked it up. "Hallow?" he asked into the receiver.

In the background, across the wire, one hour or so away, as he listened without saying anything, Paris could hear the muted sounds of a ball game on TV. He could hear a lawn mower—one of the neighbors cutting grass. He could hear the noises of suburbia. They hurt: grating little reminders of a place Paris wanted to leave behind. Calling up his dad hurt too, because—unlike every other time he'd called up his dad asking for a bailout—this time he hadn't wanted any help; this time he was cognizant of what a failure he'd become. The only thing that could hurt Paris more would be Vic connecting that bat to his head.

"Hey," Paris said into the phone.

After a moment, "Well" was all his dad had to say back.

Then, for a long beat, there was nothing. Just the ballgame. The lawn mower.

"What's going on?" Paris asked of his dad.

"Nothing special," Paris's dad responded. "Kind of hot out."

"Yeah. It's been hot."

"Gonna be hot for a while."

"It's that time of year, you know? Gets hot, stays hot."

They were like a pair of strangers, wallflowers doing an awkward slow dance, with each other only because they had to be with each other, but if there were anyone else for them to dance with they would have parted company in a second.

Paris's dad: "You know, it's funny, but I was reading somewhere about the other year, when we had that El Niño effect, and the average temperature was, I think they had said it was something like two degrees cooler than normal. Now, to me it seeeuuuuunnnnnnnhh-hhh . . ."

From there, for Paris, his dad faded into a drone of minutiae. Boring detail upon detail of little-known and largely unasked-for information that was substituted for real conversation. Any other time, Paris would have sat through it same as he had always sat through it. Any other time. But this time he didn't have time. Let the begging begin.

"Dad, I need money." It came out in a blurt. It was the only way the combo of embarrassment and urgency that Paris felt would let the words out.

Paris's dad didn't say one thing or the other to Paris's request. The ball game and lawn mower did the only responding.

Paris blurted once more, and for the record: "I need money, Dad," not even thinking about the words he was saying. He was thinking about how, after he got out of this mess, nothing even remotely like it was ever going to happen again. He was living the ultimate example of what shortcutting got you, and from now on it was shoulder to the grindstone and nose to the dirt or however those hard-work clichés went. Bottom line was: from here on out it was the long and hard and backbreaking way around things. This, all of this—the being hunted and tormented by killer Hollywood agents and being eyed as a piñata by some mid-desert redneck—all of it was just a wake-up call. Loud and harsh, sure, but when you've been asleep most your life you need a wake-up call that's . . .

Something Paris's dad said jarred him back from future thought.

"Wh . . . what was that . . . ?"

"Your mother and I just think—"

"What did you—"

"It can't go on like this, Paris. It just ca—"

"What the fuck did you say?"

"There's no need for that kind of . . . I said no."

No?

"We don't . . . This can't keep happening."

He said no?

"Every time there's . . . It's always something with you, son. We just can't continue constantly sending you money for every little thing."

Well, this just made Paris want to laugh. It really did. Every other time, every other thing Paris had gone to them for—money to cover his credit-card bills, a check to pay off AT&T—all of that Paris could've found a way around. But now, the one time he ever really, really needed their help, the last time he would need it, and here Mom and Pop were giving him the brush-off same as they would any of the cracked-up beggars who accessorized the off-ramps of LA.

"You've got to learn to do things on your own, son. That's the way you have to look at this: it's not punishment, it's a lesson. We're just trying to teach you a lesson."

Paris looked over at Vic. Vic looked at Paris. He thwapped the bat in the beef of his palm. Vic was going to teach Paris all the lesson he needed.

"This is something we should've done a long time ago. You'll come to see that."

What had happened? Had the air turned into some of that tarry goo that oozes up from the streets on one of those too-hot LA days? Paris figured that had to be it. How else could you explain how difficult it was to breathe? What other explanation was there for his brain feeling like it had to drag each thought up out of the sloth? "Dad, I need help."

"You have to learn to help yourself."

"You don't understand—"

"You say that, but I was young once, too."

"I'm in trouble."

"There's no trouble you can't handle if you believe in yourself." Paris's dad sounded like he'd just that afternoon graduated from the High School Coaches' Institute of Motivational Speaking.

Again Vic thwapped the bat in his palm. The sound of it was like a plane crash.

"Dad . . . Dad, I'm gonna die."

"It may seem that way now, but later on, one day, you'll be glad we did this. You watch and see if you're not glad."

Paris tried one last plea. It came off as a death rattle. "Dad . . ."

"I'll talk to you later. . . . And I'll tell Mom you called. Good-bye, Paris."

Good-bye. Paris couldn't recall ever hearing anything sound so permanent.

Paris hung up the phone.
Paris turned to Vic.
Paris said: "There's . . . there's a problem."
The look Vic gave Paris said: "Good."
The bat came up from and back down into Vic's palm.
Thwap!

# M

r. Bashir answered the ringing phone. "Twenty-four, Seven Mart. How is it I may help you?"

"Mr. Bashir, it's Paris."

"Paris!" There was a whole lot of relief in Bashir's voice. Then there was a whole lot of anxiety. "Is everything all right? I am very much afraid for you. I think, perhaps, the trouble you are in is very, very serious."

A little laugh from Paris: No shit. "Yeah, I'm in kind of a squeeze here. I sort of took off a little short, you know? And then I remembered I, uh, didn't get my last paycheck."

"Yes, yes, yes. I have it here. I will keep it safe until your return."

"Well, that's the thing. I was hoping maybe you could wire me some money." Hemming. Hawing. "I . . . kind of need it."

"Where are you, my friend?"

"A place called The Trading Post. In Barstow. They've got a Western Union here."

"Right, right. I will go to the nearest location and wire you the money as quickly as possible."

Paris's voice sailed ever so slightly on small, feeble wings of hope. "Thanks, Mr. Bashir. Thanks big. I owe you."

Paris hung up the phone.

Paris said to Vic: "My old boss, he sending the money."

Nena said to Paris: "Why don't you have another Coke while you wait?"

Vic clutched his bat like he was afraid he might not get a chance to use it. "What's he going to pay for it with?"

"Refills are free, Vic. At two bucks a glass they ought to be."

Paris smiled at Nena in appreciation of her being a stand-up girl, and in thanks for her jumping into things for him.

Nena smiled back, happy she was starting to get noticed.

"Just a heap under a blanket with a foot sticking out." Brice talking. "That's all it was the first time I ever saw a dead body: a heap under a blanket with a foot sticking out laying in the middle of Melrose. Who's that photographer—the guy who used to shoot all that old black-and-white stuff? A motorcycle and a half-bed had gotten it on; that's what had happened. A cycle and a pickup get it on, the pickup's always going to win. So there was this guy dead in the street, only he wasn't a guy, he was just a heap under a blanket with a foot sticking out. And I'm standing there looking at that thinking: Man, is that all being dead is? I didn't feel nothing. I didn't think nothing. What's there to think about a heap under a blanket? Weegee—he was the photographer. Bet you didn't think I'd know something like that. I'm not just tits and ass, Jackson. All his stuff was that kind of thing: dead people, but not regular shots of dead people. Cool pictures. Bodies slumped over railings, half hid by garbage cans. Legs sticking out from under blankets. Shit like that. Yeah, death wasn't so much, so I wanted to try it; see it close-up. See for sure if it was nothing. I went home and took a rock to my dog's head. Beat the living hell out of it. Blood, brains everywhere. My parents weren't too happy about it. They started in with the doctors and the therapists and all their question-asking and head-shrinking, like there was something wrong with me. Like I had a problem. Like . . . Anyway, my parents weren't too happy, but I kind of dug it—the dog and the rock and all that. Guess that's why I live the way I live now. You can kill anything you want, and your parents can't say nothing about it. It's like running through the house with scissors in your hand: your parents tell you not to, but it's the first thing you do when you get a pad of your own. Isn't it? First thing I did, anyway."

In response to all that, the actor guy Brice had picked up at the bus stop and was currently in the middle of screwing in the back of her Navigator—lost in his abilities with sexual gratification, which were impressing only himself—said: "How's that, baby? That good? Your man make you feel good?"

Brice's phone rang.

Brice answered her ringing phone.

Her trick tore himself away from his underwhelming cocksmanship long enough to say: "Don't answer it, baby."

"Shut up," Brice said back. Into the phone: "Hello?"

"Hello, Miss Lady? This is Mr. Bashir, the manager of the 24/7 Mart."

Brice rolled off the actor guy. "Hey, Bashir, baby."

The actor guy groped for her. "Hang up. I'm about to cum."

No different than the way a snake strikes, Brice's hand shot out, backhanded Actor Guy across the face, got a shocked whimper from him.

"I told you to shut up!" To Bashir she was sweet as cherry pie. "I was thinking of you. Were you thinking of me? Tell me you were thinking of me."

"Y-yes. Yes, I was thinking of you. I wanted to call you and—"

"I'm touching myself, Daddy. Are you touching yourself?"

"Uhhhh, no. As a matter of fact I am not. You see, I wanted to tell you that I have received a call from Paris."

"I have to orgasm once a day, did you know that?"

"I did not know that, no."

"At least once a day." The actor whimpered some more and Brice threw him a look that slapped him quiet even more than her hand had. "That doesn't mean I have to get fucked once a day, it just means once a day I have to cum."

"Miss Lady, please . . ."

"Hell, if I had it my way I'd never bother getting fucked. What do they say? It's not the dick I mind," she bore a stare into Actor Guy, "it's what it's attached to."

Actor Guy sniveled, then quick put a stop to it for fear of getting whapped again.

"To be honest, Bashir, I'm a do-it-yourself kind of girl." The middle finger of her right hand slid inside her. "Just the way you want it, perfect, every time."

Her middle finger was joined by another.

"But you, Daddy—you could make me dig men all over again."

"I . . . Paris . . ." Sweat trickled off the end of Bashir's nose. "I received a call from Paris."

"I heard you. Poor Paris. Where is he?"

"In the city of Barstow. He requires that I send him some money."

"Well, don't do that, silly."

"But he needs—"

"If you send the money he'll leave before I can go see him. And I want to see Paris badly." Brice sounded all sad and pathetic and un-refusable.

Then she sounded excited: "And as soon as I see him, I can come back and be with you."

"Be with . . . He said he was at a place called The Trading Post." Mr. Bashir detailed things for Brice. Anything to help get her to Barstow and back quick as possible. "You cannot help but to find his car, a Gremlin, do you know? Green."

"I'll see you soon, Daddy."

Brice hung up the phone.

Actor Guy got dumped on his naked ass in the middle of Formosa. He sat, pants at his ankles, watching Brice's Navigator pull away. Still whimpering.


Mr. Bashir mouthed again Brice's words: "As soon as I see him, I can come back and be with you." Again and again he said them, and each time they were as fresh as the moment he first heard them.

A few deep breaths.

Bashir lifted the phone, dialed. On the other end a woman answered.

"Hello, Marta?" Mr. Bashir said. "Tell the children I love them. I will not be coming home again."


Daymond answered his ringing phone. "Yeah, what?"

"Yeah, what?" Brice mocked. "Is that at all polite? I don't see how you keep any customers with that kind of phone manner."

"You crazy, muthafuckin' bitch!"

Brice Sybiled into a hellion. "What did I tell you about calling me crazy?"

"Aitte. Damn, girl. Chill. You got sumthin', or you don't got sumthin'?"

"I got something. He's in Barstow. I'm on my way now."

"How you know he ain't gonna roll?"

"He's ass-out. He's not going anywhere. Drives a Gremlin. Almost feel sorry for the kid."

"You find him, girl. You find him, and you whack him."

Brice, playful: "Maybe. I'll see how I feel when I get there."

"How you . . . Goddamn it, bitch! I'm payin' you ta—"

Daymond got dial tone. He flung down his phone. "Crazy muthafuckin' bitch!"

For a long minute Daymond did nothing but chew at the inside of his lip. Way across the room from him, on the couch, was a new set of girls. But they wasn't so new they didn't know better than to disturb the silence.

After that Daymond picked up the phone again. A cell phone. Even though there was a regular phone right there on his desk, Daymond always used a cell phone, 'cause cell phones was straight-up hipper.

As he dialed, Daymond yelled at the girls, "Whaz yo name?"

One of the girls started to answer.

Daymond cut her off. "Not you, bitch. The big-titty girl—whaz yo name?"

"Sharhonda," the girl with the big tits said back.

"Yeah, well, Sharhonda, when I git off this here phone I'm 'bout ta roll over there 'n' get busy on yo ass."

Sharhonda shrugged. She leaned back in the couch and uncrossed her legs.

Omar answered his ringing phone.

" 'Zup?" he said.

"Omar, where you at?"

Right off Omar knew it was Daymond. "Me and Kenny fiddn' ta go to Roscoe's, get our grub on."

"Oh, no. Damn that. You gonna do work. I want you 'n' Kenny ta git yo asses to Barstow."

"Barstow?" Omar angled for the curb, pulled over.

"Dat bitch Brice found da punk dat stolt my shit."

"What about Barstow?" Kenny asked at Omar.

Omar waved him off, said to Daymond: "So Brice is on the job. Let Brice handle it."

"I don't trust tha' ho. I want you on her ass. I want you making sure she git the job done. Muthafucka drivin' a Gremlin or some shit. Now, you git on his ass bef—"

"What about Barstow?" Kenny asked again.

Omar: "Shut up, nigga!"

Daymond: "Muthafucka, what?"

"Kenny, chief! I was talking to Kenny!"

"You two jus' wanna be gone, aiite?"

Omar worked up a nervous question. "Boss, what if, you know, Brice don't do work? What if she don't do like she's supposed to? Then . . ."

"Then I want you ta bust some serious caps in da bitch's ass. I'm sicka muthafuckas playin' me. She don't do right, then you open her ass up!"

"But . . . it's Brice."

"I don't give a fuck if it's that used–to–be–married–to–*Die Hard* bitch! She don't do right, she go down."

Omar got hung up on.

One more time from Kenny: "What about Barstow?"

"I'll tell you what about Barstow: the shit's about to get hectic. Serious hectic."

"**N**othing yet, sorry."

The clerk at the Western Union desk wasn't sorry. What he was, was sick of Paris asking if any money had come through for him. A little guy, the clerk looked like he ought to be in high school. But in a town like Barstow, in a place where a fellow had few if any prospects, he was probably already working on his second wife and trying to figure out how to pay off his double-wide mobile home.

The clerk said, the clerk suggested very strongly to Paris: "Why don't you go on back over to the restaurant. I'll find you when your money comes in."

Paris wasn't making friends at The Trading Post. He shuffled from the clerk back toward Katie's Kountry Kitchen. Between the two points were the doors. The doors that opened to the outside, to the Gremlin that sat gassed up and ready to roll. He wasn't a track star, but Paris wondered just how fast you needed to be to bust through some doors to a car, fire it up, and hit the road before a fat bastard like Vic even huffed his first step in your direction.

Paris's fingers fumbled at his pocket, at the Gremlin's keys. He kept staring at the doors like they were speaking his name.

"Hey!" Vic called at him for real. "Come here!"

Paris did like told.

"You ain't thinking of cutting out, are you?"

"No—"

"That what you thinking?"

"No! No, I wasn't!"

Vic was still gripping the cutoff bat. Paris was pretty sure he hadn't put it down since picking it up. It was like the bat had become a corrupt and controlling part of the big man, parasitically living off the hate he fed it.

Vic: "Where's the money?"

"My old boss, he said he would send it. I don't know what happ . . . He promised he would send it." Paris talked fast, talked like his existence depended on how well he said what he said. If Vic didn't beat the life from him, it was just a matter of time—if he couldn't get himself back on the road—before the killer music agents shot it out of him. "Look, I swear I'll get the money to you. I swear to God! But I have to get out of here."

"You people always think you can get something for nothing, don't you?"

"No—"

"Always think you got something coming to you." Vic was in a place where he couldn't hear Paris. His ears were plugged up good with his own rants that went on firebrand-strong as if he was demagoguing to a raving mob of one. "People like me got to work for a living while people like you are out drinking and fucking from noon to night."

"What are you talking about? Come on, man. It's not like that."

"Don't you 'man' me, boy. You're not going to shuck and jive your way out of this."

"You're crazy, you know that?"

The bat began to twist in Vic's hands. Hipping Vic to his own craziness was probably not the smart thing to do. Too late did Paris tumble to that.

"Leave him alone!" Nena got between Vic and the future target of his wrath. "I'll pay for him, okay? What is it, twenty dollars? Here!" Nena pulled cash from her change pocket and slapped it on the counter.

Vic promptly snatched it up, crumpled the bill, and threw it back at the girl. It bounced off Nena's face.

"You ain't paying for him. These freeloaders and welfare queens got to learn a lesson."

"Welfare quee—" Paris started.

He got stopped when Vic's hand landed on his chest and grabbed up a bunch of his shirt. The shirt and Paris got yanked for the door.

"You and me are going out back." Vic was sweaty with vicious excitement. He couldn't have anticipated an orgasm with any more glee. "I'm taking my money out of you a penny at a time."

Jerking, twisting, Paris tried to break free. No go.

Vic lifted the bat, ready to beat some submission into Paris, to beat some sense into Paris for eating his food and pumping his gas and not having the dough to cover it. He lifted it to, after for so long holding in all his delicious rage, finally send the bat smashing crashing bashing down and even the score for put-upon white guys everywhere.

There was no hiding from the blow, no dodging it, so fear and anguish sent Paris flying forward into Vic. His arms got wrapped around the big man as much Vic's girth would allow. Together the two as one sailed into tables; the force of impact sent the bat flying from Vic's hand.

Women patrons screamed. Men tried to angle around for a better look.

On the floor Paris and Vic tussled, rolled, bowled over furniture, squished through spilled plates of food, trying to gain advantage. Vic gained it very rapidly. For all the movement and violence there was very little pugilism. Paris's fighting skills ended at accepting punches to the gut, knees to the groin, and repeated kicks to the head, all of which he did expertly. Beyond that the only defense he could muster was to curl in a ball and suck up abuse, same as a black hole sucks light, until even that tactic was beaten from him. Paris's remaining maneuver was to lie on the tile and bleed. Immediately, and with great skill, he took to it.

Vic rose, chest heaving. He retrieved his bat, the wood a welcome feeling back in his mitt. Over to Paris he lumbered.

No words.

Vic just raised the bat high, a two-handed grip, ready to get to what he'd been waiting much too long for. Ready to rid the world of one more lazy, shiftless, no-good, freeloading, black piece of—

The sound could be heard through Katie's Kountry Kitchen, clear across The Trading Post, past the gift shop. Even the Western Union clerk jerked his head up. Not the sound of wood striking flesh, but of metal smacking skull.

Vic went down, his body stretching out like a redneck blanket over Paris.

Paris opened his eyes, looked up.

Above him, gripping a stainless-steel napkin dispenser that dangled hair and scalp, was Nena.

The crowd of onlookers pressed in toward the epicenter of the action.

Nena fanned the napkin dispenser before her. "Stay back!" The implied threat was the same as if she'd been waving a .45. She already, apparently, had the body count to back it up. "All of you, stay back!"

The lookie-lous planted themselves.

Paris burrowed out from under Vic. Dizzy from the beating—the one Vic had handed him, the one life kept handing him—he swayed to the waitress. And with her covering the two of them—the napkin dispenser liable to go off at the slightest provocation—they eased for the door.

Nena stopped. Back over to the cash register she went, punched open the drawer, and cleaned it out, all the while the napkin dispenser keeping a vigilant eye, daring: C'mon, motherfuckers. Start some shit.

Nobody started anything. Nobody said anything. Nobody could believe what was happening.

Paris, Nena made the door.

"You got wheels?" Nena asked.

Paris stumbled for the Gremlin still parked by the pumps, fumbled the door open. Everything was happening too fast.

Not fast enough for Nena. She shoved Paris behind the wheel, then ran around to the passenger side.

"Drive," she said.

Managing the key into the ignition, Paris turned the engine over and balled the jack out, keeping a heavy foot on the accelerator until The Trading Post was just a little something in the rearview mirror.

Literally Paris tried to shake his head clear.

Nena, still clutching the napkin dispenser, bounced with excitement. "Oh, man, do you believe that? That was great!"

Bits and pieces of the recent past began to catch up with Paris: Vic. Vic with the bat. Vic getting clocked by Nena. Nena helping herself to some severance pay.

He asked: "What did you do?"

Still excited: "I've never done anything like that before."

"What the hell did you do?"

"I let him have it, that's what. I cracked him one good." She looked at the dispenser still held firmly in her hand. "Oh, wow. There's blood on here. You don't think I killed him, do you? I didn't kill him."

Hard, Paris broke. The Gremlin wig-wagged side to side as its locked wheels rolled up on the soft shoulder.

When the car had stopped moving—before that, even—"Get out!"

"What are you—"

"Get out of the car!"

"No!"

Paris threw open his door and came around to the passenger side. That door got thrown open too. His hands shot for the girl. She got roughed from her seat.

"Get out!"

Nena's right hand dipped under the apron of her uniform and came out gripping a speed knife that she flipped open in a much-practiced move, bringing the tip of the modified *tanto* blade to rest at a spot where Paris's chin met his neck. The jugular vein, they called it.

Nena, to say the least, was upset. "I save you from getting your head beat in and this is how you thank me? Huh? THIS IS HOW YOU THANK ME!"

Paris talked soft and quiet, like he was trying not to disturb a sleeping pit bull that might wake up and decide to rip his throat out. "S-s-sorry."

They stood for a minute, the knife between them, Nena's hand on one end of the weapon and Paris's life on the other.

On the road, cars passed without so much as slowing down. There was gambling to be done in Las Vegas, and a woman about to bleed a man on the side of the road wasn't hardly going to keep anyone from that.

After a minute more, a lifetime for Paris, Nena folded down the blade into the titanium handle of the weapon and hid it back under her apron. Her look did a morph from angry to hurt.

Paris tried to explain the situation. "I am thankful you helped me, but right now I've got a lot of unpleasantness going on. A lot besides leathernecks wanting to send my head out of the park. I'm telling you, for your own good, you can't be with me."

"Well, I am."

"But you can't."

"And I can't go back to The Trading Post, and since your ass is the one I pulled out of the fire you're the one who owes me."

There was quiet between them. Except for the cars racing for The Strip, quiet.

Nena looked at the Barstow around her that Paris was going to leave her to.

She said: "I should have let Vic kick the shit out of you."

Now Paris looked, saw what Nena saw: nothing. A different kind of nothing than he had achieved in LA. Paris's nothing, back there, was built up—glamorized with palm trees, sunshine, and big-city living. But just below all that was a vapid vacuum of a hole where nothing people lived nothing lives that were set-decorated with German cars, huge houses, and the best fake body parts money could buy in order to approximate the most basal state of worthwhile being. The contrary between *there* and *here* was that Barstow wore its nothingness for all to see. It was too proud not to own up to all it wasn't.

"Get in the car," Paris said.

Sarcastic: "You're not going to grab me and throw me in?"

"Just get in the car."

"Get in, get out, get in, get out. . . ." Nena was playful. Nena was happy. Nena was leaving Barstow. Her black knight had just ridden in on a rusting Gremlin to save her.

The two of them, Paris and Nena, drove for a while—stealing glances on occasion at each other—before Paris asked:

"So—what's the knife about?"

"Girl's got to protect herself. You saw the kind of people I deal with. Make working at the post office look like a good career move."

"You got a blade, you hit people with napkin holders. You violent?"

Nena shrugged like she wasn't sure, but said: "No. The knife's for show mostly. I don't think I could ever stick anybody."

Paris wanted to know: "Why'd you do it—why'd you help me?"

"I'm not sure I did it to help you. Not in particular. It just happened. Vic was riding you; he tossed that money in my face, which really pissed me off good."

"No shit," Paris threw in, underlining the obvious.

"Next thing I know I've got my hand wrapped around that napkin holder and, wham, I give it to him." Nena looked behind her, out the back of the Gremlin, as if she was really trying to see all the way to The Trading Post. "God, I hope he's not dead." She paused a beat. "Actually . . ."

"So then you figured: What the hell, let me just clean out the register so I can spend the rest of my life on the run."

"No, that's not what I was thinking. I . . ." Nena spent a few seconds corralling her thoughts—trying to figure out, away from the heat of the moment, just what was going on in her head.

She said: "My parents were illegals—"

Paris stopped her right there. "Hey, you know what? This is way more information than I really need. Honest."

"You asked."

"I'm un-asking."

"I'm trying to tell you something. I'm trying to relate something to you." Nena went all condescending-schoolteacher with her voice. "Would you like to hear what I'm trying to relate?"

"In two minutes I'm turning on the radio, even if you're only up to how your parents sold their first oranges together at an off-ramp."

"Great, a black racist. I kill my white-bigot boss over a black racist."

"He's not dead! Just tell your story."

Nena settled into her seat. "My parents were illegals. Long as I can remember they were hiding out from the law, moving us around—I had a brother."

"Had?"

Nena didn't say anything to that, and Paris got the feeling nothing more would be said concerning the brother she used to have.

Nena went on with: "They took any shit job they could find where they didn't have to prove citizenship. And I always thought: What the hell? How bad could Mexico be that it's worth all this trouble to be someplace else?"

"This the part where they start selling oranges?"

"Fuck you. Three years ago I started working at The Trading Post. And for three years I've been dying. It was killing me. Inch by inch, day after day, it was choking the life out of me like a rope around my throat. It took a while, but that place schooled me on why my parents put up with all the crap they swallowed over the years. They may not have had much, a little money and a little less hope, but that added up to a whole hell of a lot more than they had in Mexico—a chance, an opportunity. They added up to something. I don't know about you, but if I'm going to get the life choked out of me I don't want to get choked dead for nothing."

A bug splatted against the windshield. Paris turned on the wipers, but it only made things worse.

"When I," Nena went on, "took that napkin holder to the back of Vic's head it was like . . . Well, it was like all of a sudden I could breathe again. And when I grabbed that money it was like I had one more chance to buy a life, one more chance to live for something instead of die for nothing."

Paris didn't have anything to add to the story, least of all a smart remark. Nena was right on, and his last twenty-four hours were witness to her testament. If you're going to take chances, take good ones. If you're going to die, die for something.

They rode on for a bit more, quiet, but not stealing looks back and forth like before. By now they had each other pretty well rated.

After a while:

"So where are we going anyway?"

"Vegas," Paris said.

"Vegas," Nena repeated. "That sounds about right."

**B**rice was talking to the Western Union clerk.

The Western Union clerk was smiling, like maybe he could get some from Brice. Like maybe she was the one really hot-looking chick in the whole wide world who went for guys who looked too young for their age and were stuck in a job where a name tag was the chief tool of the trade.

And while he was smiling, the clerk was responding to Brice's query about a black guy named Paris who should've been hanging around waiting for some money to get wired.

"Yeah, he was here. There was some kind of a ruckus and he took off."

"Took off to where?"

"I don't know."

That wasn't the answer Brice was looking for. "Well, you're just Mr. Fucking Helpful, aren't you? That ought to be your name: Mr. Fucking Helpful. Why don't you get that on your little tag there? Get rid of—what does that say?—'Myron'?—get rid of 'Myron' and have them print up: 'Hi, my name is Mr. Fucking Helpful. How may I be fucking helpful to you?'"

"I . . . He was . . . He drove a Gremlin. It was green, beat up."

"Hey, Mr. Fucking Helpful, you're not so shut up."

In response the clerk blinked a lot, but said nothing.

Brice put on her thinking face. She thought . . . she thought . . . On the wall, just across from her—a map. Brice stared at it: a tracker pondering the trail of an animal too stupid for thought that moved on instinct.

The map . . .

She stared. . . .

She considered. . . .

Sure. That's where Paris was going. And why shouldn't she be going back there too? Back to the place where Ned met Jude. The place where the three of them got John out of a jam. The place where most recently she handled a piece of business the night Tyson whooped Seldon's ass. Gang-related, they had called it. The end result of an East Coast/West Coast rap war.

Nah. It was none of that.

What it was, was just a girl getting work done in that place: The Meadows. Las Vegas.

Brice took off for the door, for her Navigator parked just outside.

With his left hand Omar furiously worked the steering wheel of his Lexus to stay close, but not too close, to Brice's Navigator as it raced for the 15-north on-ramp. With his right hand he dialed his cell phone. Next to Omar was Kenny, who just rode, which made Omar wonder how come it was he had to do all the work while Kenny got to sit there not doing shit.

Daymond picked up.

"Yo, Daymond. We on Brice's ass. She's rolling, but I don't know where for."

"Vegas, muthafucka. She jus' called me."

"Vegas? How we supposed to find shit in Vegas?"

"Damn, man, she goin' right after dude. All you got ta do is follow. How da fuck hard is dat?"

Kenny yawned, let the seat back a bit. For him it wasn't going to be a damn sight hard at all.

"Don't be callin' me every two minutes wit bullshit. I don't wanna hear from none a y'all until people is dead."

Omar hung up the phone. He looked over at Kenny, asleep. The motion of the car rattled his head against the door window. Omar reached over, slapped Kenny awake.

"What?"

"Do something."

"What something?"

"Just . . . shit, something. Damn."

As soon as Daymond hung up the phone, Sharhonda pressed up to him.

She said: "Let's do it again, baby."

Despite Sharhonda's extreme nakedness and the tits her nakedness revealed, Daymond didn't much notice her. He stretched out on his bed wondering when, with all these muthafuckas he got running around for him on his money, someone was going to get killed to his satisfaction.

Sharhonda said one more time: "Let's do it again."

"Get off me." Daymond shrugged her aside. The art of the cuddle was something he had never learned.

Not one to give up easily, a woman who knew the extent of her sexual powers, Sharhonda slid over blood-red silk sheets and clung to her man. The man she was going to make hers.

"Wasn't it good, baby?" a voice hot-chocolaty rich asked. "It can be good that way all day."

Sharhonda had a hand to her eye and was trembling in hurt before she even knew she'd been smacked. The blow Daymond had delivered her wasn't much hard, but hard enough that the memory of a gang of other brothers that'd slapped Sharhonda around no different over the years—long-term lovers, one-night lovers, lovers of her mother's who got good and mad when Sharhonda wouldn't give them any while Moms was at work—came double-fisted pumping back to her.

The memories dissipated, and through them came the sound of Daymond's ranting voice.

". . . Fuck a bitch twice. I don't never fuck da same bitch twice. What da fuck do I want with yo raggedy old used-ass nana? I can have any skeez I want. Why da fuck should you git a double stick from me?"

Daymond put his bare foot to Sharhonda's bare behind and ejected her from the bed.

"Now, git yo ass on up out of here. And don't be taking any a my shit on the way."

From the floor Sharhonda looked up at Daymond.

Daymond rolled away from her, muttering: "Fuck da same bitch twice, you must be out yo damn mind."

No, she wasn't. Sharhonda understood. There were some things he didn't do, same as there were some things she didn't do. Like ever again let a man get away with hitting her.

"Then you have a meeting with Dom Pepetone, A&R from Polytech/Electric. After that is a conference call with Yolly Maxwell's manager to talk about her tour dates. . . ."

Chad's secretary, Jen, was going over Chad's schedule with Chad for Chad's day tomorrow.

She went on: "Mr. Huber asked for a five o'clock. Then you're supposed to have drinks with Moe Steinberg."

Chad, nervous: "What does he want?"

"Moe Steinberg? He wanted to talk about the sound track to the movie they're doing on Pi—"

"Not fucking him!" Chad screamed. "Fucking Huber!"

"I don't know. He buzzed over and said he wanted a meeting. It was all last-minute."

Huber ran the agency. Between sticking his head-of-the-agency nose firmly up the asses of clients and record execs and studio heads, Huber was a busy guy. Huber didn't call last-minute meetings. Not usually he didn't.

Chad went to work chewing a thumbnail. "He didn't say anything?"

"He said he wanted a meeting."

"I know he . . . Important! Did he say anything important?"

"He wanted a meeting. When Mr. Huber wants a meeting it's always important."

Chad went to work gnawing on the flesh of his thumb.

Jen cautioned her way into a question. "Was there something else he should say?"

Did he say: "I'm on to that fuck Bayless"? Chad thought. Did he say: "I'm on to his creative fucking financing that came out of advances that were supposed to be going to the talent"? Did he say: "I'm going to nail that little cocksucking pisher prick to the goddamn Hollywood sign as warning to every lying, cheating lowlife who wants to make a go at show business: play to win, hide your thievery, or get ready to die"?

Chad said: "No, there's nothing else he should say."

Chad's thumb was bloody from where he'd carnivored the skin loose.

"It's just a meeting," Jen noted. "I'm sure it's nothing."

". . . Nothing . . ."

"Should I turn the air up?"

"What's that?"

"You're sweating."

"*L*ook at this again. What do you see?"

Marcus laid the picture of a happy Paris and a happy black/Asian-mixed woman next to the Las Vegas sign down on the table, slid it over to Jay.

Jay stopped eating his Katie's Kountry Kitchen deep-fried whatever, picked up the picture, and looked at it. He scrunched his face to advertise hard thinking, but came up with nothing new.

"Same thing. The kid and a girl in front of the sign." Jay slid the photo back. "All those hotels, all those people . . . How are we going to find him?"

Marcus looked at the picture. He looked at it very differently than Jay had. Instead of going tight, Marcus's face relaxed. He didn't seem to force thought, he invited it to come.

He said: "He's not in the hotels. Not in one of the big ones."

"How do you kn—"

"Works at a convenience store. And this car by the side of the road." Pointing at the photo. "California plates. Probably his. Ever see anything so busted up in your life? This Paris doesn't have much ready, can't afford anything decent. Even if he could, I'm betting about now he'd want to stay on the low pro. One of those cheap motels off The Strip, a trailer park that rents out—he's there. That's where we'll find him."

Jay was drifting. "God, the way you look at that picture. Your eyes get all deep and thoughtful. They . . ." The fork fell from his hand. "They smolder like two fires that . . ."

A shadow blotted the table. Vic, who was now cooking and making rounds since the sudden departure of his waitress, blocked the light. Hands full with plates, he pointed at the picture with his chin.

"You know that guy?"

"Him?" Marcus passed a thumb under Paris's face.

"Yeah. Him. You know him? He a friend of yours?"

"We're looking for him, but he's not a friend."

"He's a goddamn crook, that's what he is."

Marcus had to juke his head to dodge the spittle flying from Vic's mouth.

"And you missed him by about two hours."

"He was here?" Jay asked.

"Took my gas, ate my food, and didn't have dime one to pay for it." Vic answered Jay, but kept up a hot stare at Marcus. "Guess we ought to take food stamps. I got a little rough with him, sure, so what? I was gonna get what I was owed. Then my waitress hauls off, clocks me, and lights out with everything in the cash drawer. Figures. She's a beaner."

"I don't see—"

Vic gave Jay some of that piping-hot stink-eye. "What? You don't see what?" Something about Jay Vic didn't like. Something other than he was sitting around with a black guy who knew the black guy who owed him money. Something . . .

Marcus: "They leave together?"

"What do you think?" Hot stare back to Marcus. "You people stick together, don't you?"

"You people?"

"Yeah. You people. Coons. Wetbacks. Jigs and spics. What are you going to do when you find him, give him a medal for sticking it to whitey?" Vic, having delighted himself, smiled. He leaned down at Marcus. "What? You say something?"

Marcus looked up at the sign above the door. Katie's Kountry Kitchen. KKK. He thought: Figures.

Nervous fidgets came from Jay. "Maybe we should go."

Still in Marcus's face, Vic snided: "Maybe you should pay, then go."

Casual to the point of narcolepsy, Marcus took the napkin from his lap, wiped his mouth, his fingertips. "Sure, we'll pay up." With no discernible increase in speed he reached for his wallet, popped it wide for Vic to see. It was like a Ben Franklin convention in there. "Can you change a hundred? Sorry, smallest I got."

Vic rocked back. His delight left him and it took with it his stupid peckerwood smile.

"Wait. Maybe I have food stamps." Marcus made a big, Times Square–neon show of looking through his wallet for those elusive WIC coupons. None to be found. There was nothing but green. "Nope. Just

hundreds. How about that change? Hmmm?" he queried to the cook/
waiter/loser. "You say something?"

Marcus stood. Jay stood with him. While Jay quickly moved for
the door, Marcus took a bill from his wallet and stuffed it down the
front of Vic's apron.

"Here," Marcus said as he did the stuffing, "you take this. I still got
enough left over to buy the kid a medal when I find him."

With Jay one half-step in front of him, Marcus just about glided
for the door.

Dropping the plates on the table, Vic pawed the cash from his
apron, crumpled it, threw it at Marcus's back. He missed wide and the
bill hit nothing but floor.

"Take your damn money!" Vic screamed.

Marcus kept walking. Check the Bible. Lot looked back more.

"You pick it up!" It was sound and fury wan in ability to frighten.
"Pick it up, you goddamn coon! You take your money! Take it!"

As Marcus pushed open the doors, as he stepped into the sunlight,
he shook his head in pity.

"White people. How you got to thinking you're the master race
I'll never know."

The Shady Tree Inn was as shitty as the law would allow: Paint that peeled as badly as a Paradise Road stripper. An ice machine that made noise and nothing else. An exclusive but unnamable fragrance that came from each and every room. There were also no trees anywhere near the motel, which made Nena think it was shady in the other sense.

The office manager didn't help dissuade her. He was an older man who excelled at being unremarkable except that one of his eyelids seemed to be in a permanent state of partial closure. His name was Hiruss Bullum. For the rest of her life Nena would never come to know that, and never once care to.

Hiruss kind of looked at Nena and Paris as they came through the door that hung loose from its hinges. With that half-shut eye of his it was hard to know for certain where he was looking. He said: "Help you?"

Paris answered: "Need a room."

"Ten bucks."

Even for this dive, to Nena that seemed way cheap. "Ten dollars? For the night?"

"All night? Figured you just needed an hour. All night is twenty-five."

Paris went for his money, then remembered lack of cash was what started off this last little bit of trouble-filled adventure in the first place. Sheepish, he turned to Nena.

"Right. Now you need me." From her apron she hauled some bills and paid the man.

"Got luggage?"

Paris, jerking up his duffel: "Just this."

The manager's eye and a half rolled over Nena. "Sure you don't just want it for the hour?"

"No," words sliding between Paris's teeth, "we want it for the night."

Pawing in a slot behind him, Hiruss pulled loose a key. It was attached, by electrical wire, to a laminated playing card. That was supposed to amount to Vegas style.

Paris reached for the key. The manager yanked it away from his hand.

"Got ID? I mean," getting snide, "you are staying all night."

Paris produced his driver's license. Hirrus noted his name on the crumpled page of a yellow notepad. The Shady Tree Inn's registration book.

Handing Paris the key: "Round back. Nice and private." He gave a peep-show smile. "Make as much noise as you like."

The room was around back. It was private. Mostly because no self-respecting person who wasn't being chased by killers would spend more than the recommended ten-dollar hour in this place.

Paris struggled open the lock, pushed wide the door for Nena, who turned on the room light and was immediately repulsed by the collection of stains on the carpet, the collection of cigarette burns on the bedcover, the collection of bugs that slow-crawled in a corner like they owned the joint.

"Jesus Christ," she moaned.

"It's just for the night. It's cheap, out of the way."

"So's a refrigerator box in an alley."

"Then why don't you go find one?"

"Why don't you go find someone else to pay your bills?"

Yeah, well, that was the end of that conversation.

"So," Nena very smugly asked, "what do *we* do now?"

Paris sat on the bed; the rusted springs squealed under his not particularly considerable weight. He picked up the phone, a rotary, and literally dialed a number.

The other end picked up. Paris said: "I'm looking for Brunson."

Brunson spent forty minutes out of every hour slinging cards across the green felt. As far as he was concerned, breaks were for smoking. He didn't much care for wasting good smoking time yapping on the phone. Anyway, he took the call.

"Brunson."

"Brunson, it's Paris."

Here was a voice he hadn't heard in a while. Brunson marked the occasion by lighting up a cig. "Paris. Where you been hiding yourself?"

"Things have . . ." Paris explained as little as possible. "They've been a little crazy."

"When ain't they, kiddo? In this life, when ain't they?"

"Listen, I could, uh, use a favor."

Across the line Paris could feel Brunson's eyes roll.

"Christ. Favor time. You want cash or check?"

"You know I wouldn't call if I wasn't in it deep."

"Or if rent wasn't due, or there wasn't a camcorder you had to buy 'cause this week you're gonna be a director. How much?"

"Just a little up front, but this time there's a back end."

"Yeah. The back end is where I take it every time I help somebody out, and it seems like I'm always helping somebody out."

Not more than a minute since he'd lit up and Brunson had long since finished his smoke. He fired up another and had it half gone in a drag.

"I'm serious." Paris kept selling. "This one turns a profit for you."

Across the cafeteria Gayle was eating a piece of bread. Just a piece of white bread. Plain. No nothing on it. Her just sitting there eating her plain bread caught Brunson's eye. Gayle was a hot little Asian number, a change girl who worked the casino floor, having just made the switch over to Brunson's casino from the Cal. There wasn't a dealer, a pit boss, a casino host, a tourist who gambled slots while his wife was working video poker across the floor—there wasn't anybody who didn't want to get with Gayle. Word was, something or other had become of her man. Word was, Gayle had just become available. Brunson, as he watched Gayle eating that plain piece of white bread, made a mental note to himself: Get some of that.

Brunson said to Paris: "Not that I'm not interested, but right now you don't have my undivided attention. Let's make it for tomorrow. Come by the casino around three."

"Three. See ya." Paris hung up.

Nena sat next to him on the bed. "Now what?"

"Now . . ."

The skirt of Nena's uniform had ridden up a bit, displaying a touch more leg, teasing with what remained hidden just a little higher.

Paris shook himself free of a ponderous stare. "Now I get clean."

He got up, went to the bathroom, and ran a cold shower. The only kind the Shady Tree Inn offered.

Nena got up, checked herself in the mirror. Her uniform near made her nauseous, but with nothing else to wear she couldn't—

Paris's duffel.

Nena dug through it, found a T-shirt and some shorts. She pulled them from the bag, stripped out of her uniform, happy to put the last of The Trading Post behind her.

So happy, in fact, she didn't notice the small, brown-paper-wrapped package that spilled from the duffel, landed, and rolled, coming to rest half obscured under the bed.

The Monte Carlo was big and bright and very nice, and fought extremely hard to not be as tacky as Vegas usually likes its hotel/casinos to be. The staff was as polite as you'd find on The Strip, and let them smell a tip there isn't anything they wouldn't do for you. So when the reservation clerk said I'm sorry he really meant he was sorry.

"I'm sorry. We do have one room available, but it's with a king bed. Will that be all right?"

Marcus shrugged. "Yeah. We'll share. What the hell?"

Jay nearly passed out.

A 24/7 Mart. Except that this one was in Las Vegas and came with its own set of gambling addicts trying to get rich playing video poker a nickel a hand, it was no different than any 24/7 Mart anywhere else.

Brice walked in and got her usual reaction. A big, broad, God-I'd-like-to-fuck-that smile from the guy behind the counter.

The guy behind the counter said: "Can I help you?"

"Carton of Camels. Wides."

"Filter, or non?"

Brice joined in with the smiling. It had nothing to do with the counter guy. "You know, it really doesn't matter."


Across the street, in their car, Omar and Kenny eyed Brice climbing back into her Navigator.

"What in the hell?" Omar expressed his displeasure. "A carton of goddamn smokes? How the hell long is she planning on being here?"

"Ain't like we in the middle of nowhere. Vegas, baby. It's all good, dog."

"Sooner she finds dude, the better. She don't kill him, we have to go after her."

"Fuck dat bitch!" Kenny flipped a hand in the air as exclamation. "She ain't all that. If she was, Daymond wouldn't have us out here watching her crazy ass in the first place."

"That woman's spilled a mess of blood. A whole mess of blood."

Omar tried to lay things out realistically, logically, as usual, but Kenny wasn't having none of it. Wasn't so much he was a badass, Kenny was too stupid to scare.

"Sheiiit, you sound like a bug-eyed nigga. Crazy bitch. I say bring it da fuck on. Let's git this shit taken care of. I'm trying ta git my titty-bar freak on."

Omar put the car in gear and followed Brice as she pulled out of the 24/7 Mart parking lot back onto Las Vegas Boulevard.

Paris came out of the bathroom—from the shower—still kind of wet. The Shady Tree Inn towels were little and not much for drying.

Nena was parked on the bed. There was something familiar about her that Paris finally realized as his shirt and shorts she was wearing. Next to her were little piles of bills and stacks of coins, which she had neatly counted out.

"Two hundred thirty-three dollars," she said. "Minus the twenty-five we forked over for this place, plus some change." Nena had to put a little effort into not making a bigger deal out of Paris being dressed in only a tiny towel. He was decent half naked. Not as much muscle as she would've hoped for, but not much fat either. "That's an okeydoke take for a first try. Maybe we should hit a liquor store and see how we do."

Paris's hand shot for the bed. It grabbed a fistful of money and flung it upward.

"You think this is funny!" he screamed. The change plinked off the ceiling, the floor, some furniture. The bills fluttered to the ground. "You think stealing is some kind of game? It's not!"

It was a lot of rage and anger and fear that had been boiling up inside of Paris that finally got belched out.

Nena just sat a few beats among the angry words and strewn currency, watching Paris's chest heave and his moments-ago clean body drench itself in an anxious sweat.

After a few beats more, Nena picked up some bills, some quarters off the floor. Quarters could come in handy. You can always use quarters. The rest she left.

"I'll get another room," she said, her voice sounding so quiet, post–Paris rant. "I should . . . You keep the rest of the money. I'll just . . . I'll do something."

She walked past him, not really looking, but able to tell that the sweat around Paris's eyes had begun mixing with tears. Nena got as far as laying her hand on the doorknob before her exit ran out of steam.

Without turning to face him: "Want to talk about it?"

For a little bit Paris went through several abortive, nonanswering gestures. The ill-fitting towel had fallen away, leaving him naked. For the moment, for both Paris and Nena, it didn't much matter.

"I have something," he finally got out. "I took something I shouldn't have."

"Well, we've got that in common. What's so god-awful you've got to take your shit out on me?"

Paris rummaged around in the duffel, pulled out the DAT player.

Nena didn't get it. "A Walkman? You're all bent out of shape 'cause you lifted a Walkman?"

"You heard of Ian Jermaine?"

"Didn't he drown in manure or something?"

"This is the last of him. The last songs he ever sung."

Nena got it. "Jesus. How'd you come by that?"

"I stole it from him the night he killed himself. I didn't know he was going to . . . I mean, he told me, but I didn't think—"

"How did you end up—"

Paris waved her off. "How I was hanging with him is too crazy, so don't even ask about that."

Crossing back from the door, Nena stooped, picked up the towel, and handed it to Paris. She grabbed a peek as she did.

He set the player on the dresser as he covered himself again. Re the DAT: "There are people who want that. They want it bad, and they've got no problem doing things to get it."

"Whydija take it?"

". . . Not sure. Not really. I figured I could bootleg it, make a couple of bucks."

"Guess that's as good a reason as any."

"Only . . . but . . ." Paris went to the dresser, leaned up against it. "That's not the reason. Not really."

"So you took it because . . . ?"

"I took it because it was a chance. For one time in my life I wanted to take a chance."

"For one time?"

"I'm from Irvine. I came up to LA to be something. I wanted to write, direct, act—"

Impressed: "You can do all that?"

Simple: "No. Didn't matter. I didn't want any of that because I'm into art. I wanted to cash in, just like everybody else who wanders out to Hollywood figures they can cash in too. I ended up ringing up burritos and Big Guzzles at three a.m. I had a head full of dreams."

Nena shrugged. "So does the world. Nothing wrong with dreaming."

"But that's all I had. A bunch of dreams, and no way to make 'em come real. I guess I'm just . . ."

"A loser," Nena finished for him.

That picture came back to Paris. The one of Kaila screaming those very words.

This time, though, he laughed at what he saw: the truth. "Yeah. A loser. Then I heard the tape. It was like listening to the sound a sack of cash makes when it rolls off the money truck. A new day, a new chance. Turns out it's just one more fuckup. I am a loser, and a bunch of tape by a dead guy doesn't change that."

Nena lay back on the bed. Bills crunched beneath her. "No, it doesn't. That tape, the money it could bring in—they're not going to change shit for you"—pointing at her head—"until you start changing things up here."

Sarcastic: "Oh, yeah. Right. Let me just close my eyes for a second, okay?" Paris did that. "Let me just wish real hard." He opened his eyes again and made a big show of looking at a new, bright, happy world that all his good thinking had created. "Yeah, that's it, everything's all better now. Everything's perfect. You're right. It's all so fucking easy. Nena the know-it-all waitress. Where you been all my life?"

Nena rolled her eyes, not hardly down with the dramatics. "No, it's not that easy, so quit thinking everything is. Quit taking the short way. Quit dreaming and start following through. It's like I said." She lifted her head, looked straight at Paris. "If you're going to die—and guess what? we all are—die for something. Die for something, Paris."

Plain talk. Simple truth. Die for something.

Reaching to the DAT, Paris depressed the play button. The tape ran. Music played. Out of the tiny speaker of the small machine a man's life and breadth and depth bled from his soul in the form of song.

Paris laid himself next to Nena. She reached down and peeled away the towel.

They did not have sex.

They did not fuck.

Slowly, quietly, to the rhythm of Ian's soul, they made love.

*I*n a hotel room in Las Vegas, Marcus slept a deep sleep while next to him Jay gripped hard at the sheets of the bed they shared, fighting with every fiber of his body to maintain self-control.

In a hotel room in Las Vegas, Brice carefully, diligently, lovingly cleaned her .38. Take care of your weapon and it takes care of you.

*I*n a titty bar in Las Vegas, Kenny made a damn fool of himself trying to use his teeth to slide a ten-spot into a dancer's G-string. Omar didn't much join in with the festivities. All those women, and his mind was on just one chick. A chick who, somewhere in the city, was just then getting her gat ready to do work.

**P**aris finished getting dressed. Nena stared out the window at Las Vegas. The Shady Tree Inn offered a bad view of the city . . . if there was a good view to be offered in the first place. The view Nena was looking at didn't even serve up the casino-design mayhem Vegas called architecture. Nena's view was of slum houses and crack houses and houses that were mobile. Mobile homes. Why white trash wanted to keep their shit ready to move was beyond her. All that mobility, and you never hear about any of them outrunning the last flood or tornado to hit town.

Looking at the tableau, Nena said: "Never liked Vegas much."

"How can you not like it?"

"What's to like? Look at that." She ticked her head toward the window. "That place out there don't make sense."

"What are you talking about? It's just a city."

"All the money this place sucks up from gambling, but you ever see so many dirt-poor people in your life? Drinking and driving's against the law, but everywhere you go drinks are handed out free. Prostitution's illegal, but the fattest listing in the Yellow Pages is for hookers-to-go."

Paris zipped up. "Anything else?"

"How come the city of slot-machine hopes and jackpot dreams has the highest suicide rate?"

"I don't know what you've got planned for the rest of your life, but I'm sure they'd love to have you working in the tourist office."

Nena leaned her forehead against the glass, rolled it side to side. "Don't get me wrong. Vegas isn't all bad. It's clean, it's bright, and it's the only place in the world you can get prime rib for five ninety-nine. It's just . . . it don't make sense."

"Well, I like it, okay? I like Las Vegas."

"Sure. A kingdom for the King of Wishes."

Paris stood there kind of pissed, but Nena peeked over, gave a

"Come on, say something about it" smile. It looked good on her. In the process of their lovemaking Nena had gone from cute to just almost sexy. Not quite, but just almost.

"You about finished?"

Nena shrugged. "Yeah. About."

"Let's get something to eat."

"Hmm. And I guess I'm buying." Nena grabbed up her speed knife and started to clip it to the shorts she wore.

"What are you doing?"

"I told you. A girl's got—"

"To protect herself. I know." Paris shook his head, "whatever" style. "It's Vegas out there, not South Central."

Nena followed to the door, not even noticing the little brown packet, half sticking out from under the bed, that she stepped on and tore open. She noticed even less the white powder that poured out.

Paris and Nena stopped off at the motel office. Still sitting behind the counter was Hiruss Bullum, same as when they'd checked in.

Hiruss gave Nena a greasy smile, the kind of ugly leer that's usually handed over with a dollar bill to lap dancers.

He said: "Well, how was it?"

Paris let the crack pass, said: "Listen, we're probably going to check out late."

The manager's sneer went brighter, like now he was handing Nena a five instead of a single. "Really? He that good?"

Reflexively, Nena groped for her knife.

"You want the money," Paris said, "or should we go somewhere else?"

"Hell, yeah, I'll take your money. Glad to help out a couple of lovebirds."

Nena got the ten-dollar sneer. Her grip tightened on her blade.

Paris nodded his head toward the motel manager.

Nena shook hers—nothing but contempt—and dug money from her pocket. "My luck, I've got to run away with the brokest guy in California." She flipped some bills onto the counter, not wanting to hand them to Hiruss. Not wanting to risk accidental physical contact.

"Restaurant across the street okay?" Paris asked.

"The Peppermill? Good as good goes."

To Nena: "Let's go."

"Yeah. You-all go get some energy," Hiruss quipped at Paris's and Nena's backs as they left. After that he returned to his divine mission in life. He returned to doing nothing.

**M**arcus was tying his tie. Already dressed, Jay watched Marcus tie his tie. Jay had also watched Marcus shower and towel off and shave and slip on his shirt and . . .

Jay buried his face in a copy of *Showbiz Weekly*. *Showbiz Weekly* was the ultimate guide to Las Vegas excitement. It said so on the cover. Right below that was a picture of Engelbert Humperdinck. Apparently, in Las Vegas, Engelbert Humperdinck doing a stand at Bally's constituted excitement.

Marcus slid the knot of his tie up to his collar. "Want to get something to eat?" He spoke at Jay's reflection in the mirror.

"Actually, I thought I'd run over to the Mirage and try to get some tickets for Siegfried and Roy. I mean, God, if we're going to be here anyway wouldn't you like to see Siegfried and Roy?"

"No."

"I'll . . . I'll just get one ticket."

There was a knock on the door. A little voice that usually spoke Spanish said as best it could in English: "Housekeeping." The maid, like all maids at all motels and hotels, leaving zero response time for the hapless half-dressed occupant, used that magic key of hers to bust into the room like a vice cop making a raid on a sleaze den. The room was empty. Paris and Nena were off to get something to eat.

The maid got down to maid business, roboting her way through the same routine she performed in every room of the Shady Tree Inn and three other Vegas motels every day except Tuesdays—just to make the twenty-six bucks a day she made, which was all she made because she was an illegal, and illegals got paid twenty-six bucks a day.

Tuesdays, the days she didn't work, were the days she took the child that she'd had with that guy who was supposed to get her a green card but instead just fucked her and left her (welcome to America) to the doctor who was treating the kid's respiratory ailment. The doctor charged the maid a lot of money. The doctor could do whatever he wanted. The doctor was a legal. And that's why the maid worked six days a week. That's why she worked by rote, not thinking, because thinking slowed her down and a slow day meant less than twenty-six dollars.

So the maid just did like she always did. She gathered towels, she stripped the bed, she replaced the sheets with new ones that were—that were supposed to be—clean. Same as with every room. Same as with every motel. No variation.

One variation. She did have to pick up that brown package off the floor. She did have to dump it in the garbage, it was busted open after all, and she did have to vacuum that powder up off the carpet.

If she had thought about it, the maid, she might have realized the brown package was not just a package, and the white powder was not just powder. If she had thought about it she might have realized a way to not have to work six days a week, a way to pay for the best doctor in the city—the best doctor in the state—to look after her child.

If she had thought about it.

But thinking slowed her down and a slow day meant less than twenty-six dollars and . . .

The maid finished the room. One last touch before she left, that strip of paper on the toilet: THIS ROOM HAS BEEN SANITIZED FOR YOUR PROTECTION.

The Gremlin rolled into the Peppermill parking lot. Paris turned off the motor and started to get out.

"I don't want to eat here," Nena said.

Paris said: "What?"

"I don't," Nena said, "like this place."

"What do you mean, you don't like it? We haven't even been inside."

"It reminds me of The Trading Post."

"It's nothing like The Trading Post."

"It reminds me of The Trading Post."

"Why, 'cause it has food? It has food so it reminds you of The Trading Post? Is every place that has food going to remind you of The Trading Post?"

"Can we just eat someplace else? I mean," dry as the Nevada desert, "since I'm paying for it, would that be okay?"

"I'll just drive." Paris closed up his door. "Point if you like something."

The Gremlin rolled out of the Peppermill parking lot. It rolled right past an Audi A4.

The A4 parked. Marcus got out and went in to get some breakfast.

**B**rice kicked it on the bed of her hotel suite, the Complete Las Vegas Business White and Yellow Pages open on her lap. Open to *Motels. Hotels* she'd already been through. There were a lot of those in Vegas. There were a lot more motels. Motels, and motor-hotels, and RV/trailer parks that rented space, and a few—just a few—hotels that rented at motel rates, which probably meant it was just a room with shitty service.

Brice dialed.

The phone rang and picked up and a voice said: "Royal Flush Motel."

"Paris Scott's room."

The voice paused for a second, then: "Paris Scott? I'm sorry, there isn't—"

Brice hung up as soon as she heard the negative. The sentence she could've finished on her own. There's no Paris Scott here. No guy by that name checked in. Scott? Don't have a Scott registered.

It was the same response she'd gotten from all the hotels. It was the same response she'd gotten from all the motels "A" through "R."

Brice was getting tired of dialing.

Brice was getting pissed.

Brice was going to take her pissedness out on Paris when she found him.

Brice dialed.

The phone rang and picked up and a voice said: "Sandcastle."

"Paris Scott's room."

The voice said: "We have some lovely rooms available right now that—"

"Is Paris Scott there?"

"Would you like to hear about our Stress-A-Way weekend relaxer specials?"

"Paris fuckin' Scott—is he there?"

The voice choked for a second, not sure what to say, then said what it knew: "There's no Paris S—"

Brice hung up. Brice muttered: "Too much fucking trouble just to kill somebody." She took a pen and circled that motel, the Sandcastle. If time permitted she was going to stop over there, talk about that Stress-A-Way weekend. Share a smoke with whatever nimrod had been on the other end of the phone wasting her time.

Brice dialed.

The phone rang and picked up and a voice said: "Shady Tree Inn."

"Paris Scott's room."

No pause this time: "Scott? Naw, Lover Boy ain't here."

Brice felt a warm and happy glow all over. "Where is he?"

"Who wants to know?"

"Who wants to know? His wife, that's who wants to know."

Hiruss Bullum was a simple man who was guided through life by simple rules: Toilets, not floors, were for pissing in. Never pay full price for tires. And for crying out loud, if you had a woman, if you made a vow to love her before God, you didn't cheat on her . . . and get caught. A man who can't keep his cheating secret is a man in need of punishment.

Paris Scott had just broken one, at least one, of Hiruss Bullum's rules. Paris Scott had just lost Hiruss Bullum's respect.

Into the phone Hiruss Bullum said: "Figures. Wants the room for a night. Hah. Should've known he was an hour man at heart."

"You know, I really don't care who he's with or what he's doing." Brice threw in a sniffle. At the same time, done with the Motel section, she flipped over to Entertainers, which is what whores who made house calls called themselves in Vegas. In the Complete Las Vegas Business White and Yellow Pages there were 136 pages of Entertainers, Entertainment Bureaus, and Escorts. Color pictures, black-and-white pictures, and ads that just listed phone numbers. There were some decent-looking guys pictured in some of the ads. There were some not-too-bad-looking chicks pictured in them too. "I just want him to give me enough money for some baby formula."

"Baby formu . . ." Hiruss Bullum was a tolerant man. He was a forgiving man. As manager of the Shady Tree Inn he had tolerated and forgiven a lot. But even Hiruss Bullum had a point of satiation, and it had just been reached. "That suma bitch. I can't hardly get on a man for being with another woman. Don't approve of it necessarily, but that's my trade. But to leave a woman with a hungry baby . . . ? I'll tell you, lady. You can find him over at a place called the Peppermill. And when you give it to him, give him one for me."

Brice was already hanging up as Hiruss was finishing his tirade. To the cradled phone: "Yeah. Right."

There were a lot of clubs on Paradise Road. Dance clubs, strip clubs, and, well, clubs. There was a little section of Paradise Road that had a string of clubs with names like The In and Out. Beefeaters. The Bone Yard.

There was among these clubs a place called The White Swallow. A nice little club. A quiet little club. A dark little club were you could go, unseen in the middle of the day, to sit, to drink, to . . . do other things.

That's where Jay went, to The White Swallow, to sit and drink and . . . do other things. He put himself at the bar, between an overweight white guy—thick glasses, thin hair, and a permanent sweat sheen—and a black guy, light in skin tone, hair cropped tight, and features that were sharp, angular. Mixed, Jay thought, as he—with all the casualness he could force up—hoisted himself onto the bar stool.

Jay ordered a Midori Sunrise. He dug the sweet taste and pretty colors the mix of Midori and grenadine made.

While the bartender was doing the pouring, Jay turned to the black guy.

Jay said: "It certainly is hot. I mean, I'm in from LA, I'm no stranger to heat, but this is hot."

The black guy didn't have anything to say to that.

Jay said: "All dry and everything. Kind of heat that crawls all over you. Dry heat, uh-huh. Dry heat."

The black guy still didn't have anything to say to that.

Jay said: "Yeah, it certainly is hot. No other way to say it. It's just . . . hot. Good air, though. I like the desert air."

The black guy stared at Jay for a sec. The black guy said: "If you want to dance, just ask me to dance."

*B*rice stopped her Navigator at the far end of the parking lot across from the Peppermill. Out of a case she took a pair of Bushnell binoculars. Those Germans might be some crazy, genocidal, Hitler-loving bastards, but they knew how to make a great pair of binocs. She flipped open her cell phone and dialed. As it rang she focused the Bushnells on the Peppermill's big picture windows.

Inside the restaurant a waitress went over to the phone, picked it up. In her ear Brice heard the waitress say: "Peppermill."

"Could you," Brice asked, "page Paris Scott?"

"I'm sorry. We don't page people."

"I'm his mother. His father just had a heart attack."

Far away inside the binoculars, the waitress grabbed her own chest. "Oh! Oh, my God. I'm so . . . Hold on." To the whole of the restaurant: "Paris Scott!? Is there a Paris Scott here!?"

Marcus's head snapped up. French toast dribbled from his open mouth back down to his plate. Paris? Here? His head whipped around, looking for a young black man to stand up and go for the phone.

"Paris Scott," the waitress yelled again.

Come on, Marcus telepathed. Take the phone call.

Nothing. Nobody. No Paris at least.

Marcus watched as the waitress started to put the phone back up to her ear, started to tell the person on the other end of the line Paris wasn't—

The person on the other end of the line . . .

"Hey," Marcus blurted at the waitress.

She asked: "Are you Paris?"

". . . Yeah, I'm Paris."

Like it was heavy to the extreme, the waitress handed over the phone. "I'm so sorry," she said.

Marcus missed that. He was already asking: "Hello?"

Brice asked back: "Paris?"

A woman's voice. The chick from The Trading Post—the one the redneck cook said Paris had split with? ". . . It's me." Marcus kept his voice low, tried to make it indistinguishable. "Where are you?"

A click, a beat, then all there was was dial tone.

"Hello . . . ? Hello . . . ? Shit!" Marcus shoved the phone back at the waitress. "Give me my check."

"That's all right." The woman's eyes blurred red and brimmed with tears. "You just go. . . . And God bless you."

The waitress's weirdness couldn't slow Marcus down. Out the door he was flying, thinking as he moved: Paris was for sure here in Vegas. Nearby, probably, if whoever it was—the Trading Post chick, probably—thought he was at the Peppermill. So, if he and Jay could manage to—

Marcus got smacked back. He tumbled—something tumbling with him—to the hot, hard asphalt of the parking lot. In his hands, though, was something very soft. Flesh. The flesh of a very fine-looking white girl.

Marcus said: "I'm sorry." Marcus asked: "You okay?"

"I think I hurt my leg." Pain was in her voice. The white girl ran a hand over her ankle.

Marcus ran his hands over the white girl's arms. "You going to be all right?" Shit, her arms were tight. Almost as tight, from what Marcus could tell, as her ass. Thoughts of Paris didn't have a chance of staying in Marcus's head with this chick's body staring him in the face. Not meant to be salacious, but unable to be asked any other way: "Can I do anything for you?"

The white girl gave a smile. "Yeah," she said. "Kiss my boo-boo and make it all better."

At the other end of the parking lot, in their car, Kenny and Omar didn't have any fancy German binoculars. All they had was their peepers. Good enough to see Brice rolling around the ground with some guy.

Omar: "What the fuck she doin'?"

"Maybe that that muthafucka we lookin' for," Kenny came back with.

"He look like he work a damn 24/7 Mart? My man's too slick."

"Aiite, maybe Black already broke off Daymond's shit."

Omar sucked at his lip, shook his head. "Or maybe that ain't even the brother Brice is supposed to be looking for."

"So what? So she's trying to get the dick? So what about it?"

"So we got marching orders. So we been told what to do if she don't do what she been told."

"So . . . ?"

Looking at Brice and the well-dressed brother, Omar had a vision. He saw a whole lot of things going wrong and an even greater number of people getting fucked up to a monumental extent.

"So," Omar said, "we gotta pop her."

*J*ay felt joy. There was no other word for what he felt, no other word needed. Simply joy. He felt as if his entire life had been lived starved of oxygen and now, at this moment, for the first time, he had taken a breath deep and clean. For the first time he knew the pleasure of that which both gives and sustains the nature of being. Fingers closed around Jay's arms, hands gripped tighter. And with that action another breath was taken, another wave of joy raced through him.

Jay exhaled. Words climaxed from his mouth. "Your hands are just so . . . so strong, Marcus."

The black guy who held Jay in his arms rolled his eyes. "How many times do I gotta tell you? My name isn't Marcus."

Jay floated away on a dream. "Mmmmmmmmm."

In the not too terribly long history of Danny Huber—Danny Huber was only forty-two—he had distinguished himself as one of the biggest lying, back-stabbing, two-faced bastards in Hollywood, which is why he got to run a talent agency. However, Danny Huber—the last name used to be much longer and more ethnic-sounding, but early on he'd shortened it, as if it was a bad thing, in Hollywood, to be too Jewish; that was kind of like being in the NBA but not wanting to be too black—wasn't a big enough lying, back-stabbing, two-faced bastard to be able to handle running a production company. That hadn't worked out so well, but nobody talked about it. Not to Danny's face, because Danny was once again running a talent agency, where, as one of the biggest lying, back-stabbing, two-faced bastards in Hollywood, he could exact a terrible vengeance on people. People not as lofty as him, anyway.

Chad Bayless was not as lofty as Danny Huber. Chad Bayless was standing in the middle of Danny's office—an office that looked like somebody had pretty much just put a desk, a phone, and a fax in the center of a Japanese art museum; it looked that way because *Details* magazine said that style was trendy, and if that's what *Details* magazine said, then, goddamn it, that's the kind of office Danny was going to have—cold-sweating his ass off. He was cold-sweating, and he was dancing as hard as he could.

"Of course there's an expla-planation," Chad stuttered in response to Danny's question. Chad wasn't even sure what the question had been, too coked up and too scared to absorb whole sentences. He'd just caught the important words: "money," "happened to," and "what."

Like Chad had started to say, there was an explanation. He tried to think of a different one, one he could actually get away with telling, as he went along. "I mean, that sort of money doesn't just walk away. What kind of question is that—is there an explanation? Yes. Yes, there's an explanation."

Danny didn't say a word. He had learned from an E-meter audit at the Scientology church he went to—started going to when he found out that John Travolta went to the same church and, goddamn it, there has to be a way to get *that* script to John—that sometimes silence is as severe and frightening as a shout.

It was to Chad. But to Chad, high and scared, it would have been severe and frightening if Danny had dug wax from his ear.

Chad, Danny, the whole world floated along in the silence for a while.

Then, like Chad had finally gotten the meaning of Danny's lack of words: "Oh, you want it now. Well . . . fine. I can give you an explanation . . . now."

Chad stood around. He didn't do much explaining, but he did manage to get a whole lot more sweating in.

Danny stayed terrifyingly quiet.

"You know, sure, I could give you an explanation. But I think . . . yes, I think I'll just go to my office and get some paperwork that will do . . . and exp . . . tell you . . ." Chad didn't know how to finish the thought. Chad wasn't sure what the nonexistent paperwork that he'd just imagined up would or wouldn't prove. "That's what I'll . . . my office."

Getting himself together enough to leave, Chad exited Danny's office and headed for his own.

Still silent, Danny just sat, then sat some more. Then Danny reached over to his phone and dialed extension 228.

Two-two-eight was the extension for Security.


As nonchalantly as a sweaty guy—a sweaty guy who was now bawling nearly as much as a freshly ass-slapped newborn—could, Chad walked down the hall, past Jen's vestibule, into his empty office, closed and locked the door, and fell into the chair behind his desk. It didn't take him more than a few seconds of sitting before his crying went into sixth gear.

"Oh, God. Oh, Jesus. I'm fucked. I am so fucked. What the fuck am I going to . . . I'm sick, that's what I am. I am so, so sick. I have to feel better. Please make me feel better."

"How would you like to feel, Chad?" Angela. There for Chad as always. Smoke was the sound of her voice.

"I . . . I'd like to feel . . ." How would he like to feel? After so many years as a shark in a suit, as a scorpion trying to poison its way up from the bottom of a bucket of snakes; after living like his heart and soul had been safely locked away in a place whose location could not be recalled, if Chad could have any sensation to call his own, what would it be? "I'd like to feel like a child. You remember how you felt when you were a child?"

"I remember, Chad." Angela's hands were a wisp of air that swirled around Chad's shirtsleeve before it was unbuttoned and rolled above his elbow. The fine blond hairs of Chad's arm raised up beneath Angela's touch. A leather tourniquet raised his veins.

"Never worried about anything. Didn't know how to worry when you were a child." Chad was somewhere sailing. "And you always had someone to take care of you. Always."

Like God's messenger spreading her wings, Angela pointed to Chad's desk.

Chad looked.

On the blotter, between Cohibas Chad smoked but didn't like smoking and his membership card to The Sports Club LA, was a liquefied substance in a vial and a stainless-steel syringe—beautiful—that glistened even under the fluorescent light.

Artfully delicate, studiously practiced, the tip of the syringe was slid into the vial. The liquid inside, extracted.

"I'm," Chad said, "sick, Angela. I need to be taken care of. Will you take care of me?"

Pitiable as Chad sounded, Angela didn't pity him. Angela was beyond making judgments about people, their status or station in life. "You know I'll take care of you, Chad." And she would. Angela took care of everyone equally.

Chad's arm got lifted to her mouth. His skin got kissed by her lips. The lipstick left a mark, a ruby-red mark that, in Chad's mind, looked like a little target.

"Promise? Promise to take care of me?"

There was laughter in Angela's voice. "Oh, Chad. It's so funny. Sometimes I think I love you. Sometimes."

The needle of the syringe plunged into the lipstick bull's-eye. Blood was drawn back from Chad's body, mixed with a speedball cocktail, then delivered back into him.

In less than any measurable time Chad began to twitch, jump, and contort. Just as quick he stopped moving. Like clouds across a Kansas sky, bliss drifted across Chad's face. His head dropped to the side, or maybe turned, to listen to a sound a hundred million miles away. He felt himself moving closer to it and picking up speed,

He managed to mumble: "My God. It's beautiful. So beautiful."

"What's beautiful?"

"The music . . . Kid's a genius. I think . . . I think I'll tell him."

Chad, very quickly, saw his seventh birthday, when he didn't get the Big Jim action playset he wanted. He saw when he was thirteen and grabbed that girl's breast while he passed her in the hall at school. He saw himself suiting up for his first day as an assistant at an agency, ready to take on the world. Maybe not the world, but Hollywood. Chad could take on Hollywood. Sure he could. Chad could take it on and win.

That was the last thing Chad Bayless ever saw.

In a big Vegas Strip theme hotel, on the twelfth floor, down the hall off the elevator, was room 12-101. A mini-suite. The door was locked and on the handle was a "Do Not Disturb" sign hung there not in the least bit surreptitiously by Marcus. He wanted the white girl—Brice, he'd come to find out her name was—he wanted her to know that he didn't plan on being disturbed, interrupted, or impeded for the next couple of hours.

Marcus was unbuttoning his shirt, glad he'd taken time the night before to hit the hotel spa. He wasn't ripped, but he was pumped.

Brice was futzing with the Bose Wave radio, trying to settle on a tune she could groove to, having already made a full swing up and down the band. Classic Benatar, but Brice didn't work to chicks. Sting. Bryan Adams crooning his way though another movie-soundtrack song. Shit, she'd listen to Sting's fake-ass soul crap first. Didn't they play any music in Vegas? Maybe, Brice thought, they fed this garbage into the rooms to drive people down into the casinos.

"Forget that," Marcus said.

"I want to find something good."

"I don't need music."

"I do."

Brice kept scanning.

More shit . . .

More shit . . .

Journey. Journey? That was almost classic rock.

"Close enough," Brice said. She stood, turned, got a faceful of Marcus's bare chest. No hair and a fair amount of muscle. And here it was almost a full day since the last time she'd cum. All in all, it was too bad she was going to have to do an ashtray job on him.

Marcus gave Brice that "You're a pork chop and I'm starving" look. "Never hit it with a white chick before." He was practically busting out of his pants. "Don't know why. Had my shot at plenty. Just always thought there was something wrong about it."

Brice considered this. "Well, I've got good news"—her hand went to the small of her back—"and I've got bad news." It came back around clutching her piece.

All the gun got from Marcus was a little laugh. "What the hell is that supposed to—"

"You seem like a cool guy, so let's just get to it, Daddy-O. Where are the drugs?"

"Girl, you better check yourself." Marcus wasn't laughing anymore. He wasn't even smiling some. "Put your toy away, or I'll do it for you."

"Is that what you're going to do?"

"What the fuck are you going to do? You going to shoot me? You going to take your little bitch gun and shoot me?"

Brice shot Marcus. One quick tap on the trigger sent a slug ripping through his shoulder, mangling up but good a portion of bone and muscle along the way. His scream and the gun's bark just about canceled each other out.

Brice asked, bored: "Next question?"

Marcus clutched his wound; blood bubbled up between his fingers. From the back of his mind he got taunted by a little voice: See? This is what comes from trying to hit it with white chicks.

Gushing wound and all, Marcus still had some quick to him. He used it to whip out a hand, backfisting Brice hard to the face. The blow sent her reeling, sent the gun flying from her grip. Left hand taking the girl by the hair, Marcus used his right to FedEx her some shots to the head. The force of the blows pushed her teeth through the flesh of her lips. Her nose popped, not broken yet but jetting blood just the same. Punch after punch Marcus drove into Brice's skull, jaw, and temple.

"Jesus Christ," Brice sputtered with scarlet mucus, "lay off the face!" She dropped to her knees and would have collapsed to the floor except for the wad of hair Marcus used to suspend her.

Flashback. Bridgeport. The long walk home. It was coming around again to Marcus, a feeling he thought was a onetime thing tripped off of instinct and the need to survive.

It wasn't.

What it was, was a home-brewed violence long with him and left to ferment. A hate received, magnified, and returned to sender. It was the sensation that came when you knew if you had to, if you absolutely had to, you could kill. It was one simple thing: Start something with me, and you die.

"What you gonna do now, huh?" In the fraction of a second between delivered blows, Marcus realized that since the violence began his hard-on had swelled. "What you gonna do without your little bitch gun?"

This is what Brice did: Brice worked her fingers into a fist, and Brice sent that fist—using her shoulders, her hips—flying into what was right before her eyes: Marcus's massive erection.

Hurricane-hard the air rushed from Marcus's lungs. A trail of fire flashpointed at his groin and leapt wildly throughout his body. From there it was a long, fast cut-tree tumble toward the floor with a chuck to the head by Brice's knee on the way down.

Dragging herself up, rising above the stretched-out Marcus: "That's the thing about girls: we don't expose our weaknesses."

Brice stumbled over to her gun, picked it up. Into the bathroom she went. Cold water into the basin. Cupped hands splashed it on her face. The water hit like a sledgehammer. As best she could Brice washed away the blood and did a damage assessment. Her nose was swelling and would only swell more. The bone above her cheek, just below her left eye, felt cracked. Surgery would fix that, but surgery would leave a scar. Her bottom lip was a real mess, torn and fat and purple. She opened her mouth. A tooth half hung from the gum. Very, very painfully she twisted and pulled, yanked it loose along with a squirt of blood.

For a good amount of time Brice checked herself in the mirror. All the looking in the world wouldn't change facts. Her perfect face wasn't perfect anymore.

Brice left the bathroom, went back to Marcus's just-now-stirring body. Looking down at him, she sneered her new gap-toothed sneer.

"Ooooh, you are soooo fucked."

The Gremlin pulled up outside Paris and Nena's room—the room Paris stayed in with Nena, but Nena paid for—at the Shady Tree Inn.

"So who's this Brunson guy?" Nena asked.

"Dealer over at the Plaza. Friend of mine. Guess he's a friend. I just sort of know him. Spend time in Vegas, spend time in the parts of Vegas I spend time in, Brunson's the kind of guy you get to know."

"A card dealer?" Nena said, but her voice toned: Some card dealer at a low-rent joint's going to get you out of a jam?

"He's connected, hooked up with people. Figure I can get him to front some money for the tape. At least enough to get us out of here."

"Us?"

"Yeah, us."

Nena stared off out the windshield.

"What?" Paris asked. "What's wrong?"

"You say us . . ."

"And . . . ?"

Looking at Paris now. "You mean it? You really want to take me out of here with you?"

"Damn straight I mean it. I get the money and we'll go . . ." Where? Where would they go? "We'll go to Florida. Ever been?"

Nena shook her head.

"That's where we'll go; to the Keys. Island after island all strung together with miles of bridges." Paris had never been to the Keys, but just the same he spun gold with words. "We'll drive to the last of 'em. Get a place. You and me all alone. We'll be able to find something there. A house, work. A life."

Nena went back to looking out the windshield like what was out there, if there was anything out there in particular to look at, was of greater interest than what Paris was talking about.

She said to him, still looking at whatever: "I listen to you talk—"

"It's not talk."

"I listen to you, and it sounds so good: being with a guy, having a life with him. . . . Then I remember what you told me about you being a dreamer, about being full of words. I could use somebody who's going to need me like I need them. I could use somebody who's going to be there for me." Nena stopped looking out the windshield and looked again at Paris. She looked at him dead solid serious. "I can't use a dreamer."

Paris stared back at Nena just as solid, just as serious. "No more checked swings. On this one it's you and me, together, to the end of the road."

Having made his case, Paris went to close it. He leaned to Nena. Deeply, fully, he kissed her on the lips.

Nena didn't much respond one way or the other.

"Thirty minutes," Paris told her. "I make sure Brunson can do this, we trade the tape for the money, then we're out." Adding, as if his word alone wasn't good enough: "Hell, I'm leaving the tape with you. I'm not going anywhere without that."

Nena got out of the Gremlin and started for their room. About halfway there she stopped and turned back.

Paris stretched to the passenger-side door and rolled down the window.

"Like I said"—Nena didn't shout, but her voice carried just the same—"I don't want much, just something worth dying for. A life with somebody? I don't think I could want much more than that."

Nena went in the room.

Paris put the Gremlin in gear and drove off.

*I*n a big Vegas Strip theme hotel, on the twelfth floor, down the hall off the elevator, was room 12-101. A mini-suite. The door was locked and on the handle was a "Do Not Disturb" sign hung there not in the least bit surreptitiously by Marcus.

And they went very undisturbed, Marcus and Brice, for an hour and more as Brice worked her special brand of magic with Marcus on the floor, hands cinched behind his back with his own belt, as her reluctant assistant. With the aid of only a few packs of cigarettes Brice had made welts, burn blisters, and screams appear. On occasion she threw in a few kicks and punches, but that was just to add a little spice to the show—break things up a bit. A good magician's always got something up their sleeve.

"Where is it!" Brice screamed in Marcus's face. Her voice altered by her torn lip and missing tooth.

". . . I don't know," whimpered Marcus, his voice altered by some seventy-five minutes of near-ceaseless torture. The torture of the cigarettes. The torture of the kicks and punches. The torture of listening to back to back to back seventies guitar-rock tracks. Ted Nugent, Steve Miller, Bad Company. BTO. Two times Marcus had silently thanked God for Bachman-Turner Overdrive when they'd come on the radio and Brice had stopped the agony just long enough to take a dance break.

Crazy bitch, he thought, then whimpered some more.

What hurt the most for Marcus was the whimpering and sniveling and crying itself. Not that he was a hardass brother, but all that blubbery boohooing was beneath him.

So he thought.

With just her Camel Wides and her two fists Brice was able to prove to him otherwise.

Marcus bawled on: "I swear . . . I swear to God I duh-don't know what you're—"

That, like every other time Marcus didn't have the answer Brice wanted to hear, got him a cigarette ground on what little nonburned flesh he had left.

And hocus-pocus, yet again came a scream from Marcus.

"You want this to end?" Brice asked sweet and kind, playing good bitch to her bad-bitch self. "All you have to do is tell me where the drugs are."

"What fucking drugs? There ah-are no drugs!"

"Yeah. Okay. No drugs. If that's the way you want to play it, it's cool by me." Brice reached for her smokes, but the pack was empty. "Daaamn. Gone through another pack." She took a fresh one from the carton, unwrapped the cellophane with a deliberate glee. "I'll give you this, Paris: you're one tough motherfucker."

"Paris?" Thoughts were greased-eel slick for Marcus, but he managed to latch on to a few, string them together. The phone call at the diner, him taking it, the girl accidentally running into him. Marcus realized things. The realization materialized a crazy, toxic laugh.

"Am I missing something?"

"I'm not Paris."

"Denial. That's not a good sign."

Not laughing now, just screaming: "I'M NOT PARIS!"

"C'mon, man. If you haven't figured it out by now, I take my job serious." The cellophane fell away from the pack. Brice popped it open, slipped out a cigarette. "I don't like playing games."

Not screaming now, just begging: "Please, I'm telling you, I'm—"

"You took the phone call. You said you were Paris."

"You stupid bitch!"

Beat up as she was, tired as she was from the tedious work of crucifixion, none of that cut down Brice's speed. Just the sound of the B-word and she threw a gun on Marcus, and threw it fast.

"Hey," she barked.

"My jacket . . . Luhh . . . in the pocket."

Brice did nothing, not sure what to make of Marcus's request.

"Look in the pocket," he said again, a little more forceful, a lot more urgent.

Cautiously, gun still spotting him, Brice crossed to Marcus's jacket flopped out across the bed. Her hand dug through the pockets . . . dug. . . . It came up with the picture: Paris and Kaila by the Vegas sign.

From Marcus, barely: "That's him. That's Pah-Paris. I'm looking for him too. He stole from . . . from my boss."

Brice shook her head. "The kid gets around." Brice's mouth, where the tooth was missing, where the hole was torn in her lip, hurt, and was hurting more by the second. At some point drugs would be a good idea. "You know where he is?"

"Heard he picked up a girl; he's traveling with her. Thought you were her. That's why I took the call."

She didn't even know it, but Brice was starting to huff. She had gone after the wrong mark. She had made a mistake. And mistakes? Those just made Brice mad. Crazy mad. More crazy mad than usual.

"This is great." She was all full of lament. "This is just . . ." The picture of Paris got torn to pieces and tossed to the ground. "This kind of shit can't happen. It can't! I'm supposed to be a professional! I'm supposed to kill the right people!"

Psychosis was fueling her every word. The as-of-yet unreached potential of the girl's fucked-up-ness was just becoming evident.

Brice raved on. "I've got a reputation I'm trying to protect. This job's already gone on for too goddamn long. Now this. You know how bad it looks when I go around killing the wrong people?"

Marcus began to mumble.

Looking down at him: "What did you say?"

"I . . . I don't—"

"What?"

"I don't want to die." Strong, emphatic, dire. "I don't want to die!"

Her dementia dissipated quick as it had come on. Lightly Brice floated to Marcus, straddled Marcus, lowered herself to him. She stroked his face. Butterfly wings couldn't have touched more softly.

She said with a voice just as silken: "Nobody wants to die. It's just one of those things that happens."

The gun came around and settled in the middle of Marcus's forehead.

His last words came as a scream: "You biiiiiiitch!"

Out in the hall, on the twelfth floor, no one heard a gunshot from room 12-101. A mini-suite. All they heard, from a very loud Bose Wave radio, was Bachman-Turner Overdrive guitar-rocking their way through "You Ain't Seen Nothing Yet."

The Union Plaza hotel and casino—rechristened Jackie Gaughan's Plaza by its owner, most of the signs still read with the old name, Jackie, apparently, too tight to spring for some new ones— sat, simultaneously, at the top of Fremont Street and at the bottom of the world. Old, faded colors inside and out, the Plaza looked as tired as a player on an "I'm going to win it back, I'm going to win it all back" binge.

A relic; that was how you'd describe the Plaza. A ghost of a former time when it added a little extra sparkle to the Las Vegas crown.

However long ago that might have been.

No more high rollers. No more big spenders. No more whales, if the joint had ever had any. Yet, with its nickel slots and twenty-five-cent roulette chips, the Plaza held on. The army of living dead who populated it now gambled with something besides cash. They gambled with their lives and with their last chances. But, same as if they were gambling with money, the House had the odds. The House beat them down just a little lower than they were when they came through the door.

Paris came through the door. Stenciled on the glass was "The Union Plaza" in gold letters. Below that, the Plaza's slogan: "Live It Up!"

It couldn't have been more misused if it were slathered on the door of a mortuary.

Paris crossed the Omaha Lounge—where the Sunspots played as usual—passed the Omaha Bar—where the drunks drank as usual—to the gaming tables, where the gamblers did their usual thing. Behind one of the blackjack tables, slinging cards, was Brunson.

Brunson didn't shake hands with Paris. When you were a dealer in the middle of a shift you didn't shake hands with people. The eye in the sky didn't care for that.

On the tallish side and not particularly thin or heavy, Brunson was pretty much nondescript except for his face. His face was memorable. His face was like a carving board. It was as if some really old geezer had willed him lines and wrinkles and crevices. Take some newspaper, crumble it up in your hand, and open it again. Look at it. You're looking at Brunson. Just add a voice that sounded like he shot out of the womb with a cig in his mouth.

Paris sat at the blackjack table and waited but didn't play, then gave up his chair when the table filled with gamblers. You weren't allowed to take up space where people wanted to bet their money. The eye in the sky didn't care for that.

So Paris parked himself over at the Omaha Bar, near the entrance to XS, the resident stage show, featuring topless dancing girls not good enough to make the cut at Jubilee, the Follies, or even Splash; a no-name singer doing a tribute to Pasty Cline; and Baxter Fielding, a magician who would've been just as well known if, like the singer, he had no name at all.

After a while, when the shift changed, Brunson went over to the bar, to Paris.

"Well, well," he husked, "whadda we got here?"

"How you doing, Brunson?"

"I'm all right. You look like shit." That was the thing about Brunson: you got no nonsense from him. None at all.

"Thanks," said Paris.

"How about some chips? Want to lose a little?" Brunson let a few reds rain from one hand into the other. Technically a dealer wasn't supposed to be handling chips away from the table. The eye in the sky didn't care for that either. But Brunson didn't always care how the eye in the sky felt. "First taste is on the house."

"Naw. Thanks."

"Drink? Something to eat?"

Paris shook his head no to both. "It's, uh, good to see you."

Brunson smiled. The creases on his face blended like the lines on an Etch-A-Sketch. "Yeah. Okay. Sure. Whaddaya say we just get down to it? What can I do for you? Or like you put it: what can you do for me?"

Simple: "Money."

"How much?"

"Thousands. Millions. As much as you can get your hands on."

Brunson's head swayed side to side. "Everybody's got a money plan. My luck, everybody's plans run through me."

"You're hooked up. You know people."

"Yeah, I know people. Seems like fellas are always coming to me, fellas at the end of a rope that's half chewed by desperation. They're always coming around looking for help 'cause I know people, I can hook them up with people. If I could just make this connection or the other for them, well, then, everything would change. It's like, far as anyone is concerned, I'm the gatekeeper between bad yesterdays and better tomorrows."

Paris tried, poorly, to make sense of what Brunson was saying. ". . . I mean, you've just got a rep, that's all: Talk to Brunson; he knows how to help a guy out of a tight spot. He knows how to make things good again. Like you said, man. You're the toll guard . . . whatever . . . collector."

Brunson nodded a couple of times, then: "Before you go on and ask whatever it is you came to ask, ask yourself something first. Ask yourself: if Brunson's just a dealer and nothing more than that in what's probably the shittiest casino this side of the low end of nowhere, the gate he's supposed to be keeping watch over, is it to better tomorrows, or just different ones?"

Paris wasn't sure what to say to that. He had come unprepared for a philosophy class, and never would've anticipated a blackjack dealer for the professor. So Paris just reiterated: ". . . You know people."

"Wrong people, seems like."

"Look, I don't know from everybody else, but I'm being straight. You can make some for-real coin."

"I don't move drugs."

"I'm not talking drugs. Music."

"Man, if you're trying to get me to throw in with some lounge act—"

Big hand gestures from Paris cut Brunson off. "Forget that. You know Ian Jermaine?"

"Singer or something. Choked on shit or something like that out in LA."

"Yeah."

Out of Brunson came raw revulsion. "Fucking LA."

"I got his tape."

"His ta—"

"The last music he ever made: I got it."

Off in the casino, bells and whistles went wild. Someone had hit a slot jackpot and was whooping it up. Brunson didn't bother to look. He knew it was a nickel slot, nothing to get animated about. There wasn't a nickel-slot jackpot in the whole of the city that could change the life, improve the lot, turn things around for a Union Plaza gambler. All it could do was slow the bleeding a little.

"No shit?" Brunson said to Paris.

"No shit," Paris said back. "Hottest thing in music and now he's offed himself, gone, and you get the last of him. Bootleg it. Sell it off. Whatever. There's nothing but money to be made. Nothing but."

"And what's it going to cost me to make all this money?"

"Ten thousand."

Brunson gave Paris blank stare.

Barely, Paris remembered bracing Chad Bayless for a million bucks. He could just about recall all the hopped-up wild dreams that came with that kind of money. Chocolate money, it turned out to be. Money that melted away before you could even get it into your pocket. One million dollars . . .

"Three thousand," Paris said in response to Brunson's stare.

"You ain't too skilled at shakin' people down. I hear the tape, it's legit, I'll get you five."

Five. That was good. Good enough. "Thanks, man. I—"

One finger on Brunson's hand came up, wagged Paris quiet. "Whoa. A fortune in music and you're just giving it to me for five grand? What's the rest?"

"There is no rest. That's all."

Paris got more of that Brunson deadeye. Brunson was good at the deadeye look. He used it while he slung cards across green felt for eight hours a day. Five days a week. Seventeen years running. Yeah, he had the look down.

All Paris gave up in return was: "I gotta have the money. I gotta hit the road and I gotta have something to travel on. End of story, man. End of story."

A crucial need was great in Paris's voice. It wasn't end of story. Brunson could tell. There was more to things, but Brunson let it go.

He asked: "Got it with you?"

"Got it back where I'm staying. I can have it here in thirty minutes."

"I can have your money in fifteen. I'm waiting on you."

"I'll be back."

Paris got up, started to go. He didn't make hardly a step.

From out of the showroom—the show, XS, being well over—came the dancers: second-rate in skill, top-shelf in body. There was a group of them, but as far as Paris was concerned there was only one. The one with legs, thighs muscled up, that stretched out from a skirt as short as it was tight. The one with a shirt that covered so little she might as well have been wearing air, and what little it covered was a fantastic pair of tits. The one—auburn hair with blue eyes that were like a couple of X rays—who did things to a man without doing a thing.

From way far away, on a bad transatlantic connection, came Brunson's voice. "Yeah, brother. I know. See that shit every day, and it's always the same. It's like you're drowning and you don't care. Rushing headlong into a fire and picking up speed. Built like a German car, legs you'd let walk all over you and smile about while the walking was getting done. Looking at that, the whole world could drop away and you wouldn't be the wiser, wouldn't even care.

"Yeah, I know. I know. And here's the kick to the head: that girl loves her some black man."

Barely, Paris felt Brunson pat him twice on the shoulder, then: "I'll be waiting with the money."

Like Paris was caught in one of those *Star Trek* tractor beams, he felt himself pulled toward the woman with the auburn hair. Auburn hair, and fantastic tits.

He always had been a sucker for fantastic tits.

In a big Vegas Strip theme hotel, on the twelfth floor, down the hall off the elevator, was room 12-101. A mini-suite. The door was locked and on the handle was a "Do Not Disturb" sign.

Maybe, Jay thought as he arrived at the door still floating on a fantasy cloud, Marcus was napping. Maybe he had just taken another shower and was toweling off the glistening sparklets of water that clung to his . . .

Involuntarily Jay's body jerked with a shiver. He could barely stabilize his hand enough to slip the card key into the electronic door-lock doohickey. He managed it somehow, opening the door, but leaving the "Do Not Disturb" sign right where it sat.

"Marcus . . . ?"

The first thing Jay noticed was the smell: smoky. Cigarettey, and something else. Three something elses. One of the something elses was unfamiliar—kind of like a firecracker, only stronger. The second smelled oddly like cooked meat. The third . . . Had the toilet overflowed?

"Marcus, I'm back."

The ubiquitous, industrial-strength Vegas drapes had been pulled across the windows. There was nothing but dark in the room. Jay got himself to the drapes, clutched them, tore them open. Sunlight fell into the mini-suite. Sunlight fell all over Marcus's carcass. A carcass covered with cigarette burns, burn blisters, and scarred flesh. A carcass lying in its own feces, termination having slackened the body's sphincter muscles, releasing a flood of internal muck. A carcass with a mine shaft bullet-dug from forehead to skull base.

Jay looked at Marcus, but didn't make a sound. The sight of death was a gut shot that punched the air from his lungs and left him swaying, gasping.

After a period of time that measured between one second and forever, Jay went down, as much collapsing as going to the body.

"Marcus . . ."

Not mindful of blood and still-oozing body fluids or the puddled defecations, Jay scooped up what was left of Marcus, rocked it in his arms.

In an agonized gasp: "No, no, no. Don't be gone. Please . . . you can't. You can't be gone."

From deep in a pit of despair something caught Jay's eye. The combo of sunlight and teary eyes made the shredded bits of glossy paper on the floor Grail-like shimmer. Jay couldn't help but notice them. He lay Marcus down and picked the torn papers up.

Not papers.

A shredded picture. On one of the little pieces was a little face. The face of Paris.

Jay said to the body: "It was him, wasn't it? It was him who did this."

With great rapidity something inside of Jay became twisted and misshapen, then was replicated throughout him like a runaway virus. Some part of him evolved or devolved or just changed, but quite suddenly he wasn't the same as before he walked in the room. He was a different sort of human being than a moment ago, when he pulled open the curtains and the sunlight revealed his secret fantasy lover had been brutally slaughtered in their Las Vegas mini-suite. As with the story Marcus had related to him concerning his transforming walk from Bridgeport as a teenager, Jay suddenly found himself in possession of an emotion and a correlating ability he had not previously known. The emotion was undiluted hate. The ability was to kill.

"He's dead," Jay pledged of Paris. Lightly he stroked Marcus's face. "I swear to you he is dead." And then, leaning over, Jay pressed his mouth to the body's and ever so gently kissed its lips. It may have been the bastard kiss of lunacy, the manifestation of an odd and bizarre yearning, but even in its queerness there was a level of affection, devotion, and desire, a level of long-unspoken but most genuine love that most kisses, exchanged under much better, much more "normal" circumstances, would never, ever know.

The buss over, Jay immediately got up and left. No hesitation. That which he had become had things to do.

Sharhonda's shit was tight. She was looking hootchie-mama foin. She had on some thigh-highs, powder blue, that gave her a couple of extra inches in height. Matching that was a pair of tight-ass powder-blue shorts that, well, shit, they made her ass tight and all delicious-looking. Her top, what little top she had, was the same color as the rest of her gear. A sleeveless midriff thing that was tied in front with a very loose knot that barely kept her tits from busting all out.

The rest of Sharhonda was exposed. Nothing but smooth, black flesh. She was sporting only two blemishes. One intentional. At the small of her back was a tattoo, a little yin/yang thang which, if Sharhonda knew how much that shit was going to hurt to get carved into her, she would've put it somewhere where people could see it. You could see it now. Sort of. The small of her back was kinda blocked.

The other blemish? A right-eye bruise that was purple under the black of her skin. A bruise that got sent over courtesy of Daymond Evans, who chilled in his silk sheets, just where Sharhonda had left him, working the phone: cutting deals and checking profits, yelling and screaming and so forth at all his little soldiers out there doing the heavy lifting. The soldiers who made him a big, bad brother so he could lay in his silk sheets and work a phone and, when he wasn't doing that, slap around his bitch du jour.

So Sharhonda waited. She stood in the doorway, looking her fine self, and waited for Daymond to get off the phone.

*Sharhonda's pops was a barber. Not one of them hair-design cats. He was old-school, ya know? An honest-to-God barber who ran his own barbershop.*

Eventually Daymond got done with the phone.

Eventually he looked up and saw Sharhonda standing there, doing nothing, but getting shit done.

"Daaaaaaaaamn." Daymond gave the word all its worth. "What da muthafuck . . ."

"You like?"

"What da fuck do you think?" Answering his own question, beneath the sheets, something stirred. Rose up.

Sharhonda's lips parted in something like a smile. "Yeah, I think you like." It was so very, very close to being a smile.

"Git yo black ass over here."

Sharhonda did as told and was glad to. She went to the bed; the stiff heels of her powder-blue boots made what was beneath her powder-blue shirt jiggle with every step. Gently, she sailed down to the mattress.

While Sharhonda was doing all that, Daymond occupied himself by sliding a hand under the sheets, sliding a hand to himself.

To Sharhonda: "Wha's yo name?"

He didn't even remember her.

"Sharhonda," she said.

"Yeah, girl, you aiite." Daymond looked her over, inspected her like a horse to be traded. "Bitch looks that aiite, it's like she wearin' a sign: OPEN FOR BIDDNESS, or some shit. See bitches all day long with their signs hung out, then they wonder why a brother be givin' them the eye, tryin' ta roll up on 'em. They be doin' it 'cause, a brother see a sign and he don't do nothin' 'bout it, then he like some ignorant can't-read nigga, like he a turned-out punk. Brother see a sign, brother see a bitch is open for biddness, he gonna handle some biddness. Bitches got ta know dat. Like dat Tyson-raped-me bitch. You go 'round lookin' for trouble, don't be all cryin' 'n' shit when you git some trouble in yo ass. Jus' what happens when a bitch looks aiite. And you, girl"—with his tongue Daymond slathered his lips—"you aiite. Except for dat shit round yo eye. Wha's up with dat?"

He didn't even remember beating her.

*Down at Sharhonda's pops' barbershop, he had all that barbershop gear. He had them big-ass tilt-back chairs, a towel steamer, combs sitting around in that blue juice. . . .*

"You gotta do sumthin' 'bout dat shit," Daymond said.

"Yeah. I'm going to do something about it," Sharhonda agreed.

"Here's what you need ta do sumthin' 'bout." Daymond pulled back the sheets, revealing a cock, sizable, but not doing much to support the myth. "You need ta be goin' ta work on dat."

"Yeah, let me go to work on that. You just close them eyes and lay back."

Daymond did.

"Sharhonda'll take care of you," she said.

Lot of times Sharhonda would head down to her pops' barbershop and borrow things. Curling irons and straightening combs. Some relaxer if she needed it. Her pops was good about that: borrowing her whatever she needed. Today, just a bit earlier in fact, Sharhonda had gone down to her pops' to borrow something.

Sharhonda reached for the small of her back, for the yin/yang tattoo. She reached for it and pulled from the band of her shorts a very, very shiny, a very, very sharp stainless-steel straight razor.

She said: "Sharhonda'll take care of every little thang."

Payback is a slapped-around-one-time-too-many bitch.

In Nevada, selling guns was a decent and respectable business no different than selling shoes, cars. Gardening equipment. Except that guns were no good for anything but killing, it was no different. Mac Bowen's Guns, Guns, Guns was—like most Nevada gun shops—clean, well lit, and carried a variety of small arms, hunting rifles, and semi-automatic assault rifles that complied with the law but could be quite easily converted into fully automatic weapons that didn't comply with the law but made it that much simpler, easier, and more convenient to blow people's heads off.

Jay walked into Mac Bowen's Guns, Guns, Guns with his clothes slept-in wrinkled, his tie disoriented at the knot, and with a big, red stain of blood on his otherwise white shirt. In spite of all that, Jay walked into the shop sporting his best "I'm just another honest citizen who wants to buy a gun" look.

The guy behind the counter, who was not Mac Bowen, took a look at Jay, at his sweaty flinchy nature, at his unmissable bloodstain, and said, for lack of knowing what else to say: "Can I help you?"

"Yes," Jay quite casually responded. "I would like to buy a gun."

"A gun?"

"Yes."

Over in a corner, checking out cop-killer bullets, a shady-looking guy—long dirty coat and a dirty baseball cap to match—dug the scene.

". . . What kind of gun?"

"Oh, I don't know. . . ."

Jay's eyes fell over the display case before him. They came to rest on a Colt Anaconda .44 Magnum long-barrel. Jay didn't know it was a Colt Anaconda .44 Magnum long-barrel. Jay just knew it was a really big gun.

"That looks like a good one right there," Jay said, pointing at the big gun, the Anaconda.

The counter guy, skeptical: "What are you planning on doing with this gun?"

"I . . ." He was going to track down and dish out a little vengeance to a dude named Paris by putting a bullet or two or five in the back of his head. "Hunting . . . I think would be good."

In the background the shady-looking guy slipped out the door.

"Hunting what?"

"Bears."

"You don't much hunt bears with handguns."

"Birds. I'm going to hunt birds."

Counter Guy eased himself for a phone. "Why don't you wait here a second," he said, putting in his voice the same leisure with which he moved. "I got to . . . make a call."

Jay may have been in some serious post-trauma shock, but not so much so that he couldn't still read a face. Matching Counter Guy's easy manner, Jay made for the door.

He said: "You know what? I don't think I need that gun. I don't need any gun. I meant to get, uh . . . the other thing."

"Hold on!"

"That's what I need. I'm going to get that, and I'll be back."

"Hey!"

Jay gave up on being casual and bolted. He was out the door and down the strip mall flying past the used-CD shop, the taxidermist, the Cuban-rolled-cigar store—they weren't Cubans doing the rolling, they were Mexicans, but Las Vegans didn't know the difference. Didn't know, didn't care.

Jay ran and ran and ran past the shady guy who leaned up against the mall's stucco wall, leaned there like he was kickin' it waiting for a cab, a bus. He was waiting for Jay.

"Hey," Shady Guy yelled.

Jay kept running.

"Hey," Shady Guy yelled again.

Jay kept running, but said: "I have to—"

"I know what you have to do. You have to get a gun."

Jay stopped running. He turned around, stared over at the shady guy in the shadows all dressed in black, scruffy-faced and wild-haired. Something about him, just hanging there, made Shady Guy look all the shadier. Made him look like a perv outside a schoolyard peeping preteens.

Shady Guy's mien and manner might've freaked Jay a little, but once you stumble on head-shot bodies in your mini-suite, pervert-looking guys don't give you much bother.

Shady Guy to Jay: "Yeah, you need a gun. Why not? You're an American. You got a right."

"I only need it for—"

Making fly-swatting gestures in the air—Shady Guy didn't have time for explanations and logic—"Don't matter what you need it for. All that matters is you need it. 'Cept you can't get it. Not in a place like that." Shady Guy juked his head back toward Mac Bowen's Guns, Guns, Guns. "Even if they would sell it to you, which they won't, you got to wait five days to get it."

"Five—"

"Who's got five days?"

"I don't have—"

"That's my point: who does? Fucking laws." Shady Guy was doing the talking for the both of them. "Don't get me wrong, I'm not one of them militia wackos or nothing, but when the goddamn liberals get in the way of our basic freedom to strap up, then it's time for all of us to stock up on ammo and canned food."

Shady Guy was talking a little crazy, but not so crazy he didn't fit right in with the rudeness that'd been going on in Jay's life over the last twenty-four hours.

Jay, talking a little craziness of his own, hepped Shady Guy to his plight: "Marcus. I need it for Marcus. I promised."

"Sure you did. You made a promise, and now these motherfuckers won't sell you a piece. What's a guy to do?"

"I . . . What do I do?"

Next thing Jay knows, he's standing in the same strip-mall parking lot at the trunk of a '76 Granada Ghia, pea green, staring at one of the finest collections of illegal weapons one man could ever possess.

Jay, eyes wide like he was looking at a pharaoh's treasure: "Oh, God . . ."

"Yeah. Go to church every Sunday, get down on your knees, and thank God we still live in a country where a guy can get his mitts on some of these." Shady Guy waved a hand over the weapons like he was a game-show prize girl displaying a washer/dryer combo. "Nice, huh? Yeah, go on," Shady Guy prompted. "Pick one up."

Jay scanned the spread. There were Rugers and Mitchells and Charter Arms and a couple of S&Ws, but Jay's hand went to a Sig/Sauer P-226 9 mil. Just as with the Colt Anaconda .44 Magnum long-barrel, Jay didn't know the Sig/Sauer P-226 9 mil. was a Sig/Sauer P-226 9 mil. Like with the Anaconda, all he knew was it was a big gun.

Shady Guy schooled him: "Sig/Sauer P-226 9 mil. Double-action, full-time internal-impact safety. Yeah, some guy's looking down the barrel of that, all of a sudden he knows who's who and what's what. That right there'll end all kinds of social discourse. All kinds. Good choice. You know guns, right?"

"No."

"Come on, you can tell me. Guys who know guns go for the S/S."

Slightly flattered: "No, really—"

"But it feels good, don't it? To the hand, having a gun—that shit feels real good."

It did. It did feel good to Jay. But feeling good wasn't enough.

Jay asked: "Is it good? I mean, is it a good gun for me?"

"Depends on what you want it for."

"Payback is what I want it for." Dark clouds sailed over Jay. "I want it to put somebody on a one-way train straight to hell. I want it to make sure somebody never sees this side of six feet of dirt again."

A beat, a shrug: "Yeah, it's good for that."

"How much?"

"Uh . . . you know, let's say two-fifty."

"You take credit cards?"

"I'm selling guns out of the back of my car." For emphasis Shady Guy pointed to the guns in the back of his car. "What do you think, I take fucking credit cards?"

"Okay. Two-fifty. I can handle that."

"It's yours. Welcome to the wonderful world of the Second Amendment."

Jay looked over his new possession. He asked: "You have a silencer?"

"A si . . . ? You don't need that. That's movie shit."

"I want it."

"Yeah," Shady Guy laughed, "a silencer. Why don't you get yourself a laser sight while you're at it?"

"You have one?"

It was dusk in Las Vegas and it was fairly quiet. There was traffic on the 15—there was always traffic on the 15. People racing the devil to get their gamble on—but other than that it was quiet. Most of the noise, along with most of the action in Las Vegas, took place behind the walls of the fake castles and phony pyramids and make-believe tropic isles.

It was quiet, also, at the Shady Tree Inn. Just the sounds of the old wood settling, and of Nena splashing through the pool she hoped was at least as clean as it looked. She broke the surface, swept back her hair—made richer by the water—and rested poolside. From a towel she took her watch, which lay next to her ubiquitous speed blade. It had been an hour and twenty minutes, nearly that, since Paris had left. Thirty minutes, he had said.

"Thirty minutes," Nena scoffed.

She heaved herself out of the pool—the water dripped and splattered on the concrete, loud in the quiet—toweled off, and wet-foot splatted back to the room.

It was dark in the room, dusk and all, shades drawn. Nena turned on a light and toweled off some more and didn't notice the blond woman with the battered face sitting in a chair in the shadows until the woman said:

"Hey."

Nena sprang back into the nightstand, knocking the lamp, but not knocking it over.

"Whoa, careful," Brice said. "You're going to break something." Flipping her head toward the bed: "Have a seat."

For a second Nena did nothing except try and figure out who this woman was. Even simply resting in the chair there was something about her, something besides her mangled features—her manner or her tone—that carried with it a considerable nastiness and told Nena it didn't matter who she was. *What* she was, was no good. Quietly, cautiously, Nena sat.

Brice let a moment or so pass, and as it did she checked Nena out.

"Turn your head a bit."

Nena did.

"Back the other way."

Nena did that as well.

"Pretty. Real pretty. I can see why this Paris guy goes for you." That came off as a compliment. "I can definitely see why someone would go for you." That came off as simply lurid. "What's your name?"

". . . Nena."

"Nena. Nena, did you know I have to orgasm once a day? Of course you didn't know that. How could you? Well, I do. Once a day. At least once a day. And I don't mean I *like to* cum once a day, I *have to* or I just get seriously bent out of shape. Most times guys are good for it, for getting me off. Most times. But when there's no guy around . . . Well, then, you just gotta make do, know what I'm saying?"

As dim as the light in the room was, the gun resting quietly in the crotch of Brice's lap seemed to glow.

Nena's body jerked with a shudder. She became unbelievably nauseous, more so than she had ever been anytime previously in her life that she could recall. It was a sickness so intense and severe it made her want to both puke and cry. Fear kept her from doing any more than give off another jerk, another shudder.

"Now you're probably asking yourself: Why is this bitch telling me about her orgasm cycle? I'll tell you why, Nena. Because it's time for you and me to get to know each other. Just us girls."

Down Sahara Avenue were the Sahara Lake Apartments, the lake being a man-made algae-filled pond the apartments were built around. They were okay, the apartments. Just okay. The kind of inexpensive drywalled and bad-carpeted rooms a girl who danced in a low-end Vegas revue at a low-end Vegas casino could afford. The Sahara Lake Apartments were where Willia lived. Willia—her unbelievably true name was Willia Desire—being the long-legged, auburn-haired, blue-eyed, hot-bodied dancer who, good to Brunson's word, had a thing for brothers. A thing to the point where pretty much all Paris had to do to pick her up was stick his face in front of hers. Some weak gibble-gabble followed that, which was followed by Paris in his Gremlin following Willia to the Sahara Lake Apartments. That's how he ended up in her pad, on a chair, watching Willia sitting on her bed— naked head to toe—combing her hair. Long, even strokes that just about lulled Paris into a trance.

Willia's amazing body was only made more amazing by its lack of clothes. She was a smart gal, too. Not that she was a graduate-level reader, but at least from the bit Paris had rapped with her she didn't seem to be as stupid as he figured a showgirl would be. For sure she wasn't as stupid as the couple of strippers he knew. So—a kinda smart chick with a good body . . . How, he wondered, does a girl like her end up in Vegas?

Paris asked: "How does a girl like you end up in Vegas?"

"That your line?" Willia's hair-stroking didn't stop.

Confident: "Didn't know I needed one. I'm already in the door."

"You're in the door, but you're not in here." Her hand disappeared down where her thighs met.

At a distance Paris heard, at least he thought he heard, the squish of moistness. No, he wasn't in there yet. His confidence went down. His anticipation rose.

Willia sensed it. Willia dug it. Willia smiled. There was nothing so fine, as much as she wanted to get off herself, as wielding the weapon of sex against a man.

She said: "What do you want to know for? Ten minutes after it's over you won't blow pocket change to send me a postcard."

"What makes you so sure?"

As quick as it came Willia's smile went away. "Because a girl like me ended up in a place like this." Willia stopped brushing her hair. She turned, looked in Paris's direction. Not at him, just in his direction. Her story began.

"It seemed like," Willia said, "a good idea at the time—Vegas. I used to dance back in Indianapolis. One day these guys from a casino came through looking for new talent. I figured, I'm not beautiful enough to be a New York model, can't act good enough to be a Hollywood star. But I've got enough to be a Vegas showgirl. Well, I did after the boob job anyway."

"Looks good."

"Thanks. So what the hell, right? I was seventeen. I dropped out of school and hit The Strip."

"Your parents freak?"

"I promised them I'd make a little money, then finish school." Once again Willia's brush went to her head and made the long sweep down her hair. It was a programmed movement.

"I lied."

Paris tried to do some cheerleading. Partly to make Willia feel better. Mostly to keep the possibility of sex alive. "Well, so what if you never finished school? You came to Vegas, you're a dancer. It's like a dream come true."

Paris finally got Willia's eye, but the look that came with it was: You dipshit. "I never dreamed about being a showgirl. This is just where I ended up.

"It was fun at first, you know? Dance, hang out, be one of the girls. There's always next year to do something else; always next year to get your life together. But every year the new girls come in a year younger, a year prettier. A year better. Then one day you wake up and they're not just a couple of years younger, it's five and eight, and you're not dancing to dance anymore. You're dancing to keep up, you're dancing to pay the bills. You're dancing to stay alive. So here I am. Still in Vegas. Still a showgirl. Still alive. Barely."

A vision of failure, a vision Paris was very downright friendly with, got up in his face.

"You wanted to know," Willia said.

Paris sort of nodded.

A very depressing moment took its time in passing.

In an "enough about that" fashion, very much as if the previous conversation belonged to two other people, Willia got up from the bed. She crossed to Paris, straddled him in the chair.

Paris's anticipation rose a little more, along with the meat between his legs.

In conjunction, Willia's smile found its way back. "I like black guys. You think it's weird I like black guys?"

"Right now I think I really don't care."

"Just something about black guys."

Paris's hands fondled their way down Willia's back, over her lats— no fat there, just the curve of pure muscle. Dancers. "You got some kind of slave/plantation-wife freak?"

"No. I don't think it's that deep. It think it's muuuh . . ." Willia straightened, lost her breath. Paris's fingers had slipped over her ass. Bingo. "It's more like a," she labored to continue, "a good-sex freak."

She put her lips to his ear. Words got carried on hot breath. "If I'm not careful I think I could just about fall for a black guy." Pulling back, looking Paris in the eyes, prolonging the tease: "You got somebody to love?"

". . . Not really."

"Not really yes, or not really no?"

"Well . . ." Nena. Did he love Nena? Was this cheating on her? Did her and him have a relationship to cheat on? He had picked her up, or the other way around, and he dug her and she dug him—except that he was costing her money, but he was going to cut her in on his score. And there was that talk about going away together. And Paris had meant it too. Really he had. But . . . Willia. This wasn't cheating. Was it?

Willia mooted the whole issue. "Doesn't matter. I don't believe in love."

"You don't be—"

"I don't believe in love," she stated again.

Paris waited for more. No more came, so he asked: "What do you believe in?"

"Lust and fear. I think people get together with someone because they lust after them. I think people stay together because they're afraid of being alone."

"That the only reason you're with me, you don't want to be alone?"

"If I said yes would it bother you?"

"Like I told you: right now I really don't care."

Paris went back to work on Willia's ass.

Willia went to work on Paris's fly.

Gayle liked to walk home at night. After spending her days locked up in a casino like a lab rat doing experiments on secondhand smoke, the cooled-up desert air felt good to her lungs. Toward the back of the Plaza was the employees' entrance. Employees of the Plaza weren't supposed to use the front of the building. Didn't look professional. Wasn't good for them to mingle near the marks off the street. Gayle didn't care. It was quicker to head out the front than it was to make her way around from the back of the building. Too bad for the management if they didn't go for that. Gayle was getting to the point in her life where she was her own boss.

Brunson, who'd gotten hepped to Gayle's leaving out the front ways, hung near the main doors doing double duty: waiting for the girl and waiting—with five grand in pocket—for Paris, who, knowing Paris, might or might not return for the money. Where he'd spiked himself gave Brunson a ringside seat for peeping a rainbow of degenerates—bankrupt in every sense of the word—flow into the Plaza, then, shortly, flow out again slightly more bankrupt than previously. Every once in a while some well-dressed cat would make his way into the casino. Brunson figured them to be Strip rollers who, curious, were coming around to see how the other half lost their money, or heading for the video poker at the bar to pick up a prostie who serviced at downtown prices.

From in the casino came Gayle, who passed Brunson with all the indifference she could subconsciously possess.

Brunson took her by the arm to slow her down and got a surprise from the amount of muscle the sleeve of her shirt hid. Fast as he could, Brunson let her go. Something about Gayle told him that she was the kind of woman who wasn't afraid to use the gifts God had given her, arm muscle no exception.

"You want something," Gayle said more than asked, and said in a way that was more bored than solicitous.

Brunson hoped her boredom was just symptomatic of the malaise that came gratis with eight hours' labor, and not an instant assessment of him.

"I'm Brunson," he introduced himself.

Gayle responded to that no way in particular.

"You're new here."

Gayle's lack of responsiveness only increased.

"I figured, you being new, you might not know too many people, and maybe I could . . . show you things."

"Show me things," Gayle repeated, her features arranging themselves into a very thoughtful grimace. She nodded a couple of times, took a beat like she was putting together ideas, then: "I don't really want to have a baby," Gayle said and Brunson flinched at, getting a little more information from her than he'd been expecting.

She went on: "I don't really want to have a baby, and when a woman doesn't want to have a baby, then, other than rotating her tires or moving furniture, a man doesn't really figure into things."

Brunson thought up an argument for that quick-style. "You don't want to have a baby, but that don't mean you can't have fun."

"Fun like bowling?"

"Fun like fucking."

"Yeah, well, the nice thing about being a woman is you don't need a man to have a good time."

"What, you dyke? That ain't the word on the street, but you gone dyke?"

Gone dyke? That would imply Gayle didn't dig fucking men. She dug fucking men, and had the men in her past to prove it. There was John, who, after eight months of spending up her money and bedding down other women, disappeared, never to be seen or heard from again. Not that she was busting out in tears and torch songs over it. And there was the other one, the one whose name she couldn't even recall, who talked tough and acted cool, but who possessed all the resilience of damp tissue. Good riddance to him, too.

And now there was this guy coming around, Brunson, trying to get Gayle to buy what he was selling. But from all she could tell, besides his barely passable looks and his I-don't-know-you-but-you-owe-me-sex attitude, he didn't even have what little her last two men had to offer. So, no, it wasn't that Gayle didn't dig fucking, it was just good and hard to find a man she dug *worth* fucking. And knowing that she didn't really care if she found one or not, that made for a real liberating feeling.

In answer to Brunson's question: "Naw, I haven't gone dyke. I've just gotten free."

Brunson saw how things were. There might have been a time when he could've sweet-talked his way into the promised land nestled between Gayle's legs, but that time had long passed. Gayle didn't need anybody's shit. Gayle didn't take anybody's shit.

She moved on from Brunson.

Gayle headed out the door and into Las Vegas.

In a big Vegas Strip theme hotel, on the twelfth floor, down the hall off the elevator, was room 12-101. A mini-suite. The door was locked and on the handle was a "Do Not Disturb" sign. In the mini-suite, on the bed, sat Jay with a phone in one hand and the Complete Las Vegas Business White and Yellow Pages in the other. On the floor was Marcus, still dead and moment by moment becoming deader.

Jay dialed the phone. He'd spent the last three years as an assistant to one nameless, faceless, soulless, don't-know-how-to-talk-except-for-yelling agent or another, and in three years a guy can rack up a lot of dialing. A whole lot of dialing. Never before had he dialed with so much intent.

The phone rang . . . it rang . . .

"Las Vegas Lodge," the voice on the other end answered.

Jay asked for: "Paris Scott's room."

A short delay. "I'm sorry, there's no Paris Scott registered here."

Jay hung up. "Shit!" Still, it was a brilliant little plan, call all the motels, the little dives where a guy—where a pathetic troll—like Paris was bound to crawl into. Call them, ask for him, until Jay found the worm he was looking for. Brilliant. No one else would ever think of a plan so beautifully simplistic. No one who didn't have the icy, shrewd heart of a killer. Jay laughed at his brilliance . . . laughed . . . cried, then laughed again.

A knock at the door: "Housekeeping," someone said.

"No," Jay said back. His index finger drew across the next number to dial.

The person outside the door knocked again. Again the person said: "Housekeeping."

"I DON'T NEED ANY GODDAMN HOUSEKEEPING THANK YOU VERY MUCH!" Jay screamed at her.

"¡Hijo de tu puta madre!" the maid screamed back.

Jay dialed.

The phone rang . . . rang . . .

"The Lucky Six Mo—"

"Paris Scott's room."

"Scott . . . ? I don't think there's anyo—"

Jay hung up. At the phone, as he dialed the next number: "You're dead, you little bastard. I'm going to find you, and when I do you're dead! Dead!"

So brilliant.

He laughed some more . . . he laughed some more . . . he cried again, then laughed some more.

$\mathcal{D}$usk had become night, but other than that not much had changed in Nena and Paris's room at the Shady Tree Inn. Brice was in her chair flipping through a Victoria's Secret catalog. Nena was on the bed scared to death that the next moment might be her last moment, and if not the next then the one right after it.

Brice put the magazine aside, checked her watch, saw that it was late and getting later.

"I don't know. Doesn't look too good." Her head shook. Brice sounded disappointed, like she was talking about a guest of honor tardy for dinner.

"He s-said . . ." It took Nena two tries just to get that out. "He promised."

"A guy making an empty promise. There's something new. What'd he tell you?" Derisive: "He looooves you? He neeeeeds you? He'll take you with him wherever he goes? Sheeeyeah. A guy like that needs to get shot."

Brice's ridicule, on top of the intense terror Nena was sinking under, made her want to cry. But she wouldn't cry. Nena knew that's what this woman got off on: humiliation. Maybe she was already as good as dead, but Nena wasn't going to give her any pleasure about it. She wasn't going to cry. Her eyes teared, her nose ran, but she wasn't going to cry.

Outside the door a drunk wailed. "Spennnnncer . . . Spennnnncer!"

Brice looked toward the sound.

Nena, as she had been doing for the last hour whenever Brice looked away, millimeter by millimeter micro-moved her hand toward her towel and the knife that lay hidden in it.

Brice looked back to Nena. "It's kind of tough. Which way do you pull? If this guy doesn't come back for you, that makes him a lying sack of shit. If he does come back, then he cares about you, but I gotta kill him. Sometimes you just can't win."

"You don't have to kill him." For Nena, keeping her voice steady was like riding a bull. "He didn't do anything."

"Stealing drugs ain't much, but it's something."

Utter surprise splashed over Nena's face.

"Ohhhh, he didn't tell you about that? I guess he is a lying sack of shit."

Outside, again: "I'm sorry, Spennnnncer. Just talk to me, baby."

And again Brice looked.

And again Nena moved her hand.

"Men," Brice said, sister to sister. "They're nothing but a bunch of walking, talking assholes. Every one of 'em. My last man, he was a loser like your guy. When we first hooked up we didn't have nothing. Not a thing. Just a fast car and a couple of guns. But when you're young and in love that's all you need. Ned was never much into the life, not at first. I did all the heavy lifting, and did it happy. There was nothing I wouldn't do for my man. Nothing." Something slowly, little by little, crept into Brice's voice, same as an animal afraid to venture into a dark place. It was just about the last thing anyone who had ever met Brice, especially those whose acquaintanceship with her had concluded in death, would expect to hear from the girl. It was something that sounded very much like pure, genuine heartache.

"I took care of him. I supported him. I luhh . . ." Now it was Brice who had to fight to keep her voice from shattering. "Then he runs off with that twist Jude. She shows up smiling her smile, wiggling her ass, and Ned goes love-simple. You know what he told me when he skipped with her? He told me I was losing it, that I was going mad dog 'cause I gave the bitch a bullet in the leg as a going-away present. She shouldn't've been fucking with my man. She's lucky I didn't blow her goddamn . . ." Brice felt the weight of the gun in her lap, the weight of body piled on top of dead body smothering her. "I didn't used to be like this. I didn't used to be nothing but a . . . Now look at me. I'm not even . . . I'm not . . ."

"Human," Nena finished for her.

Nena took a chance saying what she said, but Brice didn't receive it badly. Nena spoke nothing but the truth.

"I was until she . . . The bitch. She's the crazy one. I mean, okay, I've got my problems, but that girl's messed up. Hope she kills him."

The declaration came off as the weak rage of a woman scorned but still in love. Brice said it again and tried to make it stick. "Hope she kills him dead." It sounded as feeble as the first time.

Fragile, vulnerable to her own emotion, Nena saw one last chance to talk Brice out of things.

"Couldn't . . . couldn't you just let him go?"

"I've tried to forget about Ned. I can't."

"No! Paris! What if he just gave the drugs back? What if—"

"Oh, I'll get the drugs back. That's not the issue. The issue is pain and retribution. Actually, damn the retribution. The issue is pain." Brice was forgetting the past and returning to her old, irrationally com-bustible self. "I'm going to hurt the guy like he doesn't know hurt. I'm going to hurt him, I'm going to hurt him, then I'm going to kill him."

The drunk, outside: "Spennnnncer . . . I still love you, Spen-nnnncer!"

"Would you shut up, you freak!" Brice screamed at the door, at the drunk. "She doesn't need you!"

Brice turned back to Nena. She came throat to blade with Nena's speed knife.

"That was quick," Brice admired.

Nena didn't respond with anything more than a narrow stare. She was ready to kill, but hesitating just beyond the unpleasant chore.

"Well, see, now you've got a problem." Brice spoke with the countrified drawl of an antebellum lawyer pointing things out to some slick carpetbagger. "Stab me in the throat, it'll take me 'bout twenty minutes to bleed to death. Twenty minutes' time to put a bullet in your little bitch head. Don't much care for that option, but I think I can handle it. I go, we go, you know?"

Nena two-hand-gripped her knife like she was serious about traching the girl.

"You want to kill me quick you've got to stab me in the heart, shut that sucker down. Go on. Put the knife at my pumper."

Even with two hands Nena all of a sudden couldn't keep the knife from quivering.

"Well, go on. You want to kill me, don't you? Put the knife over my heart."

Nena's quivering turned into shaking.

"Let me help you out." Her hand to Nena's, Brice lowered the blade to the nipple of her left breast. "There you go. That's better. Except . . ." A drawback became, or at least she made a big show of it becoming, apparent to Brice. "You'll probably snap that little poker off on my ribs. Yeah. It's a fact: God built these bodies Ford Tough. You know what? You know what you want to do?"

Again Brice took Nena's hands and moved the knife. This time the tip of the blade came to rest just below Brice's sternum.

Nena didn't try to stop her redirecting. Nena was in the middle of losing it.

"Right up under the breastbone, that's the ticket." Brice sounded genuinely happy about Nena's assisted choice of location for making a sharp-force wound. "Smooth sailing up into the heart. Now you're ready to get some killing on. Just jam it on in there. Go on," she prompted. "Shove it in."

Shove it in? Kill? Nena couldn't hardly even see Brice through all the water in her eyes, let alone stab her. And she couldn't hardly move either. Her hands, her body—this whole experience belonged to some other girl in some other cheap motel in some other hell besides Las Vegas.

And all the while Brice kept coaching: "What's the matter? Stab me! You wanted me dead, so do it!"

Shivering. Quaking. Crying.

"Kill me!"

Trembling. Quavering. Sobbing.

"KILL ME!"

Nena let loose with a banzai yell and a full-force lunge that Brice put the dodge on by slipping to one side and landing a roundhouse to Nena's head.

The knife dropped from Nena's hands to the floor, and she collapsed on the dirty carpet next to it.

To the pile of Nena below: "You cunt! Jesus Christ, you were gonna cut me! You were really going to cut me!" Brice reached down, picked up the blade, felt the dull tip with her finger, then tossed it onto the nightstand. "I'll give you an E for effort. You've got balls. Sort of. This Paris fucker doesn't deserve you. 'Course, he's not going to get you. See, killing isn't something you can do half-assed. It's serious business. It's my job. And now it's time to go to work."

Nena, barely, raised up her head. The inevitable got asked. ". . . What are you going to do?"

Sitting comfortable, smiling slightly: "There was a little girl who had a little curl right in the middle of her forehead. When she was good she was very, very good. But when she was bad . . ."

Out of Brice's pocket, onto the arm of the chair, came a pack of Camel Wides. No filters.

". . . she was horrid. Tell me something," Brice asked, "you like music?"

*I*f their lives had been a movie, Paris and Willia would have been basking in the afterglow of lovemaking: smoking cigarettes and looking beautiful despite the sweaty minutes of passion. But life wasn't a movie, it was real. Paris was drinking out of the one can of Diet Coke Willia had left, Willia was wiping between her legs with a towel stolen off a Union Plaza housekeeping cart, and both were wallowing in the secret shame that comes free of charge with sexing strangers like the complimentary stench included in a sack of dead fish.

"So, after"—Willia tossed away the towel; it landed half on a chair and dripped down to the floor, where it would stay for a good, long time—"you get this tape to this guy Brunson, then what?"

"Take the money and run."

"Where to?"

"Florida. The Keys. That's what I'm thinking."

"With her?"

Paris didn't answer that, so Willia asked again.

"With her?"

She still got no answer for her asking. She drank up what was left of the gone-warm Diet Coke, looked down into the can. Nothing but nothing was in there.

"I've never been anywhere," Willia said. "Not really. Won a trip to Milwaukee once. Got sick. Couldn't go. Even if I had gone to Milwaukee I never would've been anywhere. I'm tired of being here, Paris." She was matter-of-fact about it—the tiredness that was a constant in her life. "I'm tired of this place, I'm tired of prancing around half naked for a bunch of drunks marking time waiting for their luck to change. I'm just tired, and mostly . . ."

Paris finished dressing, and when he had, he drifted for the door.

"You don't have to tell me yes or no," Willia went on, making Paris stop and hover just this side of stepping from her life. "I know you don't love me. And you know I don't care. I just figured . . . Like I started to say: mostly I'm just tired of being alone."

He'd started things with Nena, Paris thought. He'd started things with her, and he should follow through with her.

He should.

Willia's rack just about shouted at him.

Paris said: "Half an hour. Get the tape, get the money; it'll take half an hour. Have your shit packed."

Willia was already putting her shit in a bag before Paris was out the door.

*O*mar folded up his cell phone and jammed it back in his pocket.

"Still no answer," he said.

"Well, where da fuck Daymond at?" Kenny asked, all indignant. Staring through the Lexus windshield across the parking lot at the motel room door Brice had long since disappeared through: "How long she been in there?"

"A couple hours. A few."

"So what do we do?"

"Don't know."

"I say we kill her." Kenny spat out the window. "Dat's what Daymond had told us."

"He said if she didn't get the job done."

"Well, muthafucka, look what time it is." Kenny pointed outside. "It's dark, dat's what time it is. It sure da fuck wasn't dark when we started. Now, I say dat ain't getting the job done."

"Sheiiit" was all Omar responded with.

"Man, since we got this gig, you been the one always logicalizing and shit 'cause you think I ain't nothing but a dumbass nigga."

"I don't think you're no dumbass," Omar lied.

"Well, I'mo drop some science on yo ass: every time shit starts gettin' wild, Daymond brings the bitch in. Every muthafuckin' time. Now, we put a cap in her, in this Paris muthafucka, 'n' we get Daymond's shit for him, who you think he gonna dial up next time there's drama?"

"We get the call."

"Muthafuckin' right. We ain't errand boys no more. We serious hitters."

"Sheiiit."

"And I tell you who should be number three on our get-whacked list, right behind Crazy Bitch 'n' Stealin' Drugs Muthafucka." Kenny looked at Omar sharp, hard, and straight for real. "Daymond."

One more time Omar got with "Sheiiit," then added: "Fuuuu-uck."

"You 'n' me, bro. Ain't no reason we can't be goin' for ours."

"You talking crazy."

"I'm talkin' 'bout where it at now, and where it at now is you 'n' me breakin' off a piece for our own selves. Daymond ain't nothing but soft anyway. Ain't nohow his shit shoulda got stolt in the first place. Lettin' his fucked-up cuz deal—dat ain't nothing but asking for trouble."

In the short span of seconds, Omar got down to more hard thinking than he had before in his entire twenty years. His mind was a hot car that raced him down a two-lane fantasy blacktop of money, power, and the females who came around when the two were mixed. Omar liked where his mind was taking him. Omar made the easy choice to get himself there for real. It was time, high time, for Daymond to take a fall. Maybe Kenny wasn't such a dumbass nigga after all.

Aiite, Omar was about to say. Aiite, let's do it. He was about to say that when a beat-up Gremlin pulled into the Shady Tree Inn parking lot.

Omar saw the car.

Omar: "Sheiiit." He watched Paris get out of the car and go into his motel room. "There's that."

"Don't gotta be."

"Brice is going to tap him."

Kenny shrugged. "Let her. She come out, we tap her and take the drugs. We play it right, Daymond ain't even gonna be 'round longanuff ta be askin' questions."

Omar sat. Did more of that hard thinking.

Kenny did some prompting. "Why you scareta da bitch?"

"I'm not—"

"We ain't never gonna git nowhere with you goin' around scareta bitches all the time."

Omar took another ride in his mind car, which was picking up speed, moving faster by the second. The soundtrack on the stereo: You ain't scareta no bitch. A couple of seconds of that, and Omar said what previously he was thinking. "Aiite, let's do it."

Simultaneous, both men got out of the Lexus. They started after Paris, for his motel room. Kenny sidetracked over to the Gremlin.

"Lookit dis shit, huh. You believe dis shit?" Kenny opened the passenger door.

"What are you doing?"

"We got time. Brice ain't gonna be killing him in no hurry. How many times you get to sit in shit like this?" Kenny eased himself in.

Yeah, how many times, Omar thought, and got in too, putting himself behind the wheel.

Kenny: "Now, dis shit be tore up. Muthafucka better off dead than gettin' spotted in shit like this."

"I don't know, bro. When we move up I might make this my ride, ya know."

"Aw, shit." Kenny busted up. "Don't even play dat shit."

"For real. I'd be rollin' on the serious DL. And you peep all that space up in back there? A brother could freak himself all kinds of bitches, know what I'm sayn'?"

Kenny did more busting up all ignant-Negro style: feet-stomping, gut-grabbing, into-hand "Aw, damn" in no-you-didn't disbelief at what Omar—usually serious Omar—had just said.

Then the two slapped hands, grabbed fingers, and pulled at them until they snapped. Generally, there was a coonish good time to be had by all.

Unexpectedly, in the middle of the festivities, Omar's head split open. Ripe melons dropped from a train trestle should splatter as much. Just as suddenly Omar became aware of nothing, and would remain that way for the rest of forever.

Kenny took a 98.6-degree facial of internal skull matter.

"Oh, shit!" he started to say. Started to, but did not finish, because of a bullet that entered his throat. Not too far off, as it turned out by coincidence, from where he'd previously taken a bullet to the throat years ago. Following that a second bullet, like with Omar, very severely blew open his head. And then Kenny, again as with Omar, shared an awareness of nonexistence.

Jay came running up to the Gremlin, Paris's Gremlin, with the freshly dead black guy behind the steering wheel. A black guy who was not Paris.

"Fuck!" Jay screamed, not so much caring that he'd just killed the wrong guy and an extra one to boot, but more upset that he'd missed the right one. "Fucking shit!"

Even though he'd only used three bullets, Jay ejected the clip from his gun and inserted a fresh extended clip of Teflon-coated, armor-piercing, hollow-point bullets into the Sig/Sauer P-226 modified with a laser sight, silenced flash suppressor, grip sleeve, extended slide release, and the extended magazines that carried the bullets that had emptied the heads of Kenny and Omar of all thought and, if Jay had his way, would do at least that much for Paris.

"You're dead, you son of a bitch." Jay worked the slide on the Sig/Sauer, chambering a round. "I swear to you, Marcus, this time he's dead."

Gayle finished the walk from Fremont to her apartment building on Sahara—she'd sold her house and was saving her money to get the hell out of Vegas, she'd had her fill of it, thank you very much, and move herself to Maui quick as possible—in good time. Today she was feeling extra energized, extra self-strong. As she made her way around the man-made algae-filled pond to her apartment, she saw her neighbor, whom she'd never been particularly neighborly with, standing around outside.

It was sorta late to be standing around outside.

Gayle asked her neighbor: "What are you doing standing around?"

"Waiting."

"For?"

"Met a guy."

"Yeah?"

"Yeah. Met a guy, and he's going to take me out of here. Going to Florida. The Keys. He's got money."

"Yeah?"

"Yeah. Well, he doesn't got money, but he's going to get it. He's going to get some money, then we're going to go to Florida. The Keys. We're going to live like the Czar and Czarina. So I'm just waiting for him. Waiting for my guy."

Gayle didn't have the heart to come straight out and tell her neighbor to get comfortable. If she was waiting on a man, she'd be waiting a good long time.

Instead: "Why don't you c'mon inside for a sec, have a little coffee. You and me can talk about things."

"Can't. Don't want to miss my man."

Fuck it, Gayle thought. The girl'll learn. She had.

Gayle went into her apartment, counted out her tips, and put the money in her get-me-to-Maui jar.

aris fumbled open the door to the room, stumbled in the dark over to the nightstand calling out Nena's name a couple of times along the way. He turned on the light.

It took a second, a few seconds, for Paris to figure some things out. Nena was sprawled on the bed. She was sleeping. Paris was sure she must have been sleeping. But if Nena was sleeping, why were her eyes wide open, hazed over, and staring so blankly at something just beyond the ceiling? If Nena was sleeping, why did she look all beaten up and burned and . . . and dead? What it took Paris those couple of seconds to figure out was Nena looked as she did because she was beaten and burned. Nena was dead.

The unreal coalesced into the real. Paris as much gasped as said: "Nena . . ."

He was about to gasp it again when the door imploded before Jay's Florsheimed foot. Terminator-style, he bum-rushed the room.

"You sick son of a bitch!"

Paris collapsed to the floor, ducking splintered wood and driven down by fear.

"You little animal!"

The laser sight's red dot floated up Paris. His throat, mouth, eye. Forehead.

Paris jammed himself up into a corner—"Oh, God"—a bug trying to put the dodge on a can of Raid.

"You don't feel, you don't care, you don't . . ."

"Please . . . please . . ."

Soft: ". . . You don't even know what love is." Hard: "All you know is how to hurt and kill and ruin. Not anymore." The red dot fixed bull's-eye steady. "It's time to die."

Paris, screaming for his life: "I didn't do anything!"

"Didn't do . . . ? You killed Marcus!"

"I didn't kill—"

"You murdered—"

"Jesus Christ, man, I didn't kill anybody! I'm the wrong guy! You got the wrong guy!" Shaking, wailing: "You killed her for nothing!"

The crazy, thrashing world Jay had been trying to ride for the last half-day slowed up some. "Her . . . ?"

Her. Nena. Stretched out dead and blistered. Same as Marcus.

Jay's Sig/Sauer lowered.

Paris's head dropped down crash-landing in his hands. Yowling: "You didn't have to kill her. Jesus . . . you didn't have to . . ."

". . . I didn't kill her!"

"Fuck you!" The words on fire.

"I swear I-I didn't kill her."

"You killed her! You killed Buddy!"

"Who?"

Long pause.

Paris's jukin' and jivin' world calmed up some too. "Buddy. You killed . . ."

From Jay, Paris got nothing but blank stare.

"You didn't . . . ? But if you . . ." Fear hopped in the backseat and let logic do the driving as Paris tried to suss a few things out. "Something messed-up's going on here."

"I didn't kill her. . . ."

"Something real messed-up."

". . . Never touched her."

"Sure . . . sure you didn't. There's something else. Some other . . ."

Jay did some thinking too. Jay came up with an idea: "There is some other—"

"There is?"

"It's so obvious."

"Wha—"

"If I didn't kill her . . ."

"Yeah . . ."

"If I didn't kill her . . ."

"Go on . . ."

"Then you did, you goddamn psycho!"

Jay's gun jerked up.

Paris screamed. "No!" His hands shot in front of him, useless against a bullet.

The gun's black eye got ready to wink Paris out of existence.

"Hey, dumbass!"

Jay looked toward the new voice.

A blonde. Jacked-up face and sporting a .38. "He didn't smoke your friend." Her torn lip smiled. "I did."

A processing delay, short but too long. Jay swung his S/S around. Brice had him beat. Had him beat bad.

Mini-explosions. Three, four of them. Lead punching flesh, cracking bone thud-thud hard, jerking Jay's body with each hit. Fountains of blood. Splash patterns swirled and splatted on the walls, the floor, the ceiling. The fresh cordite smell canceled out the aroma of Nena's molten flesh.

An ugly thwap: Jay's way-dead body head-smacking the ground and head-smacking it hard.

Quiet now. Half the people in the room were too dead to make a sound. One was too shocked. For the fourth it was just another day at the office.

Brice went to the dead Jay, picked up his Sig/Sauer, looked it over—looked over its silenced flash suppressor, grip sleeve, extended slide release, and extended magazines.

"What the hell is this supposed to be?" she asked at his practically smoking corpse before pocketing the S/S.

Paris fought off body quivers, started to stand. "Thank you. You s-saved my—"

A flash of nickel plating cut him off. Paris took Brice's gun in the face. That was quick-followed by a mouthful of busted tooth chips. That was followed up by a mouthful of gushing blood. Paris sank back down to his reserved spot on the floor.

Brice, no nonsense: "Where is it?"

"Wha—"

Brice's Timberlands, Paris's gut.

Brice's Timberlands, Paris's head.

More busted teeth, more blood.

"I am way too tired to fuck around." Another kick punctuated that for her. "Just tell me where it is."

"Aiieee . . . I don't—"

A kick, a kick, a kick to the ribs. Stomp to the head.

Brice: "I could care less if I find Daymond's shit or not." Stomp, kick, stomp, stomp. "All I have to do is get you dead. That's plenty fine by me."

Boot to the rib, Paris flipped.

Boot to the head, one eye lost vision. His face cracked, swelled. The violence kept coming. Instinct carried Paris for the bed. He struggled up against the nightstand. His head lolled, and his last good eye looked at Nena.

"Yeah, say good-bye to your little friend." Brice taunting now, winding herself up for the kill. "Real sweet."

Paris's head sloshed with thoughts. Nena . . . Should've been there for her, should've been there for Nena. Could've gotten her away from all this. Could've been safe and free and clear. Could've . . . Should've . . .

His hand, wet with blood and sweat, slipped on the nightstand. The lamp got shoved over. Light shot around the room at odd, sharp angles.

"She was a piece of ass, boy, I'll tell you that. You know what the last word out of her mouth was? 'Paris,' you shit! 'Paris,' she said."

She'd said "Paris."

Nena. Help me, Nena, Paris prayed to the dead. A prayer begging of forgiveness and redemption. He called out from his heart for absolution of prior misdeeds, and shielding and protection from current harm. He called out to be saved. Same call Paris had been making most of his life.

Help me, he cried. Just this time. Just this one, last time.

"Hey, bad boy, do me a favor. . . ." The gun hammer clicked.

Something on the nightstand glinted right before Paris's eye.

"When you see your girl, give one for me."

Grab, flick, turn. Wild scream. Across the room in a frenzied tear. Paris against Brice. Brice against the wall. So close their breath mingled. She smelled . . . she smelled good. She was soft to the touch. Not hard and icy like Paris would've thought. Soft.

Brice got with a little smile. She leaned forward as if to touch lips with Paris.

He stepped back.

She looked down.

She saw the hole the knife, Nena's knife in Paris's hand, had opened in her left side. She saw the blood that gurgled out. Brice's eyes rolled back and she slid to the floor, not dead, not even dying, just cut wide open.

Paris took the gun from her hand. She didn't much have the strength to stop him. He didn't much know what to do with it. He just kept holding it.

Brice said: "Whoa." Then she said: "That hurt." She stuck a finger in the wound and it disappeared to the third knuckle. "Guess this means you're not going to give me the stuff, huh?"

Paris was fast over to the dresser. He ripped open the drawer, grabbed up the DAT player. "You want it? Take it!" He threw it down into Brice's lap.

She grimaced as it hit.

The player sank in blood.

"TAKE IT! I'm sorry that shit ever got into my life!"

Brice fished out the player, looked it over. "What the hell is this?" It slipped from her fingers back into her lap.

"It's the tape. It's the last of Ian Jermaine. It's what you've been chasing me for. It's what you killed all these people for, you lousy—"

"Ian Jermaine?" Brice puzzled. "The guy who died in the pile of shit? What do I want with this?"

"The . . . the tape . . ."

"I want Daymond's drugs."

". . . Drugs . . . ?"

It was two people doing a verbal jig, trying to put together what in the hell the other was talking about.

Brice did a quick read of Paris's face. There was truth in his ignorance.

She said: "You really don't know about—"

"THERE ARE NO DRUGS!"

An odd sort of lazy, dopey breath wiggled its way out of Brice. Call it a laugh. "Oh, man. It's days like these that make you want to quit the business."

"You don't want the tape?"

"Ian Jermaine? Who the hell listens to that crap? If it was Lynyrd Skynyrd . . ."

"Jesus Chri . . . All this . . . all this for nothing."

Paris stared down at Brice and Brice stared back up at Paris, and for a good bit neither had anything much to say.

Moments faded one into another into the next.

Eventually Paris made a decision that involved reaching down, slowly, and picking up the DAT player from the puddle of blood in Brice's lap. There was nothing he could do about the things that had passed, the dead would never again be anything more than that, and in time, in a great deal of time, Nena and all of this would be gotten over. But there was still a chance to salvage a future. The tape—that could still be sold. The money—that could still be spent. Willia and the Keys—they could still be had. A life, an easy carefree life of sunshine and companionship with a beautiful girl, could still be lived. And after the life he'd endured the last two days, didn't his next one deserve to be better?

And it would be.

It was there for him just outside the door. All he had to do was simply walk from the room and—

"Where . . ." Brice managed to ask, "where are you going?"

"Somewhere. Anywhere. Anywhere I can forget. This shit is over."

"It's not over."

Paris turned back to the woman, "but I'm telling you" written all over his face. "You got the wrong guy. I don't have your drugs. It's ov—"

"It's not over. Wrong or right, I don't hunt someone across two states just to let 'em walk."

Someplace, somewhere, someone took a stroll on Paris's grave.

"And if you think you can gut me and just fade away you're dead wrong. This is the way it works: you gotta finish things up."

"I . . . what? I didn't . . ." Paris struggled with the basics of communication, wrestled with it, trying to squeeze out words that made sense. All that came to him were more of the same he'd used before, but this time they were spoken in a frantic plea. "I'm not the one! I didn't steal the drugs!"

"Doesn't matter." Brice was as calm as Paris was animated. "It's my job, and I always do my job. Makes no difference how things started, it's the way things ended up. Shit . . ." A cough, a spurt of blood from her side. "Shit like this just happens."

Shit like this? Murder, she was talking about. She was talking about murder.

"Please . . . I don't want to—"

"Hey, I'm trying to give you some square advice, Jackson. Do it. If you don't, one day I'm going to heal up. One day I'm going to find you. You know I will. One day I'm going to find you, and one day . . . if you don't do me, I'll do you."

Murder.

"I can't. I . . . can't!"

"Got to, my man. Have to."

Murder.

To snuff out a life. Even hers, even this thing down below him, monster that she was, how could he? How could he possibly . . .

And yet . . .

Paris looked to Nena, lifeless on the bed. He looked at Jay, who was of equal deadness.

He thought of Buddy.

Dead.

Ian.

Dead.

The guy Jay bust through the door yammering about, saying that Paris had killed. He, whoever he was, was dead too.

And were there any others? Any more bodies stretched out between LA and LV?

Probably.

Probably.

And how come they got that way? Because first off Buddy wanted to steal some drugs for cash to impress Alf, and Paris wanted to rip off a tape for cash to impress his ex. Because whoever owned the drugs wanted to get even, and whoever had claim to the tape needed to get it back. And at the end of the day nobody got the money or the drugs or the tape or the girl or anything except for killed.

Everything else, the getting of things in life, was hard. Very, very difficult. Dying, making people dead—that took no effort all. No more effort than the little bit of lazy bother needed to slide back the trigger of a gun.

There was, real suddenly, no sensation to the weapon in Paris's hand. It seemed—like hair and fingernails. Like flesh—quite naturally, quite comfortably, just another part of him.

"First time's the tough one." From below him, spindled awkwardly in the crotch of the floor and the wall, Brice gave Paris a walkthrough. "But not hard like you'd think. All it really takes is a good try. Tell you this: a spoonful of music helps the medicine go down."

Brice kept her smile going. There wasn't a fucked-up second of this fucked-up event she wasn't completely digging. She asked: "Like music, Paris? Me, I'm a Bachman-Turner Overdrive girl myself."